SUPER AWKWARD

SUPER
AWKWARD

BETH GARROD

■SCHOLASTIC

First published in the UK in 2016 by
Scholastic Children's Books
An imprint of Scholastic Ltd
Euston House, 24 Eversholt Street, London, NW1 1DB, UK
Registered office: Westfield Road, Southam, Warwickshire, CV47 0RA
SCHOLASTIC and associated logos are trademarks and/or
registered trademarks of Scholastic Inc.

ISBN 978 1407 16640 7

A CIP catalogue record for this book
is available from the British Library.

Printed by CPI Group (UK) Ltd, Croydon, CR0 4YY
Papers used by Scholastic Children's Books are made
from wood grown in sustainable forests.

5 7 9 10 8 6 4

www.scholastic.co.uk

To my family, old and new.
And to everyone who has ever felt super awkward.
You rock.

CHAPTER

ONE

So. It's official. My life sucks. I'd always thought it, but this whole caravan trip has confirmed it. I, Bella Fisher, am on a one-way road to Loserdom. And it's not even the kind of road where you can pop into a petrol station and buy Haribo to make yourself feel better.

Is it normal to have such a high embarrassment-to-days-alive ratio? I've only been around for fifteen-and-a-half years, and four of those I can't even remember (except for that hour when I was three and a half and got my tongue stuck to a box of Calippos in Sainsbury's, but that doesn't count) and already I've ticked off way too much stuff on the cringe list. Going to school with a pair of pants stuck in my sock – check. Calling our deranged geography teacher 'Mum' by accident – done.

Twice. And he's a man. Getting hit in the face by a rounders ball which bruised my chin and made me look like I had a beard – achieved, the day before our school fashion show.

Why do these things happen to me? Every. Single. Time. Yes, it's entertaining for everyone else, but imagine *being* me. The world's a terrifying place. I wouldn't be surprised if one day I opened the drawer under the kitchen sink – the one that Mum stuffs with old birthday cards, half-burnt joss sticks and dead batteries – to find some weird life contract that she'd signed me up to:

> *Dear Ms Fisher, I appreciate that birth is*
> *a tricky business, but within the first thirty*
> *seconds of life, your daughter managed to hit*
> *me, an incredibly esteemed doctor, in the eye*
> *with a jet-like urine stream. It is still watering*
> *now. So, I have no choice but to issue you with*
> *the following rules that her life must adhere to.*
> > *Many thanks,*
> > *An Important Doctor*

Bella's Life Rules:
- Bella shall emit a weird smell that any

vaguely fit boy can detect, causing them to treat her with deep suspicion. It will probably smell a bit like the farty waft at the end of a packet of salt and vinegar crisps.

- Bella will accompany every laugh with a snort. And in extreme cases, hic-burps.
- Whenever there is a party that literally everyone is going to, Bella must be otherwise engaged on a dreary family holiday. Suggested 'holidays' could be long stints in slightly damp caravan parks, interspersed with Mum lectures about the benefits of pelvic floor exercises.
- Bella will be a geek. And not in a geek-chic kind of way, but in a secretly-caring-about-failing-maths-and-science way.
- Bella will always fail maths and science.
- Finally, whatever Bella does or says to try and impress anyone will always, ALWAYS, backfire.

Urgh, it all seems so very possible. Must check that drawer as a matter of urgency. On the plus side, it would mean none of my life-tragicness was technically my fault. It was just destiny, and Mum says you can't argue with that (although she does use red biro to change bits of her horoscopes she doesn't agree with).

If Mum was just one shade less unhinged, we'd have been spared this horror in the first place. My mum + the internet = worse combination than tuna ice cream.

Last year she bid on a model of Benny from Abba for her band memorabilia collection. She never wondered why the postage cost was so high for a 1.8 centimetre cardboard model. It never crossed her mind it would be 1.8 METRES. Now whenever my sister, Jo, and I go to the downstairs loo, we're eyeball-to-eyeball (or eyeball to pant-region, depending what stage of the weeing we're at) with a life-sized model of a bearded Swedish man. Mum only moves him when she gets him to answer the door to freak out salespeople, or to scare off potential burglars.

Her favourite lecture to me is not to talk to strangers on the internet. If only she'd done the same then right now we wouldn't be travelling miles to a fun-sponge of a place on the advice of some randomer called MysticBabs, who she met on a forum called HippyAndHappy. Alarm bells, anyone? Mum said Babs is 'a deeply spiritual guru' – I think she's a twelve-year-old boy having a right laugh. She (or he, depending on whose side you're on) persuaded my mum that the answer to inner bliss wasn't a Saturday night spent perving on the tight-trousered-mum-magnet Dermot O'Leary, but realigning her chakras (or Shakiras as Mum calls them). One dubious internet search later and Jo and I have been bundled into the car on the way to spending our last bit of half-term holiday freedom being dragged to Black Bay Caravan Park for a 'Meditat-YAY-tion' retreat.

I still can't accept we're going. Not even now as our brown Mini that's older than Jo (Mum says 'vintage', we say 'health hazard') is pulling off our drive (I've already seen one neighbour peeking to check the sound wasn't actually an aeroplane taking off). I have to give it one last try.

"Mum, I know the state of your chakras are on the line, but can't you go without us? Pleeeeeease..." She cranked up 'Dark Pipe of The Moon' – her Pink Floyd panpipes cover album – to show her mind was made up.

"And what would you get up to, Bells? Tell me what marvellous reason you've got to make me break the law and leave you on your own?" She checked her bright pink lipstick in the rear-view mirror. Turns out she didn't think 'being at extreme risk of actual death from boredom (DFB)' was a marvellous reason. "Wave to Benny, girls!"

I shoved my hands under my bum in anti-waving protest.

"Jo'll look after me ... WON'T YOU, JO?! She's got that uni athletics trip she needs to get ready for. I bet she's got loads to pack. And, er, shorts to iron, and, er ... trainers to lace?" The world of voluntary sport was a mystery to me. "RIGHT, JO?" Jo's vertical bun wobbled as I kneed the back of her seat trying to vibrate the right answer out of her. She always got the front seat. Way to make my short legs feel even worse about themselves. As usual, Jo leapt to my un-defence.

"Have you got enough room there? You seem to be accidentally, repeatedly kicking me." Sister loyalty means nothing to her. "Oh, *how weird*, it's stopped. Anyway, I'm all packed, thanks for asking. I did it days ago – you know I like to be prepared. Means you don't forget stuff. Talking of which, did you remember to bring all that homework you were trying to get me to help you out with?"

Eye. Roll. Jo was my age once, but I swear Mum's alternative carob birthday cake turned her thirty on her thirteenth birthday and she's been stuck there ever since. Sure, I was going to have a terrible time on this holiday, but there was NO WAY I was going to make it productive as well. I'm not a total idiot.

"I've done it all already, *actually,* thanks for asking.

6

What do you think I was doing in my room all of yesterday?" 1–0 to me.

"Sorting your nail varnishes into rainbow order, spending hours taking selfies that look as if you've done them spontaneously, and making a collage of quotes from Anna Kendrick movies?" Game, set, match to Jo. That was entirely what I'd been doing.

"Stalker," I hissed through the headrest.

"Loser," she hissed back, and flicked her long brown hair in my face.

"Come on, girls." Mum wasn't having any of it. "We've got a four-hour drive ahead of us. Apparently Black Bay is like the St Tropez of Wales, so I don't want to hear another word about it, OK? Loads of people would love to be in your position."

I disagreed.

"Name one person, Mum, one person."

She thought. "Well... Benedict Cumberbatch is a massive fan."

"WAIT. You're telling me Sherlock is a Black Bay regular?!"

"Well, the person that works in his dry cleaners is, and apparently they've got very similar tastes in trousers. And probably holidays too."

There was no point in arguing.

Seven hours and three wee stops later, we arrived in the dead of night. The only thing still lit up was their proud welcome sign, 'BLACK BAY CARAVAN PARK, WHERE WE PARTY LIKE IT'S 1999'. First impressions were that it did indeed resemble St Tropez – if St Tropez was less golden French yacht paradise, and more one hundred per cent muddy British field. Our tiny caravan had more shades of orange and brown in it than a fancy dress night where the theme is otters eating fish fingers. It was everything I'd worried about – with added floral.

How on earth was I going to make it through the next five days? Isn't there some sort of government committee to prevent massive misuse of school holidays that could rescue me? But unable to find enough phone signal to check/send urgent request for help, I gave in to Mum's demands for us to unpack.

Turns out my definition of unpacking – keep my clothes accessible by emptying everything out of my suitcase in a heap, while rummaging for a ring I hadn't actually packed – is way less mum-friendly than Jo's traditional 'coat hanger' method. So, surprise surprise, suck-up sis got rewarded with the sofa bed and I got left with one that spent daylight hours folded up into a coffee table.

By the time I'd flipped it out, Mum was already asleep, snoring.

I wriggled my way between the sheets, trying to ignore that my pillow smelt of ham (the linen cupboard doubled up as our food cupboard), and plugged in my headphones that I'd hidden in my pants. But even 5 Seconds of Summer and the 1975 couldn't cheer me up. Because being trapped in a human tin full of mum-snores, fragranced with Eau De Piglette, wasn't even the worse thing. Something far worse was looming. The most awful thing since Mum accidentally posted her camera roll to my Instagram.

Being stuck at Black Bay for the rest of the week meant missing Saturday. The event of the year. My best friend's sixteenth birthday party. Mum couldn't see what the big deal was, as the day before we left, on Rach's actual bday, the three of us had spent an awesome day together, completing her fifteenth year bucket list by having pizza for breakfast, lunch and dinner. But Saturday was The Big One. An epic night, complete with parentless house, a playlist that's been six months in the making, the most Ben and Jerry's ever seen in one freezer – and absolutely, completely zero me.

I pulled my duvet further over my head to hide the

glow of my phone as I tried to load Maps again. Even if I'd started walking home this second, I wouldn't make it back till two days after the party finished. And that was without time to sleep, eat or share pics of my epic journey (while probably doing impressions of Frodo Baggins). My fate was sealed. Half term was officially now barf term. So instead of adventuring across hill and dale, I ventured across rug and small pile of my pants to retrieve the sock full of caramel Digestives I'd smuggled out from the house. As silently as I could, I munched my way through four toes' worth of biscuits, wondering just how bad party FOMO was going to be.

But little did I know that at that very same moment someone else was thinking about the party. And their perfect plan to make it the biggest disaster of my life.

TWO

Can weather laugh at you? Because as if this holiday, or more precisely hell-iday, hasn't been bad enough, it's been raining for four days solid. NOT FUNNY, CLOUDS. You've turned my bob into head pubes.

Why couldn't Black Bay be one of those parks that Lou (a girl in our year that got boobs two years before anyone else) goes to every summer that sound like a real-life version of *Hollyoaks* (but in a good way, without the sporadic multiple-murders). I'm the youngest person here, except for children (and they don't count, as I'm not hanging out with anyone who eats nose-morsels). Eurgh. I swear the best entertainment here has been the daily food-poisoning gamble of eating the buffet. Still, on the bright side, I did an excellent job of getting out of the life drawing class that Mum and Jo are at. I pleaded that I needed to work on my fancy dress outfit for tonight. It sounded slightly more dignified than, 'AS IF I'M GOING TO SAY YES TO SEEING MY FIRST EVER MAN-DANGLE IRL IN THE COMPANY OF YOU TWO?!'

I stabbed at the cardboard cereal boxes I was using for my costume, as if they were to blame for this evening. We've been looking forward to Rachel's sixteenth ever since I met her. Which was basically birth.

Rachel, AKA Rach, is one half of my two best friends, Tegan and Rach. (She's obvs the Rach half). Three's an odd number, but so what? It works for us. They're my person-equivalent of breathing and have kept me sane since for ever. I sometimes wonder if I know more about them than I do about myself. Like, Tegan is so on-it and brilliant, she'll probably run the country one day. And she can do the splits both ways. Not that she'd do that if she was Prime Minister – she only does it when she's competing with her gymnastics team. And she wears socks that have days of the week on them (she sews on the days herself, but never wears the same day on each foot).

Rachel is always happy and always smiling (and

always looking like a search result for #lifegoals) and she makes us laugh every single day. She's constantly doing dead arty things, like painting pictures of dogs, but only using triangles. Our art teacher saw one and put it forward for an award, which it won, even though they hung it upside down. When Rach isn't sketching, or painting, she'll be curled up with her head in a book, which is weird because for all the words that go in, some really nonsensical ones come out. She also has an extreme phobia of when fork prongs get stuck together in cutlery drawers, and can't walk past squirrels (she says she was once bitten by one, but her dad insists it was their neighbour's hamster gone wild).

Rachel has The Best parties too, and that's when they're just normal ones. This one's been a full year in the planning. She's got an insanely great house, and her mega-loaded parents will make sure it's the kind of evening Kendall and Kylie would turn up to. I'd die for parents like that, instead of a mum who thinks the height of hospitality is splashing out on upgrading to non-supermarket brand cheese puffs. Eurgh. It's more gutting than a fishmongers' convention.

I checked my phone. No pre-party update from either of them. I put it back on the floor, trying to will it into action with threatening glances. Mum reckons

I'm chained to my phone, but it's not my fault no one had invented interesting technology in her day. She just had wood and washing machines and kettles and boring stuff like that.

I chopped open another cereal box. If Tegan and Rach were here, we'd have found a way to make Black Bay fun. Props to Jo for trying. She's in on tonight's Project: Survive The Evening, and once she gets back from her class she's taking me to the campsite's Pop-Swop Night to take my mind off the party. It's fancy dress karaoke, which isn't exactly an amazing house party with all my friends, or the *X Factor* tour at Wembley, but it'll do. It's not as if anyone else has to ever find out; what happens at Black Bay Caravan Park stays in Black Bay Caravan Park.

Must. Not. Look. At. Phone. It's so hard, though; my eyes are magnetically drawn to it. Lucky they're attached, or they might fly out and cling to it, like some sort of freaky all-seeing iron filings. It's not even a phone any more, just a ticking torture device. Last time I looked it was 8.28 p.m. – *if* I can just hold off looking till 10 p.m. then I'll have made it through the first third of the party. Based on pre-party gossip (Mikey told Rach who told Tegan who told me), Luke's probably going to cop off with Lou, the school trophy snog. Bothered? Me? Well, yes, obvs, but I'm not going to admit that to anyone. I wish I wasn't even admitting it to myself, but I'm hard to lie to.

I can't believe I used to go out with Luke. He puts the 'ex' in 'extreme idiot'. That doucheball was my first actual proper boyfriend. I'd been so excited to get together with him, but turns out he's a total disaster that should only be available to girls who have successfully passed the level five boy-handling exam. I haven't even graduated from level one, which is just the basics of non-sweaty hand-holding, and understanding the appeal of cricket. I am a boyfriend first-baser, and Luke is the sort of boy Taylor Swift could get at least three songs out of.

Luke and I haven't spoken since just before Christmas when he'd responded to my suggestion that maybe we needed to see each other a bit less, by laughing in my face and telling me I'd been a joke to him all along. Word soon got round, and I ended up getting actual high-fives in the corridor for being the first girl ever to turn the tables and dump him. I was so fuming at Luke, I never bothered to correct them. Eurgh. I would like to Ctrl-Z his whole existence please.

*

15

8.30 p.m. DammitIlooked. I'm so rubbish at keeping promises to myself. I must promise to do better in future.

I wonder what was already happening? Was Lou already functioning as a human mirrorball in one of her trademark glittery boob tubes? Was Mikey finally going to tell Tegan how he felt? Had Rach already accidentally broken someone's heart? It's not that she means to be mean, she couldn't be mean if she tried, it's just what happens when you look like a walking version of a Disney princess. Her hair looks like it's blowing in the wind, even when she's indoors. Although she'd get a U for common sense. She once said to me, 'I know April Fool's Day is the first day of a month, but I can never remember which one?'

8.32 p.m. Argh. How has only two minutes gone by since I last checked?! Will this torture never end? At least I know what missing out on the most important social event of the year feels like. Kind of like being too ill to get out of bed at Christmas, but multiplied by one million.

Hurry up, tomorrow, when I can be back home. It's cringe that I'm excited about going back to Appleton. It's my dive of a nothing-to-do and nothing-to-see village, whose only highlight is that we have a weird rock, which if you look at it from an exact angle resembles William Shakespeare. Sadly, that is only interesting for 0.5 seconds, and I've had to live there for 15.5 years, which is quite a lot of seconds more. Thank goodness the others live there or I'd probably have already become Britain's Youngest Hermit, which sounds like the name of a TV show I'd probably watch while being one.

I picked off a rogue cornflake which had glued itself to my knee and tried to focus on tearing up the cereal boxes for my DIY costume. It should really be called BPDDIY – Bella Please Don't Do It Yourself (as it's potentially the worst idea I've had yet). As I glued down flaps of cardboard, blobbed on spots of nail varnish, I reassured myself that this bad idea was a good one.

BEEP.

FINALLY! Information from the outside world. But the name on my screen hit me like a tennis ball in the boob. Luke. Why oh why did God invent mobiles?! And why does He enable intermittent reception in caravan parks when He can't manage decent hot water or food that isn't beige? Priorities, please, beardy one. Maybe he'd bum-messaged me by accident (Luke, not God). I opened it up. Two words.

Guess who? 😉➤

There was something else. A picture. A picture that made my insides knot before my mind had even figured out what was happening. Proof I really do think with my stomach.

If only there was an emoji for throwing up on a caravan floor. There on my phone, invading my space, my eyes, was Luke. Doing what he does best. Thumbs up. Winking at the camera. Not paying any attention to the poor girl he was kissing, cos as always, it was all about him. *Was it Lou?* All I could see was the back of a wide brimmed purple hat, which was more fabric than Lou would normally wear on her whole body. But why send it to me? We hadn't managed eye contact, let alone phone contact, since we split up, so why start messaging me all of a sudden? Did he think I'd be bothered? I totally am, but how dare he think that! None of it made sense.

I rang Rach. Answer machine. No replies to my messages either, same for Tegan. I even called Mikey, even though he can't form sentences if it's over a verbal communication device. Crapballscrapballscrapballs.

I shouldn't care what Luke does. It wasn't like I liked him any more. So why did I feel so gross about it? Out of everyone in the world, it should be easy to understand myself, but I swear there's a secret bit of my body that hides away information from my own brain, eurgh.

Whatever happens, I MUSTN'T reply. He'd think I cared. And it doesn't matter what I *really* think, but it really *does* matters what he thinks I think. WWBD? What would Beyoncé do? Yes, I was a strong, independent woman, who could rise above being stuck in solitary caravan confinement while my ex prods at my pride.

Guess who cares, more like.

Oops. As soon as I sent it I regretted it. Well, I regretted it before I sent it, but it takes more than concrete logic to stop me making bad decisions. So, I was a strong independent woman with the willpower of someone who once threw up after eating an entire tin of Quality Street. I don't even like strawberry creams.

My phone beeped.

Hope ur ok. Don't panic but Luke telling peeps he snogged T ☺. Not true. Repeat NOT TRUE. Long story – explain when ur back. DO NOT WORRY. Battery dying. Miss u. R xxx

WHAT THE WHAT?! When World War II erupted, did Winston Churchill, or whoever, just text the UK saying, 'Ooh, look out, there might be a spot of trouble brewing?'

How could Rachel drop a text-bomb like this on me? She knows I'm a sensitive (by that, I mean unbalanced) individual. What 'long story'? And why couldn't she plug her phone in?!

I studied Luke's picture. Last time I looked, the hat was just a piece of headgear; now it was an evidence-obscurer. Who *was* he kissing? And why pretend it was the one person in the world who we both knew would never snog him? I ignored the niggling doubt that made me zoom right in just to see if I could spot a glimpse of Tegan's black hair. But there was nothing to be seen except Luke's smug face. I forwarded it to Rachel.

**WTW is this? I'm FREAKIN out. Ring me!
RING ME.**

I waited about fifteen seconds. I sent the same to Tegan. Nothing.

Are you getting my messages? Ring me! It's urgent x 1000000000.

Didn't they understand the urgency?

NOW.

Was that too demanding? I messaged an extra 'please' just in case. But no matter how much I wafted my phone, no delivery notifications would come through. Had they even sent?

In frustration I slammed the nearest thing to me down on the table. Unfortunately, it was an opened box of Cheerios, which flew over me like breakfast-based confetti.

But as I flicked off the main offenders, I was oblivious that I'd still be picking them out of my pants when I met the boy of my dreams.

CHAPTER

THREE

"Er, please tell me that isn't the most disgusting rash I've ever seen?"

Jo has a habit of choosing the worst moments to show her face. And her grey eyes were wide open, staring straight at a clump of Cheerios stuck to my armpit.

"And why are you standing on a chair with your arms in the air?" She eyed me suspiciously. I flicked the armpit Cheerios on to the table. Totally still eatable.

"Sending a message." I continued to wave my phone above my head, ignoring the alarming watercolour of a naked man she'd casually thrown down on to the sofa. She really had paid attention to detail. Too much detail.

"Right..." She gave me the slightly disapproving-yet-patronizing look that makes up eighty per cent of her entire look repertoire. "What's up *this* time?"

"Just party stuff. . . It's complicated." Still no signal.

"What kind of complicated? I'm currently averaging 92 per cent in my degree; I think I *might* be able to get whatever it is." Then it dawned on her. "Ohhhh. Is it boy-complicated?"

"Maybe."

"Maybe yes, or maybe no?"

"Maybe yes, all right! I just got a weird message from Luke and it's making me lose my mind a bit."

She looked me up and down, which is easy to do when someone's standing on a chair. "Did you lose it *so* much you didn't realize you seem to be rocking a combo of cardboard, comedy pants and *my* vest top. Which I can't seem to remember us ever talking about?"

"They're pug pants."

"It's *my* vest top."

"It's the start of my costume."

"And it's *my* vest top."

She was so annoying.

"Cowbag."

"Thief."

"Sssshhh. Can't you see I'm having a breakdown?

Stop nagging me, and start telling me everything's going to be fine."

"Everything's going to be fine."

"No! With conviction."

"I don't lie. Nothing is *ever* fine with you . . . and it's *my* vest top."

I pulled out a chair and sat cross-legged so she couldn't spot my de-furred legs and figure out I'd finally found where she'd hidden her razor. The distraction worked, and I avoided discovery. She sat down beside me, and I took a deep breath.

"So, apaz Luke's saying he snogged Tegan."

"No way!" Her genuine shock reassured me.

"Way."

So it *was* weird. Jo knows as well as I do that Tegan's one of the good people. The kind that have nice eyes and play wing defence in netball. She's also the person who can always be relied on to sort party drama, not cause it. Jo doesn't know, but I do, that Tegan also calls Luke 'Puke', and surely you can't willingly put a tongue in someone who is human vomit?

"I can kinda see why you're freaking out."

"I'M NOT FREAKING OUT!"

Jo raised her eyebrow at my frantic phone wafting.

"Of course you're not."

24

"Look, there's probably a logical explanation. You know what it's like when parties get out of hand."

"Not really. . ." Unless she meant Mum's overnight Pilates parties, but they're just full of foot smells and people offering us green tea.

"Stupid stuff *always* happens. That's what parties are for. For things that would never happen in real life."

I walked the one metre across our caravan and lay on the sofa, closing my eyes like I was in an American therapy session.

"Pleeeease tell me I'm the subject of a hidden camera show, just that there aren't any cameras and this isn't funny?"

"I . . . can't do that. Have you tried ringing them?"

"Obvs. No answer."

"Ahh, so is *that* who you're messaging?"

"Can see why you're doing so well in your exams."

"Oi, I'm *trying* to help. Show me your phone."

I showed her the crucial messages, carefully obscuring the slightly manic ones I'd sent since.

"Look, it's probably not that bad. I was once in a similar situation."

"You were?"

"Well, not quite, cos I've only really been out with boys that have liked me more than I've liked them."

THANKS FOR THE REMINDER, PERSON WHO EVEN LOOKS GOOD SLEEP-DRIBBLING. She carried on oblivious to my mental gagging.

"Anyway, a boy I once liked – you know, Owen, the actor one? – well, after we'd been out a few times, he ended up pulling Rosanna."

Rosanna was Jo's best mate, and one half of their award-winning cross-country running duo, RoJo. This *could* actually be a useful insight for a change.

"We ended up talking it through, and seeing the funny side – that we'd both been taken in by a man whose day job was dressing up as a hamburger." She laughed at the *hilarious* memory. "So always remember the rule. BFs before boyfs."

Am I seriously the only person alive whose sister is basically a walking talking personification of inspirational internet quotes, which people like, but no one actually does? I rolled my eyes under my shut eyelids.

"No offence. But you two are not normal. And anyway, Tegan didn't even snog him, 'member?"

"Either way, there's nothing you can do about it from here, so there's no point obsessing over it."

"I'm not obsessing. I'm just thinking about it. Deeply. A lot of the time."

"Well, why don't you deeply think about something you *can* control, like taking off my top, or at least putting on some more of your costume so I don't have to look at your bum any more. Or . . . you could stay in on your own and wave your phone for the next three hours, but I doubt you've got the upper arm strength for that."

What a choice. Rock. Hard place. But if Jo wasn't going to let me wallow privately, I'd just have to do it publicly. I looked at the rest of my cardboard creation, which was taking up almost all of our floor space. A giant arrow shape, taller than me, constructed out of all the red cereal boxes I'd dug out of our bin (and maybe some other people's bins too), with a special circle cut out for me to poke my face through. Despite my best efforts, it not only looked a bit rubbish, but smelt a bit of it too. Oh well.

When I'd strapped the prototype to my body earlier, Mum didn't instantly guess that I was obviously dressed as 'a tribute to the beautiful memory of One Direction'. Although, maybe she just wouldn't know a giant comedy pop reference if it hit her. Which it then accidentally did. Oh well, if I did have a full-on breakdown, at least I was basically an easy-to-find walking version of Google Maps.

With my phone in constant line of sight, I opened up three fresh roles of sellotape and began securing the creation to my body. One hundred and twenty-four phone checks, five Beyoncé power anthems, four Cheerios in surprisingly difficult to reach places, three emotional breakdowns and an unhealthy amount of talcing and vertically backcombing my hair later, I was ready to go.

If messaging Luke was my first big mistake of the evening, throwing myself into this look was my second. I tugged at my outfit, feeling like a cross between a lamp post and a red Monopoly house. I'd had to do up Jo's belt so tight to help secure it, I was risking oxygen deprivation.

"Jo. Be honest. Are you *sure* people will get it?"

Jo looked at me like honesty wasn't the best policy.

"Look. The worst they can do is stand and point. And you're already kinda doing that anyway."

I nodded as if this was reassuring but almost knocked the ceiling light off with my giant pointy head. This must be how aliens feel.

"Guess the only way is up? Isn't it time you got changed?"

"Into what? You've nicked the red top I was going to wear. I'll just go as one of last year's *X Factor* rejects."

"But no one here will remember who they are?"

"Exactly." She'd picked up her arguing technique from Mum – confuse and conquer. "Trust me, you'll feel loads better when we're there, and everyone's all dressed up. You *know* that weirdo family who always wear matching trousers will have gone way more OTT than you."

Feeling entirely self-conscious, but also desperate to distract myself, we headed out. We were both in Jo's shoes – easy for her, harder for me, who is two sizes smaller. We walked/tottered (Jo/me) our way out to the events hall, unaware that witnessing tone deaf OAPs gyrating to Brie-anna (a cheese-based tribute duo) would soon be the very least of my worries.

Words cannot express how embarrassing it was walking through the heavy wooden double doors into the way-too-brightly-lit party room. If there was an Olympic medal for Simultaneous Conversation Stopping, I would currently be on a podium collecting it. The door even creaked extra loudly just to help focus everyone's attention on me. Not that you need any help getting attention when you're dressed as a giant arrow. Of the hundred people gathered there, not one other person had gone in fancy dress.

A woman in office-wear scurried over, an enthusiastic smile plastered on her face, the exact opposite of the horrified one on mine.

"Ooh, loves, look at you." She said 'you' plural, but clearly meant 'you, the girl in the cardboard monstrosity'. "Don't you just look ... *something*. So sweet of you to make the effort, even though we posted that memo about fancy dress just being for the staff."

Standing in the middle of a multitude of ageing couples who were very much not wearing giant arrow costumes was not the ideal time to discover this. MEMO TO THE ROOM – I DID NOT GET THE MEMO. Office-wear woman continued.

"We decided to call off fancy dress for the guests when our most enthusiastic family had to head home after one of their children got concussion running repeatedly into a brick wall."

Oh. My. Cod. Matching-trouser-child had managed to hospitalize himself in what was surely an ingenious escape plan. Why had I not thought of this?

Over-friendly office-wear lady did a slow 360 spin. "I'm Mariah Carey, see?"

I did *not* see, unless Mariah had a second job as a doctor's receptionist. I shot daggers at Jo. How could

30

she not have checked?! "And full marks to you for your fab arrow outfit. Are you a . . . Pointer Sister?"

I was shaking so much with rage and humiliation that I looked like a wobbly compass needle.

"I. AM. OBVS. A TRIBUTE TO THE BEAUTIFUL MEMORY OF ONE DIRECTION."

Oh excellent. My volume control had taken a mini-break along with my dignity.

Jo mouthed 'sorry', but unless she had Doctor Who skills, 'sorry' was not going to wipe the memories of everybody in the room. Even the mini sausage rolls looked like they were laughing at me. My eyes prickled the pre-cry warning.

Two options. Stand and cry, or storm off.

I kept it classy, and did both, scoring extra loser points for my staccato hiccup crying voice as I yelled at Jo for not reading the memo.

Back home my real life was being ruined by my ex-boyf, and now my holiday life was an utter shambles too. Sympathetic looks coming in from all angles, I bent myself sideways out of the wooden door (taking out one entire line of bunting in the process) and stormed back to the caravan. All I wanted to do was crawl into my table/bed and hide from the world.

Now, I don't know how I forgot that I didn't have

any keys, but I did. Probably something to do with having the worst night of my life. So I had to do an extra half a mile detour stomp to the restaurant where Mum was meant to be enjoying 'Losing Your Veg-inity' (their annual vegan dating night). It's actually quite exhausting doing a long distance storm-out, but I had to keep it up in case Jo saw me walking normally and figured I was over it.

I would NEVER be over this.

Luckily, there was hardly anyone in the restaurant block. Unluckily that included my mum, who was nowhere to be seen. Sweeping the floor was a disinterested waiter, who chose to ignore what I was wearing, and that I had more mascara down my face than on my eyes, and reeled off a message from my mum. Apparently 'she was out all night, with her phone off, finding inner peace practising "Yoga through the Menopause", and there was some tuna in the fridge if I was hungry'. Why did I have to have the maniac-fifty-something-hippy mum, not the totally-normal-taking-us-to-Spain-for-a-week-in-the-summer mum?

I stomped back out into the freezing night. Now what?! Was going back to the warmth of Pop-Swop better or worse than slowly dying of hypothermia? I hobbled to the hall to assess the options. A man was on stage announcing that they were moments away from the delights of Pearls Allowed (the OAP girlband), Oldplay (clue's in the title) and BigMacFly (a Weight Watchers cover band). Hypothermia won. Resigned to waiting for Mum to finish posing like a post-menstrual panda, I trudged back to the caravan.

The park seemed foggier than usual. Or was it just talcum powder billowing out of my hair? There was also a gross smell of pickled pear drop. I sniffvestigated, only to discover it was me. Wow, embarrassment sweats had upgraded my Loserdom to 4D. Still, I had to keep warm, or I might die, and then all over the world they'd publish my underwhelming life story alongside one of my awful school photos.

Maybe I could try some basic PE stuff. That could help? I flung my arms and legs around trying to remember what Mrs Nyatanga taught us. What was it . . . grape vine? Spotty dog. Yeah, this was working. And the way my costume was bobbing around was kind of funny. Ski jumps. Jumping Jacks. And I did feel a *bit* warmer.

But one simple high kick later and I'd frozen solid.

One simple high kick later and I was staring at a life in jail.

Exercise is bad for your health. Fact.

CHAPTER

FOUR

"Your elbow's in my groin." A man-voice was coming out of my ribcage. Surely not even the most advanced stomach could rumble sentences?

"Sorry, could you possibly move? Your elbow really is in my groin."

Argh, it wasn't a man-voice. It was an actual man. And it just said the word 'groin'. To me. As if strangers should ever say 'groin' to each other.

Sorry, Bella. Back up. What *had* happened in the last fifteen seconds? I thought back. One particularly enthusiastic jumping jack – yup. Heel stuck in the mud – check. Losing my balance like a comedy cartoon character – done. Sailing through the air, legs akimbo – achieved. Shoe flying off like a glittery missile – kap-ow. And the final cherry on the cringe-cake? Landing full force on a big boney cushion – AKA an actual human. Oh excellent.

I looked like a mad woman – and one who thought it was OK to play spontaneous horizontal musical statues with strangers. But who, *or what*, was beneath me?

I looked down and freaked out as I couldn't see a thing. Had the fall knocked out my sight?! But as I felt around in the dark, I realized with massive relief that the giant arrow bit had just fully flapped over the hole for my face. Phewphs. I yanked it off and squinted at my human landing pad, trying to make out some features. It had hair. Scruffy, brown hair. It had a face. A squashed and wincing face. And as it came into focus, I made out something far more terrifying. It had a squashed, wincing and undeniably *fit* face. WTWOMG.

Was my man-mattress actually Louis Tomlinson? Had I squashed The Tommo to death!? Harry was going to kill me. Who knew they holidayed in Wales? The news report was totally going to use that school photo of me now.

"Err, it's actually starting to hurt quite a bit."

I lifted my head up off my landing cushion, chest,

whatever, and assessed the crime scene. My elbow was digging into something sort of warm, squishy, and . . . in his jeans. The area that shall not be named!! Mortification! This is not how my first boy-part contact was meant to be. I plucked my elbow out of the danger area and scrambled to my foot. It would be feet, but only one of them was in contact with the floor, the shoeless one could only dangle two inches above ground.

"Ughghgorry."

Instead of apologizing, I sounded like I was trying to simultaneously gargle while getting tickled. As the attack-ee stood up, I got visual crush confirmation. Attack-ee was a lean, mean, scruffy haired fit-machine – and I'd potentially caused him organ damage. Not ideal. Must try again.

"Ughghgorry. I'm gory. Soggy. Sorgy. I'm sorry."

Attack-ee was patting down his jeans, so luckily didn't see my face giving my mouth evils for being so lame. Come on, guys, work together, you're a team.

"Don't worry about it, these things happen."

They do? Shoe projectiles and spontaneous mountings might be a common occurrence to him but it's deffo a first for me. But if he could play it cool, so could I.

"I was just doing some jumping jacks. To keep

warm. Because I'm locked out. And I'm only really wearing cardboard. Which might sound a bit like cardigan. But is nowhere near as warm. And is a terrible choice of clothing. Unless you're an actual cornflake. Which I'm not."

He didn't reply.

Must knock 'playing it cool' off the list of talents I previously wondered if I had. I looked up. Wow, he was proper tall. About six inches taller than me. (Even wearing one heel. Me, not him.)

"And I wasn't throwing myself at you. On you. I just tripped. I promise. I wasn't . . . being a weirdo or anything."

Attack-ee looked bemused. Argh. Had I left gaps between those words, or just delivered the world's longest mono-word? Was he going to dial 999?

My fate hung in the balance as he calmly straightened the collar of his denim jacket and brushed down his grey jumper that was peeping out underneath.

"Well, that's good to know. All makes perfect sense now." He laughed like a horse warming up pre-neigh – but in a hot way. My stomach lurched like when my mum goes 25mph over the small bridge by our house. Had I made a real life discovery of a specimen of Boy-Shouldus-Be-In-A-Band-Ius?

I tried not to stare at him as he picked bits of grass out of his ruffled hair. Out of all the no-hopers at Black Bay, why did I have to achieve my most mortifying accomplishment in front of this unique specimen?

"I'm so embarrassed. I didn't mean to do *any* of that. And now look – you've soiled yourself." His eyebrows shot up. "Not soiled! I meant like, earthed. Like grounded. Like dirted..." Someone invent a mouth filter for me, please.

"MUD!" I shrieked. "Yes, I meant you got mud on yourself." We both flinched. Him because I bellowed in his ear. Me at having a Eureka moment remembering a three-letter word. Could I pretend English wasn't my first language? Sure, if I had the ability to think of a single country more obscure than France. I don't.

"Are you OK? You look more weirded out than me. And I've just been hit in the face by a shoe..."

Oh great. The flying shoe had hit him. I'd been hoping things could get even more cringe. He looked me up and down.

"... all while dressed as a giant ... Cheerio?"

The horror of being labelled as the notorious Black Bay's Sex Pest Shoe Attacker had made me numb to what a total dork I must look. Without the arrow bit, I was basically just a lone-girl dressed as a cereal box and smelling a bit of bins.

"I'm SO sorry. I'm not a complete loon. Promise. This is fancy dress." It should really be called no-one-will-ever-fancy-me dress. "I don't normally wear food packaging." Hope that was stating the obvious. "It *was* an arrow. Now it's pointless." A bit like me trying to explain myself. "I was just pretending to be One Direction. As in not *them*. Not the boys. I mean, I can't even grow a beard. Or dance. Or sing. I'm just their name. Well, I was until I squashed half of the arrow off. I mean, are you even OK? Please don't report me."

Attack-ee pointed at the large purpley bruise above his left eye. Some shoe glitter twinkled on it. Was that glitter embedded?! Oh great, I'd not only injured him, I'd permanently accessorized him.

"And who would I report you to? I don't *think* the police have a department for crimes of landing on people." He smiled. He must be pretty laid back to be taking this in his stride. "Although you do kind of look like a cereal killer. . ." Oh ha, very ha. ". . . and if they've caught it on CCTV, it'll be a most excellent YouTube vid."

Oh, the relief! Attack-ee wasn't going to press charges! Attack-ee watched terrible videos too! I

39

giggled. It came out like a three-year-old child's, so I lowered it to sound more alluring and sophisticated, but sounded like Father Christmas instead. Attack-ee took a more traditional approach to silence-filling and made conversation.

"So . . . have you only just arrived? I haven't seen you about?" Aaaah, a Liverpool twang to his voice. Northern accents make me all melty like a human toasted cheese sandwich.

"No, I've been here for a few days – but haven't seen you about either." Obviously, as one sighting of him and I'd have been sleeping under his caravan. "We're leaving tomorrow – THANK GOODNESS."

He looked fake hurt.

"All right, Black Bay's biggest fan?! It's my fifth time here. . ."

Cringe. Why couldn't I be less insulting with my insults?

". . . and none of them have been near death experiences for me – yet. Although more recently some stranger attacked me in the dark with some footwear. Don't know if you remember that one?" He looked even cuter when he was teasing me.

I shrugged my shoulders back at him, although all he saw was my arrow bob up and down.

40

"Nope, no recollection. Sounds awful though. You should let someone know, they sound dangerous." I smiled. Maybe I *had* been too harsh. If Black Bay was good enough for this McFittie's biscuit, it was good enough for me. "On second thought, you know, thinking about it more carefully, maybe it's not *that* bad here."

"My gran's been coming here since she was little. That's why we come back every year for her birthday. So ... putting your total overwhelming-under-enthusiasm to one side, it *would* have been a nice change to have had someone to hang out with who was born in the same decade as me. Or even century."

Did he mean me? Was this fit boy saying it would have been nice to have hung out with *me*? Could I somehow get him to repeat this – on camera?

"Sorry, do you mean *me*?"

It splurted out.

"Erm, yes?" He'd definitely noticed that I wasn't normal.

"Cool."

'Cool' was the understatement of the century. Ten minutes earlier I'd been counting down every second till we left, now I reckoned I could permanently live in a place where my bed played hide and seek. Plus, he thought I was his age, whatever that was.

"Aaaaaanyway, let's start at the start. What's your name – or can't you tell me as you're a highly skilled undercover agent, disguised as a box of breakfast?"

"Ha. Ha. I'm Bella. With zero special skills. Although I can get all five of my foot toes in my mouth." Overshare. I hadn't even attempted it since I was seven. "People call me Bells for short." Luke also calls me Blobfish or Fishy Balls, but I didn't feel I needed to offer all options.

"Well hello, Bella slash Bells slash foot chewer. . ." He put his hand out. Making full contact with his brown eyes made me all limp inside, like a school canteen baguette. "I'm Zac."

So the love of my life was called Zac. Good to know who I was going to be obsessing over for the next for ever. I smiled up at him.

"Nice to meet you toooooo." I accidentally did a ghost impression, as my body involuntarily shivered, like a little human earthquake.

Zac didn't flinch and flicked off his jacket.

"Here." He swished it over my shoulders, as if him catching hypothermia for a girl he'd just met was no big deal. "In the words of someone very profound, the cold never bothered me anyway."

I swooned so much I even felt it in my liver.

"And if you're locked out, how about we go somewhere a bit more sheltered? I could show you a spot that none of the oldies ever make it to? Kind of my own personal hideout."

I nodded slowly and tried to squeeze out a normal reaction, but I was so overwhelmed with the excellence of this idea that I just sounded like Siri.

"Yeah ... seeing a ... new bit of Black Bay ... sounds ... good." By 'good' I meant, best idea ever suggested in the world ever, including the invention of Daim Bar Dairy Milk.

So, off we limped – him from injury, me because I only had one shoe on. As we meandered towards the wood, I figured that with such a disastrous start things could only get better. But the only destination I was hurtling towards was the capital of Cringe City, population: me.

CHAPTER

FIVE

So here I was. Just casually picking my way through a tiny forest path with the world's fittest man. As you do, Bella, as you do.

"So, er, what do you do when you're not being hit in the face by strangers?" Fingers crossed he wasn't going to say 'kidnapping people in forests'. Or line-dancing.

"Well, that's kind of a full-time thing." Oh, great. Fit AND funny. "But, when I *do* take a break from it, I'm mainly at college." Soooo he was at college. He did look older. "Or working on some prints. I spend half my life covered in paint."

So he was a hottie arty type. I got a body tingle – bingle – in a way I'd never felt before. Probably the lesser-sighted-sexy-art-boy bingle – very hard to come by in Appleton, where the majority of boys think the highest form of creativity is weeing a pattern into snow.

"Oh, cool." I said, ducking under a branch that he'd stopped to pull out of my way. "What kind of, er, prints do you print?" I was completely clueless, but knew the golden rule is to always show an interest.

"It depends really. Kind of abstract stuff, expressionism. You know."

"Yeah, yeah." Obvs I had no clue. The only expressionism I knew was the intelligent expressionism I hoped was currently on my face. If only Rachel was here to help; she's got a room full of books all about art (that up until now I've artfully avoided).

"Enough about me. What do you do?"

Gulp. What *do* I do?! I could hardly say that most of my time is spent making gifs of animals sneezing.

"You know. Stuff... Life stuff." I nodded as if this held deep meaning. "And, erm ... listening to music?" Could I *be* more generic?

"Me too. Obsessed." His eyes sparkled, real-life dimples peeping through on his cheeks as he smiled. He must love music as much as me, which is a relief as it's kind of a deal-breaker when I'm deciding if a person is excellent or not. Although those dimples could probably renegotiate any deal. "What was the last gig you went to?"

Oh no, straight back on to shaky ground. Does being forced into accompanying my mum to an ABBA tribute count as a gig?

"Wow, last gig?" I pretended to be racking my brain through all the totally awesome gigs I'd been to, while blocking out the glimpse of Pearls Allowed attempting to twerk. He *definitely* thinks I'm older than I am. "Think it was All Time Low." By *think*, I mean, *definitely wasn't, but I have watched enough of them on YouTube to probably carry this off*. Same could be said for 1D, but Zac didn't look like a coordinated-canoe-paddle-dance-move kind of a guy.

"Nice. I could *not* get tickets for their last tour. You must have friends in high places!"

"Yeah, it was pretty amazing." Not technically a lie, as the videos were definitely taken by people in very high places – like one or two rows from the back.

"So, what do you do at college?"

Uh-oh. The college clanger. There was no way I could come clean about still being in school. I didn't want him to add 'being younger than him' on to the ever-growing list of reasons that he is way out of my league and should not be speaking to me.

"I, er, do all sorts really. I mean, what *don't* I do?" Could I rhetorical-question my way out of this? Mum and Jo had taught me well.

"I know what you mean. It's crazy busy, isn't it, way too much like hard work for my liking." He stopped to brush some moss out of his hair. "So what *don't* you do then?"

"Well, I *don't* do French." This was true. I didn't do French at college. But I also didn't do anything else there, what with me not being at one.

"Wise choice. I kind of had to give up on the whole French thing when I discovered French cows say 'meuh' not 'moo' and then my mind was blown." What?! I really had never thought of this. Do animals say different things in different languages? How has this never come to my attention before?

Uh-oh. Panic. Bella, stop thinking about what dogs say in German. I can't pick anything he's studying in case he asks me about it. Could I gamble on science?

"I take, erm, c..."

WHACK. Ouch.

"OOOOOWWWWWW."

Saved by a massive branch in the face! Result! I'd been so paranoid about making his jacket smell sweaty that I'd kept my arms rigidly by my side and had somehow missed a branch the size of a sideways tree dangling at head height. Thank you, forest, for your tree-mendous work.

"Are you OK?!" Zac rushed to my side, brushing my hair back off my forehead looking for any sign of damage. Concerned-Zac face was maybe even more fit than happy-Zac face and teasing-Zac face combined. I must injure myself more often.

"I'm fine. I promise... It sounded worse than it was." I rubbed my head, even though it had already stopped hurting. "I was just a bit slow to twig on to it."

He laughed. I MADE HIM LAUGH.

"You all right to carry on?"

I nodded and followed after him. He was making an extra effort to make sure there were no hazards dangling in my way, like some kind of sexy safety superhero. We chatted about nothing and everything, although I was glad he dropped the college questions. I found out he was deffo seventeen (fit), lived in Wolverhampton (my new favourite place) and had a guitar called Keith (strangely alluring). Keith was also the name of his dog (a girl dog), but he couldn't pick which Keith was his favourite. He found out that I was almost seventeen (exact details seemed unnecessary), lived in Worcestershire, was obsessed with my camera

(I like arty things too! Love me!) and had a weird crush on Aslan from *The Chronicles of Narnia* (an unplanned panic blurt out that I would like to take back, please). He clearly won.

Ten minutes later, after squeezing our way through a falling down fence, we came to a stop. We were in the prettiest clearing overlooking a tiny lake. Who knew Black Bay could be so beautiful?!

"What did I tell you? The perfect place to hide from the organised fun." He stretched out on a rickety bench near the edge of the water. Did he know he was a walking album cover?

Right, me. Let me get this straight. On Tuesday when I'd been stumbling through a Zumba in the Dark class with my mum (where I may or may not have broken Jo's toe), this fittie had been minutes away looking all brooding and moonlighty? Life is so cruel.

I sat down, at what I hoped was an appropriately casual distance away. As he chatted, his face lit up by the moonlight, I took in every detail. He had an insane bottom lip that seemed to pout out, even when he was smiling. Just above his left dimple was a tiny scar that looked like he'd had it added on just to make his face less perfectly symmetrical. And his brown hair looked so good I had to stop myself from sniffing it. Now, I'm all for personality over appearance, but oh my gosh. He was *so* fit. Like, uncomfortably fit. He must have never had a normal conversation with a girl, ever. It's scientifically not possible to casually chat to a boy of such hotness. He didn't even seem aware that he shouldn't be wasting his time talking to someone like me. Instead he talked away about when he once messaged his mum about a game of Cluedo, telling her he was going to kick her butt, but it got auto-corrected to 'lick'. And how the first song Velvet Badger, his band (HE WAS IN A BAND, SWOON x 1 MIL), recorded was 'V is for Viennetta', an electronic-guitar ode to their love of ice-cream-based desserts. I laughed along, loving every second with him. Despite my severely lacking conversational skills, he made talking/listening feel easy. Even if I did bring it all to a stop by saying, "What's brown and sticky? A stick."

I'd only known him for under one earth hour, but felt able to talk to him about anything. That's probably why, despite everything in my brain saying 'no', my mouth ended up pouring out full deets about the message from Tegan. I'm not totally devoid of sense, though – obvs I pretended that the whole scenario was actually about Jo. He didn't need me verbally confirming I was boy-repellent. His man-brain perspective was useful, though. He said the same as Jo – I was reading too much into it. But when *he* said it, it felt like he meant it, and wasn't just trying to shut me down.

Zac shifted nearer to me on the bench giving me a full waft of his amazing man-smell. He smelt like how an underwear model holding a puppy looks. I bet all he's thinking about me is why am I shivering so much that I'm like a human phone on vibrate.

I rubbed my hands on my arms to warm myself up, catching an unwanted sight of my watch. How long could I ignore that panicky feeling in my stomach? It was almost midnight and Mum was probably having a very un-zen post-yoga meltdown. But I could hardly admit that to Zac and risk looking like I was either fifteen, or a seventeen-year-old whose mum had attachment issues. Could honesty be the best policy?

"Zac, sorry if this sounds lame, but I should probably be getting back." Well, half honesty. "I need to get up for dawn yoga with my mum." One quarter honesty. His eyebrows raised.

"Wow – dedicated. You must be pretty good?"

"Well, some people might say so." I wasn't sure who those people might be, as I wasn't even flexible enough to tie my shoelaces without sitting on the floor. "You know, downward dog, and pose of a, er, pigeon and all that."

Zac nodded like he'd never had a mum that had made him bend in such ways. My mouth continued to speak without sign-off from my brain.

"Every session ends in an argument, as Mum refuses to wear deodorant. She thinks it's a government conspiracy theory. It's mortifying. I die whenever we have to put our arms over our heads. Which is like, all the time."

Zac laughed.

"Everyone knows what it's like having a crazy family. Especially me."

"No offence, but I doubt they can be as bonkers as mine."

"You have *no* idea. You have nothing on me. Seriously." He shoved his hand in his pocket. "And I will use my last two per cent to prove it!"

He pulled out his phone and scrolled down the screen.

"Here you go."

THE TIME YOUR MUM COMES TO YOUR
FIRST COLLEGE ART EXHIBIT AND SHOUTS THAT
THE BIGGEST SCULPTURE 'COULD
HAVE BEEN DONE BY A YEAR 7'.
IT WAS DONE BY MY TUTOR.

What. I didn't get it. Was this him?

"Wait – is this *your* mum?"

He nodded. "Uh-huh. You want more?"

He swiped across.

THROWBACK THURSDAY:
THAT TIME WE ARRIVED LATE TO THE
CINEMA AND MY MUM SAT ON AN EMPTY
SEAT – THAT TURNED OUT TO HAVE A SMALL
CHILD ON IT. HE CRIED SO MUCH THEY
HAD TO RE-START THE FILM.

I snorted.

"Are these for real?"

"Yup, they're real and they're my life."

EVER TAKEN A LOVED ONE TO A&E
ONLY TO FIND OUT THE REASON THEY'D
PASSED OUT IS BECAUSE THEIR HOLDING-IN
PANTS ARE TOO TIGHT?

How had he turned out so normal?!

"Enough, enough! I can't believe you put this on the internet!"

Zac grinned. "Nah, it's just a silly app. All anonymous.

My mum's too funny not to share with the world, especially since Dad left and she's become a wannabe-cougar." I looked at the screen – 'PSSSST'. I hadn't heard of it.

"I waste loads of time on here, it cracks me up." I searched the screen for his username just as his screen disappeared. RIP battery. "Anyway, you're right. We should get back before your phone dies too, and I'm stuck alone in a forest with no one to save me from your next shoe rage."

He clearly couldn't read my mind that getting stuck alone with him, anywhere, was probably the best idea in the world.

I pushed myself up from the bench in a weird sideways style to try and shield him from my bum, which was currently eating my trousers. I'm so prone to buttock wedgies that Jo calls me 'Hungry Bum', or 'Bumgry' for short.

"Thanks for the jacket, now I feel a toasty minus 25 degrees, not minus 105."

"My pleasure. It was the least I could do for . . . for probably giving me some sort of massive face bruise?"

I laughed it off, which felt more reassuring than saying 'yes, it's officially ginormous'. He really didn't know the half of it. Thank goodness there weren't mirrors in woods.

"Hold up, if there was *hypothetically* a tiny, miniscule bruise, it *would* give you the perfect opp to think up a whole new story. Make out it was all part of some insanely brave deed?" Oh crapballs, I said 'make out'. Had he noticed? Change subject. "Shout if you see any hazards. I'm paro about stepping on a slug in my bare foot."

"Worry not, I'll protect you . . . or abandon you with slug oozing between your toes. One of the two."

"Prepare yourself for a full-on freak-out then."

He raised his eyebrows, as if challenging me. "Sounds interesting."

I tried to smile back, but his direct eye contact had paralysed my reacting muscles.

He lowered his voice.

"In fact, I think I'd quite like to see a full-on freak out. . ."

He put his hands either side of my arms. Now, I've seen this on *Hollyoaks*. Unless I was very much mistaken, he was either about to try some basic judo moves, or – and it was hard for me to possibly imagine this – or . . . or he was about to try. . . And. Kiss. Me. *An actual kissing situation.* With me. A random boy, a hot boy, an older boy, an extremely cool boy, a boy who had a guitar/dog called Keith, a boy who looked like I'd designed him on some kind of BoyfGoals app. A boy who definitely knew how to do kissing very well. And me. Who definitely didn't. Could I run away? If only Rach and Tegan were here for moral support. Although maybe a crowd of four would not make this less awkward. His hands didn't move. His eye contact didn't budge.

My heart was beating so hard he could probably hear it. I am NOT equipped to deal with kissing of boys. If I wrote a kisstory book, it would be one page long. And that's if I used really large font. And it had small pages. Zac CANNOT find out how tragic and inexperienced and not able to kiss, and not seventeen, I am.

Auto-pilot-Bella-panic kicked in. Talking absolute nonsense at double speed. If I talked with wild enthusiasm, it would be harder for his lips to hit a moving target.

"Sorrydidyounothearmeabouttheslug? Nothing's worsethanstandingonaslug." Breathe. "Becauseit'shard enoughtoknowwhenthey'realivewhenthey'realive, let alonewhenthey'resquishedonyourshoe." Breathe. "Andlikewhatdoslugs*do*anyway?"

Lucky boys are not like animals and can't smell fear. And they're not furry and don't have six nipples (I assume). MUST NOT think of Zac's nipples. This will not help anything.

He stepped nearer. What was wrong with him?! Did he find slug chat sexy? What a weirdo. I *knew* he couldn't be normal.

He took another step. His belt buckle pressed into one of the many cereal boxes that was stubbornly still hanging on to my body, making yet another piece of sellotape ping loose. Could I fake death? Or actually die. Anything other than him kissing me and me messing it up and him being embarrassed for me and me being even more embarrassed for me and us never speaking again.

He moved a hand to the back of my neck.

I needed days, weeks to prepare for this sort of thing. This was NOT FAIR. When had I brushed my teeth? Was it ages since I had put on my strawberry lip-balm, or was it too recent and I smelt like pudding? I hadn't breathed for thirty seconds; why hadn't I fainted yet? Why was my saliva the consistency of nail varnish that I'd left the lid off?

He pressed his lips into mine.

KISS ALERT. KISS ALERT. We had contact!

I, Bella Fisher, was being officially being kissed by the Grand High Lord Of Hotness and his sexy pouty bottom lip and equally as hot but less pouty top lip. Award for Happiest Moment Of My Life goes to NOW. (And also Most Terrifying, in a double winning twist.)

It felt soft, and warm, and amazing, and way better than two people just touching talking apparatus should feel. My head span with all the magazine tips I'd ever read. 'How to guarantee your first kiss won't be your last.' 'Be natural.'

BELLA.BELLA.BELLA.

'Don't use too much tongue.' 'Don't use too little tongue.' 'Lean.' 'Close eyes.' 'Don't bash teeth.' 'Don't panic about those weird suction noises or who was making them' (it was deffo me). 'Follow his lead.' 'Make your own leads.' 'Remember everything.' 'Don't overthink it.'

BELLA.BELLA. BELLS.

Jo?

BELLA. BELLINGTON BOOT.

I opened one eye to work out what was happening. All I could really see was Zac's stubbly (eek, stubble!) face so near mine he looked like one big fit blur. But something glinted at the edge of the clearing.

Something was pushing through the trees. Oh, holy meatballs. I knew EXACTLY what that something was.

"WOW – sorry. I didn't know I was interrupting anything."

Zac stepped back, confused. Probably his first ever sub-three second snog.

A hugely annoyed Jo crossed her arms.

I willed myself to disintegrate.

I'm pretty sure number one on the list of things not to do when snogging a hot boy is bite his tongue off. And number two is be interrupted by an older, and totally raging, sibling.

"Bella – I've been looking for you for HOURS. I've been worried sick."

Yup, Zac, I'm the kind of hot, independent girl who has to be babysat by her big sister. I couldn't bring myself to even look in his direction. I was so hot with embarrassment I worried I could ignite the last few bits of cardboard still clinging to my waist.

"Go. Away." I spat my words out.

Zac shuffled awkwardly. He made a little cough.

"Erm, sorry to be a bit slow. But what's going on here?"

"Good to know you can speak when you haven't got your tongue shoved down my little sister's throat."

AS IF SHE JUST SAID THAT. Could she BE any more awful? Please don't let my ears have heard right.

"Don't be such a cowbag. I'll see you back home." But she didn't move. ". . . OK?!"

Despite Jo being way out of order, Zac tried to break the tension.

"We *were* about to head back anyway?"

"Oh, were you? Cos Bella is coming back with me. NOW."

Jo grabbed my arm and tried to pull me away. I wrenched it free, but the damage had already been done. I was a total loser, and Zac had only needed ninety-five minutes to work it out.

Jo hissed "Come on" and ducked under the first branch.

I paused for a final glimpse of Zac. How had it gone so wrong so quickly?! Best moment ever had nose-dived to the worst. This was the first proper silence we'd had since we'd met.

Zac put his finger to his lips and whispered.

"Maybe it's a bad time, or whatever. But . . . lunch? Tomorrow?"

OUT-LOUD GULP. Sorry, what? I was not expecting that?! Has Fittie McFittington, who I'd kicked, talked to about slugs, half-snogged, and just been sister-shamed in front of, just asked to see ME? For a second time? I pinched myself to check this was real. Ouch. It hurt more that I meant it to. I looked up at Zac. He'd totally seen. He kindly pretended not to have seen the thing we both knew he just saw. "Up to you . . . no pressure?"

Maybe no pressure from him, but serious pressure from my future self to not make the worst decision of my life. I checked Jo was far enough away to be out of convo-range.

"Deffo. Let's do it." If it was 'up to me' I'd happily chain myself to his ankle on the spot, but that probably wouldn't help raise his opinion of me.

"Main block. Midday." Perfect. We weren't leaving till five. He gave me a short one-handed wave. How could he even look hot in silhouette?

I waved like a robot as I ran through hilarious options of what to say back. My first impression had been terrible, so I should make the last one a high. But Jo reappeared and grabbed at my wrist, nearly toppling me over a badly placed tree stump.

"WIX." I shouted back after him as I got dragged out of view.

No, Bella. No. Tell me your final word hadn't been an abbreviation of 'wicked'?!

Jo and I marched back to the caravan, hurling insults at each other. She couldn't believe I'd been 'soooo selfish', I couldn't believe she had deliberately ruined any chance I'd had with Zac.

When we finally got back, Mum was still out moonlight meditating, so Jo pushed me for details on exactly who Zac was. I told her I didn't want to talk about anything. She ignored me and asked me where her other shoe was. I told her I was a footwear freedom fighter and had returned it to the wild. I was going to be in big trouble when Mum was back.

Despite never feeling more awake, I climbed into bed, pulling the duvet over my head and pretending I couldn't hear Jo drone on 1.5 metres away. It was hard to be alone in a room which was three people's bedroom, kitchen and lounge.

I'd just had the best and worst night of my life and all I wanted to do was replay every Zac second – Zecond – that had happened. The way his hair got ruffled by all the twigs. The way his scar wiggled when he laughed. The way his jacket smelt. The way it felt when he'd half-kissed me... Although, I never wanted to replay the look on his face when Jo arrived. Was there *any way* he'd ever want to attempt an actual full snog ever again? Maybe if I made an amazing impression at the lunch. I looked at my watch. I did still have twelve hours to practise interesting conversation topics. I could even steal Jo's perfume so I smell a bit older.

I set my alarm for the picnic and drifted off to sleep, Zac running through my mind. But it wasn't my clock that woke me up, it was Mum – with the most alarming news.

CHAPTER

Six

11.30 a.m. – thirty minutes until the scene of the biggest-crush-crammed-total-love-packed-mind-meltingly-so-dreamy-and-hot-that-a-bit-of-sick-almost-comes-up-in-my-mouth-whenever-I-think-about-it moment my life will ever experience. AKA Zac time.

I should be counting down the 1800 seconds until I get to witness his fitness.

I should be planning how I can redeem myself for last night.

I should be putting the finishing touches to my mascara and checking for black eye bogies.

I should be getting Jo to take a video of me doing various everyday poses so I can check I haven't got VPL.

I should be about to meet up with the only boy who has ever swept me off my feet. (Well, technically, I swept him, but that's just detail.)

But I'm doing none of these things.

I'm panicking.

I'm losing my mind.

I'm on the verge of tears, but they're not coming cos I'm so angry they've got blocked somewhere in the system.

And I am SO mad at Mum.

Yesterday's snogteruption scores a ZERO in relation to this. This isn't just a step too far, it's a gold-medal-winning triple jump past the boundary of acceptable motheringdom. Today is the day I know for certain she officially doesn't care about my life.

Instead of what I *should* be doing, what I'm *actually* doing is staring at the back of Jo's head feeling sick because of the combination of Mum's bad driving and dealing with my life being ruined.

Can hearts actually stop when they realize there's no point in carrying on, cos the one chance they had at being happy in life has been abandoned in Wales?

NO work emergency is a good enough excuse for Mum waking me up at six a.m.. NO life crisis gives her the right to herd us out of the caravan in a frantic departure fifteen minutes later. I'm not a pot plant – I have rights! I can't just be transported against my wishes! Mum always nagged me to enjoy Black Bay, and now I finally was, we're 280 miles away.

"Come on, love. You have to say *something*. Or are you planning on keeping silent for the rest of your life?" This was Mum's fifth attempt at talking. Considering all of her spiritual development this week, she was still exceptionally bad at reading minds.

"I have nothing to say."

"You just said *that*." Eye-roll. How dare Jo say *I'm* behaving like a child, when she says stuff like that? Was she nineteen or nine? I kneed her chair. I hate them both right now.

I had a date. A real date. Well, sort-of date. With the best person I've ever met. And they're making *me* stand *him* up. Which doesn't even make sense, as I'm not even standing, I'm sitting, really annoyed. And I bet he is too. This was meant to be my chance to win him back round, not annoy him so much I got relegated out of both the friend AND casual-acquaintance zone. I don't even have his last name.

I pulled Jo's red top out of my bag and stuck it under my nose. I'd stashed it for the journey, just in case it had any of Zac's smell left in it from his jacket. I might not have his name, or any way of speaking to him *ever* again, but I *do* have a fifty per cent acrylic top that kind of smells a bit of him if I try and block out my sweat.

MMMM. Zac. If I was less selfish, I should probably let a museum know, so they could pickle him and exhibit him for all to see.

As I inhaled, Jo reached around the headrest and grabbed it out of my hands.

"I'll be having that."

She has no respect for priceless artefacts. Heartifacts.

"Oi, it's mine . . . Sort of."

Her annoying face reflected back at me in the mirror.

"If by *yours*, you mean *mine*, then yes it is."

Mum cleared her throat. The signal she's about to say something mum-y. She was fed up of us arguing all morning.

"You *do* need to be bit more careful of your sister's things, Bella. I heard what happened to her shoe last night."

No, Mother, you heard a Zac-less version of what happened to that shoe last night. Still, I was in no hurry for Jo to tell her the full Bella-met-a-boy-she-likes-and-so-you'll-ask-over-one-million-questions story.

But I figured there was no way she was going to risk a retaliation blab about her semi-losing me.

"You're going to have to put some money towards a new pair, you know?"

I grunted. Luckily they didn't know the shoe was actually priceless. A foot-shaped cupid's arrow, without which I would never have met/maimed Zac. I'd happily sell my left arm to be with him right now – in fact, I'd give it away for free. Although I'm not sure who'd want a spare left arm, especially as it can't throw anything beyond 3.5 metres. It even disappoints our dog, Mumbles.

Zac *will* see that our caravan had been packed up and we've left, won't he? I *should* have left a note. Even if it only said, 'Sorry for saying wix.'

I think I might actually love him.

But what does it matter. I'm never going to see him again. I should try and put myself off him to make this thought more bearable.

I did the 'think about him having a poo' trick. But picturing his scruffy morning-hair in combo with a loose white T-shirt that he'd probably slept in just made me fancy him more. PJ-upped Zac = hotness, poo or no poo.

What about the LOVE test? I got my phone out and

typed in what I had of our names. 'Bella Fisher LOVES Zac'. I counted up the letters. Forty-six per cent. But if I knew his last name I'm *sure* it'd rocket up into the nineties. Especially if it's Voles. Bella Voles – that works for me.

Although hang on. There was *one* thing I knew about him.

Over a dodgy motorway phone signal, I downloaded *PSSSST*. But my heart immediately sank as I realized you could only get a live feed of posts. There was no way to search for what he'd shown me yesterday. Another Zac dead-end.

But as I went to delete it, I paused. Maybe, just maybe, if I read it every day I *might* see one of Zac's posts. Recognize his mum stories. Be able to send him a direct message? Eurgh, it would be like trying to find a camouflaged needle in an anonymous haystack, but any chance was better than no chance.

I punched in my details and up popped the anonymous name it generated for me – PruneFlapper. It sounded like the kind of job I'd end up in. Next it suggested a random list of people to follow. If *only* I'd got Zac's username. I clicked away and soon anonymous secrets started to scroll past. But as I started to read them, a message filled up the screen: *'Don't just stare, you gotta share!'* Ew – I can't just laugh at other people's misfortune on *PSSSST*, I was going to have to share my own?!

I looked at Jo bouncing up and down happily to Mum's panpipe musical torture. Suck-up. Maybe *she* could help *me* out for a change.

MY STRAIGHT-A SISTER THOUGHT THAT WHEN
A FILM SAID 'PRESENT DAY' IT WAS SOMETHING
TO DO WITH CHRISTMAS.

I pressed post. But it came back with an error message as it wanted a profile pic first. As tempting as it was to put up a bad picture of Jo's annoying face, I figured that, as Zac said, the best thing about it was it being secret. I scrolled through my camera roll and chose a nice non-descript pic of my feet up on the caravan windowsill.

UPLOAD PIC. UPLOAD PSSSST.

Ha, not so cool are you now, Joanna? She caught my eye in the mirror. She knew I was up to something. I smiled back sweetly enough to make sure I unnerved her, and got back to staring out of the window. What she didn't know wouldn't hurt her.

With Black Bay gone for ever, and probably Zac

too, my life outlook was fifty shades of bleak. When Zac was around, the total mess of my real life hadn't seemed so important. But as the black and white sign of APPLETON flew past the window, I couldn't pretend any longer. Mum and Jo had ruined the one good thing about the holiday, and now I was going to have to face up to reality. First stop, Rachel's house. Like it or not, it was time for me to find out what really went down at the party.

CHAPTER

SEVEN

Why is it when you stare at your phone for incoming friend messages it never, ever beeps? Even when you look away in an effort to fool it, it STILL does nothing. It's like it *knows*.

I grabbed it off my bedside table and ran downstairs.

"See you later, Mum." AKA Killer of Dreams. "I'll be back for tea."

They were the first words I'd said since we'd been back. I knew when to take the high ground, and when to take the pie ground. I marched out the door and towards Rachel's. She lives a ten-minute walk away, and despite hating all forms of exercise (except sass-waving my nails) I love the amble there. I normally take Mumbles and do the route at least twice a week. I'm not a keen dog walker, but I AM a semi-professional boy spotter, and the journey takes me past the playing fields where I'm often treated to a sighting of MIAGTM – Man I Am Going To Marry. I don't know his name, but he's a bit skatery and I've crushed on him since I spotted him three years ago. Although, *crisis*: now I've met Zac, do I need to change his name to MIMPM – Man I Might Possibly Marry?

MIAGTM is my old faithful. I dial my crush levels up or down on him to fit whatever boy drama is happening in the rest of my life. He's like the Jay-Z to my Beyoncé, he just doesn't know it yet, and I'm assuming neither of us can rap.

As I walked past the playing field, I rang Tegan's house phone again. Her mum picked up. Apparently Tegan was teaching at one of her mammoth day-long gymnastics classes. That meant she'd have zero reception, which made more sense than my network just selectively blocking her messages. I'm so in awe of Tegan's dedication to stuff. Hardly anyone at school even knows she does gymnastics, let alone teaches or competes. For her it's never about what other people think. If I was as good as her at *anything*, I'd probably get it printed on a T-shirt. And matching trousers to be on the safe side.

But Tegan was off-radar all day, and to make

matters worse, there was also a total lack of MIAGTM/ MIMPM sighting. He was probably off saving a puppy's life, or trying out for a professional football team or something.

I rang Rachel's doorbell and waited for someone to make the trek to the front door. Their house is mahoosive. Maybe that's why rich people tend to be thin – they get their daily exercise just going to the kitchen and back to make tea. It was Mrs Waters who opened the door.

"Oooh, Bella, you, erm . . . startled me there."

Note to self, must work on my enthusiastic hello-parent face. I stopped the manic smile.

"Haven't you just come back from holiday?" She looked me up and down searching for the faintest hint of a tan.

"It was just a week with my mum and sister."

"Oh, a lovely beach holiday?" She nodded, as if willing the answer to be 'yes'.

"Sort of, we went to Wales."

Her nodding stopped. I put her out of her misery.

"In a caravan."

Her smile remained, but her eyes screamed, 'Is *that* what people call a holiday these days?'

"Bellllllaaaaa!!" Rachel's long red hair swooshed

round the door. "You're here! MUM, why didn't you shout for me?" She pushed past her mum, opening the door wide enough to walk through. "We have SO much to talk about."

Rachel's manicured hands grabbed my arm and pulled me in. I couldn't help but note her fingers were 1.2 centimetres from the exact spot where Zac's had been fifteen hours earlier. New favourite bit of skin, beating my previous favourite of a weirdly smooth bit next to my armpit.

Taking my shoes off, I looked for evidence of the party. Nope, still a gleaming show home. I could murder someone here, and it would be so spotlessly clean the next day that the police forensic team wouldn't be able to find a single clue. Good to keep in mind if Jo ever snogterupts me again. Or tells that story again about me taking a selfie with a waxwork nun in Madame Tussauds, only for me to discover it was a real – and quite annoyed – old lady.

"Sorry about my mum, you know what she's like. She can be so cringe sometimes."

"As if! You've met *my* mum. You have NO NEED to apologize. Your mum isn't the one who once sent you to school with a cheese sandwich – made from human breast milk."

Her already massive blue eyes got even wider.

"Oh yeah! I still can't believe Mikey ate it?!"

I laughed. I'd forgotten about that bit! He really would do anything to impress Tegan.

"Someone should have let him know the way to Tegan's heart isn't via 'eating lady cheese'."

Rach faked gagged, looking a total contrast to the professional photoshoots of her fam we were walking past.

"Pure vileness! On a total level with my mum telling Mr Lutas that in her day he would have been a hottie. I wished the ground would open up and hollow me."

If it was anyone other than Rachel, I'd probably point out it's 'swallow'? But best not add to the already difficult thought of why her mum would crack on to an art teacher who always had suspect chalk marks around his groin from where he was 'adjusting' himself. He's prob the only teacher in the UK that still uses a blackboard to make notes.

We went into Rach's room, which had real-life framed modern art on the walls, and crashed on her bed. It was big enough to lie widthways on. I stared up at her big wall, which was covered with floor-to-ceiling bookshelves. It never failed to amaze me. The top shelves were stacked with the ones she'd inherited (mainly dull, but there were some well-funny ones of naked people in giant champagne glasses we occasionally got down), the middle shelves were the art ones her mum had got for her, and the bottom shelves were full of the well-thumbed ones you never saw her without.

Rachel prodded me with a glittery nail.

"Come on then, how was your holibobs?"

Deep breath, me. Play it casual. Maybe don't even mention Zac for a while? Perhaps seem cool for once by making out the biggest deal ever was, like, not that big a deal. Yes. Good plan.

"OMGItwasAMAZING. I SNOGGED, well semi-snogged, the FITTEST boy and it was probably the GREATEST moment to have EVER happened to anyone on record EVER, give or take a flying shoe, but that's NOT IMPORTANT, cos what IS important is that he is INCREDIBLE and has great teeth and loves his gran and laughs like an strangely alluring horse." The words couldn't have come out of my mouth any faster. Rachel's jaw officially dropped – and stayed there as every single tiny other detail spilled out, in such rapid fire that I forgot to breathe and had to lie flat on her bed to avoid a fainting incident. It was *never* me who had these kind of stories – and it felt good.

Rach reacted just how I hoped, even jumping at the key moments, causing tiny tidal mattress waves.

"So, let me get this straight. HE apologized to YOU because HE wanted to kiss YOU?"

"Uh-huh."

"And right now, at this second, he thinks you've stood him up, cos you're not interested, even though also right now, at this second, you're seriously considering leaving my house and walking 379 miles just to say sorry for saying 'wix'?"

"Correct."

She waggled her long arms and legs around like an upturned ladybird.

"And his last words before he semi-snogged you were about . . . slugs?"

"Uh-huh – a whole new meaning to talking dirty."

"Bells – this is one hundred per cent insane. I love it!!!"

We squackled – squealing mixed with cackling – with the sheer brilliance of my achievement. Maybe the world *had* changed. Maybe now I, Bella Fisher, was the kind of girl who had stories about snogging boys, rather than just tripping up in front of them.

Riding high on this life revelation felt like a good time to broach the subject of last night.

"So, er, now I've fully splurged about my hottie-day, it's time for you to spill the beans on last night."

She beamed. So it *had* been a good night.

"I wish you'd been here. OBVS, *soooo* much happened."

Exactly what I didn't want to hear. 'Absolutely nothing happened and it was so boring that we all made a pact to never have a party without you ever again' was more along the lines of my ideal response.

"Go on then . . . spill." PleasepleasepleaseletthisbeOK.

"OK – major headlines." She paused, rummaging through a whole head-full of excellent stories. "Well . . . our toaster's now broken because Lou's chicken fillet flopped into it and we didn't know until breakfast this morning when it melted on to mum's bagel. . . What else. . . I met this dead nice guy, PJ, but might have ruined it as I introduced him to everyone as BJ and no one told me. Oh, and Mikey did a BRITS-worthy rendition of 'Shake It Off' complete with major sass moves."

Rachel chatted away enjoying having someone to relive it all with. I'd normally be heartbroken I'd missed out, but this time, if I'd have been there, I'd never have met Zac, which made it way less painful to listen to. I'd swop a toasted-fake-boob for a Zac-hang any day. But what I was lacking in FOMO, I was making up for with a nagging worry. She hadn't mentioned the Luke-and-Tegan-shaped elephant in the room. And it was making me panic. She knew how much I'd freaked out – she'd been on the receiving end of my messages. Was she avoiding it on purpose?

I waited for a pause in her story of how Mikey had almost knocked himself out headbanging, literally, into their grand piano. It was time for me to wave and point at the elephant. It was time for me to get the truth.

CHAPTER

EIGHT

"Raaaaaach." Gulp. Here I go. Stay casual. And properly casual, not like my last attempt.

"How *weird* were those messages from Luke last night? I mean, like, *SO* weird."

She bent her long arms over her even longer legs and picked at her fluffy rainbow slippers, avoiding eye contact. I ploughed on with my fake 'totally mentioning this in a completely unplanned way' casual act.

"And then . . . then I got that one from you. Which was like, also a bit weird. And you and Tegan have both been off-radar all day." She wasn't filling in any blanks. "Pretty weird, huh?"

Her face flushed. My heart sank.

I needed to come up with some less weird words for weird.

"Oh yeah . . . *that*." She looked sheepish. So I wasn't being paranoid – she *had* been deliberately avoiding the subject.

"Yeah – *that*."

Rach walked over to her full-length mirror and pulled her hair up into a messy topknot. Unfortunately for her, she'd forgotten mirrors tend to do quite a good job at reflecting things, so I could see was stressed. Her perfect world wasn't very good at dealing with un-perfect. I felt like I was waiting for an exam result.

"OK, if I tell you, do you promise not to get mad?" She didn't give me a chance to answer, carrying straight on. "I mean, I *said* we shouldn't invite Luke in the first place, but it was *you* who had said that we had to or it'd look like he was still getting to you. And we all agreed."

She still hadn't told me anything I didn't know already.

"Aaand?"

She fiddled with a body spray, making a rhythmical 'pop' with the lid, buying time as she searched for the words.

"And. Well. Fine. Right. So, er, well, we were all sitting around and stuff, and Luke was chatting to those girls from Joggies. You know the ones." Figures. JOGS, or James Owen Girls' School, is a posh girls' school round the corner from ours, where all the girls look like they've just come back from an incredible skiing holiday, all the time. Does snow even exist in the summer?

"Anyway, one of them starts getting all cosy with him. They're on the sofa – the one that Mumbles weed on?"

It was leaf patterned! She thought she was outside!

"And he's got his arm round her and stuff, and they're *obviously* about to snog. They had that, 'Oh, are you *ticklish*?' thing going on?"

I knew it all too well. It'd been me once. Classic touchy-feely faux-friendly Luke. So predictable.

Rach lay back down next to me. I had to keep the convo on track.

"So was that the girl in the picture? The one Luke sent? Purple hat girl?"

She thought before answering, as if trying to place her before she confirmed.

"Yeah . . . exactly."

If she had a mirror on the ceiling, I'd have been able to check if she had anything crossed. On the flipside, she'd also be really creepy, so I probably wouldn't be lying here in the first place.

It was annoying, but the thought of Luke being all over Purple Hat Girl in front of my friends did sting a bit. Is it factually impossible not to care a bit about ex-boyfs' new girlfs? Hopefully they both got a waft of Mumbles' wee mid-snog and thought it was each other.

"So then what?"

"Well, not much. I left them to it, as I figured that was what you'd want."

Phew. It was. No drama.

". . . until I got your message with that pic Luke had sent."

Uh-oh. This sounded very much like it might be drama.

"Which kind of annoyed me. Big style."

The drama dial shot up.

". . . so I kind of showed Dan."

One hundred per cent deffo drama. Dan was Rachel's law-studying, eye-wateringly-hot, rugby-playing brother whose arm was the same width as Rach's head. We'd made him measure.

"Rach, don't leave me hanging."

"And then Dan kind of threw Luke out."

SOUND THE DRAMA KLAXON.

This was exactly what I didn't want. Actual Luke drama. Because of me. ARGH! Mouth, brain, do NOT freak out. Yet. Maybe nobody saw? Rach carried on.

"Luke made a right scene. I didn't know faces could go that red. He looked like the Rothko on my wall!" Rachel gestured at the picture of a red square that she was given a print of on her ninth birthday. It was the same year I was given a second-hand horse pyjama case that neighed when you pulled its tail. "Honestly, it was like a film!"

OPTIMUM DRAMA ACHIEVED. The backfire was complete. My 'invite Luke to the party to show I wasn't bothered' had ended up with me sending him snarky messages and then getting him kicked out – just like someone who was completely and utterly bothered. ARGH! And now I'd got Rachel and Tegan dragged into it too.

"He's SUCH an idiot. Why can't he just get on with his own life, instead of messing with everyone else's?! And what's he got against Tegan?! I mean, if he was going to talk rubbish about anyone, why make out he was making out with Tegan – who never makes out with anyone, or makes out that she does?" None of this made sense. What was I missing? "Any ideas?"

Rachel shrugged apologetically. I carried on thinking out loud.

"AS IF he thinks I care who has the misfortune of snogging him. I feel *sorry* for them if anything." A tiny white lie, as much to Rachel as to myself.

EURGH. My tired brain couldn't handle this conundrum. I splatted, starfish-shaped, across the duvet, getting my phone out to look back over his messages. Stupid Luke. Stupid Purple Hat Girl. Rachel titled the screen towards her, looking for clues too.

"OK, Bells. The thing we *do* know about Luke is that his brain doesn't work in normal brain ways. That's quite something coming from Rach, who once dislocated her shoulder trying to prove you could lick your elbow. "So it's hard to know why he does *any* of the weird stuff he does. Remember that time he put loads of pegs on his face and leapt out of a cupboard in the middle of maths? That isn't normal behaviour. So we have to think un-normal to even get close... I reckon he was just trying to get into your head while you were away."

"But at that point I was having the worst holiday in the world?"

"Yeah, doofus, but that's not what friends say to ex-boyfs, is it? We kind of made out it was the party capital of Wales, with a hot-boy-to-Bella ratio of 100:1."

I smiled – good friends really were the best liars.

"Bella, darling. . ."

I froze. Why could I hear my mum's voice?!

Was she here? Had she taken to hiding under my friends' beds for one of her mother-daughter bonding exercises? I peered over the edge of the mattress.

"Hello? Hell-oh-oooo. Daughter! Is that you?"

Rachel gestured at my jeans. I'd not only bum-answered, but bum speakerphoned too. Cheers, bum, you refuse to enable me to do a squat without wobbling over, but you have mastered basic technology.

"I'm just at Rach's." I used my 'don't forget I'm still in a mood with you' voice.

"Hi, Ms Fisher," Rachel shouted at my bum.

"Hi, girls," my mum/bum chirped back. I couldn't be bothered to fish my phone out of my pocket. There was nothing she could say that Rachel couldn't hear (although the denim had muffled her a bit).

"What do you want?"

"Glad to see you're still a ray of sunshine, darling." Eye-roll at Rachel. "Now, I know you're out, and having lots of fun with your friends, but please can you get back here in the next half an hour? I'm on my way out to Pilates with Puppies and noticed you'd left your keys at home, so I want you back before I go, OK?"

"But, I'm just..."

I didn't get to finish. She interrupted with that unfair mum tactic – pretending not to hear and talking over you in a voice that says 'this isn't a question, it's a fact'.

"Greeeatt. I *knew* you wouldn't mind. Anyway, I need to get the kohlrabi out of the oven, so must dash. See you in fifteen, lovely. Bye, daughter, bye, Rachel! YOLI!"

Mum always liked to end phone calls with motivational thoughts. I found getting my mum off the phone motivational enough.

A confused Rachel waved at my bum. My bum didn't wave back.

"Er, YOLI?"

I was hoping she hadn't noticed that.

"Don't ask. Mum's going through a reincarnation phase. You Only Live Infinitely."

Rachel laughed but I wasn't in the mood to find anything funny. Except maybe baby pandas sneezing.

So that was that. One bum-move and my last night of holiday freedom had disappeared. I pulled on my jacket and shouted my goodbyes to Rach's fam in the kitchen, accidentally yelling "Bye, HOB" at Dan, as I'm too used to referring to him as Hot Older Brother. He looked at me like I was saying an emotional goodbye to their cooker. Hurrying to the door, I got Rachel to agree to convince him I didn't have feelings for appliances, and also to promise to urgently ask him about emigration laws for my potential relocation. I trudged home, thoughts of Luke, purple hats, kitchen appliances I *would* say goodbye to, and hot guys called Zac all swashing round my head.

When I finally closed my bedroom door for the last time this holiday, I should have dealt with the homework I'd been putting off all week. But instead I used my last moments of freedom much more wiscly, alphabetacalizing (new word, look it up in the alphabetacalized dictionary) my books, painting rainbow stripes on my toenails – and accidentally some carpet too – and re-reading some magazines. Time flies when you're procrastinating.

If only today had worked out differently, I could be reliving my second date with Zac, instead of wondering how on earth I could make up for my shameful sister summoning and subsequent disappearing act.

But there was *one* thing I did still have. I opened up *PSSSST*. Wow, fifteen likes on my Jo comment! That was more than my picture of Mumbles dressed as a gherkin got on Instagram. What if one of the likes was from Zac?! I should post again. I racked my brains. It was a bit sad to realize I had way too many things to choose from.

MY MUM BEGGED ME TO SHOW HER PHOTOS OF
A BOY FROM UNI MY SISTER LIKES. SO I SET HER
UP AN ACCOUNT, SEARCHED FOR THE GUY AND
LEFT HER SCROLLING THOUGH THE PICS. I DIDN'T
REALIZE SHE KEPT TAPPING AWAY, TRYING – AND
FAILING – TO ZOOM IN. WHICH ENDED UP IN
HER ACCIDENTALLY LIKING OVER FIFTY OF HIS
PHOTOS. FROM THREE YEARS AGO. UNDER HER
REAL NAME. MY SISTER IS YET TO FIND OUT.

Jo was going to kill me for allowing this to happen.
But it's not my fault Mum can't even use a phone and
calls likes 'hearting'.

I scrolled through all the new *PSSSSTs*, willing,
hoping something to pop up on my timeline that I could
trace back to Zac. Maybe he'd post about Jo's totally
embarrassing display yesterday? But there was nothing.

Disappointed, I plugged my phone in to charge, and
flicked on the torch under the covers. The inevitable
had arrived – a long night of pretending to be asleep,
while doing my homework under my sheets. But with
what school was about to throw at me, beauty sleep was
going to be the very least of my worries.

CHAPTER

NINE

Isn't it weird that the second your alarm goes off for the first day back at school it feels like you were never not at school? Parents moan about going to work, but they're obviously forgetting lessons are way worse – and we don't even get paid for being there. If I could buy two hundred and fifty Toffee Crisps for every day I dragged myself to St Mary's then it really would be much more worthwhile.

Getting ready today also took way too long, as I wasted fifteen minutes pulling everything out of my wardrobe searching for my jumper only to discover it in the bottom of my school bag, along with two unsigned letters and a really miserable looking apple. The good news was I must have looked so miserable in my gone-off-fruit-scented crease-ball uniform that Mum ended up giving me a lift.

"Here you go, chick-a-dee, door-to-door service."

I opened the car door quietly trying to make a quick escape before anyone spotted me. Keeping a low profile and a brown car that has a sticker saying 'Hippies do it braless!' didn't really go together. Mum leaned over.

"Now, remember what Jo says, 'Believe and achieve!'"

I grunted.

"I *believe* today will be awful, and I will definitely *achieve* it." I slammed the door shut. "Bye."

Beeping, she drove off. At least she'd got through her phase of replacing the horn with an electrical cow moo. Small mercies.

I hoisted my school bag on to my shoulder and walked towards the big wooden double doors. Positive-thought time. All I had to do was get through the next eight hours with the required mix of attending lessons, seeing Rachel and Tegan, eating lunch, and not seeing anyone else – especially, definitely not Luke. Simple. I could do this. Game-face on, Bella. Maybe no one will even be thinking about the party, let alone talking about it?

"Beellllllllllaaaaaaaa." I jumped as unexpected arms

threw themselves around my back. I didn't need to see a face to know that gentle voice. My long-lost friend had just become un-lost. And she sounded pleased to see me.

"So you're alive then?!" I turned to face Tegan, who had chosen to ignore the five per cent annoyed-ness in my voice. Her new braids had been pulled up into a bun, and they looked even better in real life than in the photo she'd sent last week. Whereas I looked like a human jumble-sale stall, she looked like every single bit of clothing had been perfectly placed. Although how her skin glowed so much without make-up was the kind of thing I wish we could study for GCSE.

"Yes, I am. Sorry about that. Although teaching that gymnastics class yesterday, with a nine-year-old boy who already fake tans and plucks his eyebrows, almost finished me off." She put her arm around me (2.2 centimetres away from where Zac's had been) and gave me a squeeze. "We've missed you. Pleeeease *never* go away on a family holiday again without inviting us?"

Tegan is one of the most uncomplicated people I know – in nothing but a great way. I always know where I stand with her. And right now it was arm-in-arm. Lots of people in our year think she's too serious, maybe even intimidating, but if she's your friend, you see a whole other side of her. As we walked, linked-up, towards our lockers, I felt part of a team again.

"Next time, Tegan, I'm putting you in my suitcase, OK? You're bendy, you'll fit."

"Er, well last I heard Black Bay was basically the Black Death, so can we negotiate on the destination before I'm human hand luggage please?"

The moment I'd been waiting for. Telling her all about Zac and getting to relive it all over again. I pulled her to a standstill.

"Stop. Right. There. I have big things to tell you. Black Bay turned cray!" I couldn't help throwing in one last dig before we were quits. "Although if you'd bothered to reply to any of my messages in the last day and a bit, you'd already know all about it." I pulled my best angry teacher face.

She wrinkled her nose.

"I'm sorry, I'm sorry, I can explain!"

"And the party?"

"That too. It's all no big deal."

Her sorry-ness was like a reassuring blanket giving my worry-brain a cuddle. Yes, Rachel had explained what happened, but hearing Tegan back it up was the final thing I needed to stop worrying.

Tegan and I met at playgroup, a few weeks after

her family had moved from Zimbabwe. It's a matter of dispute between our mums, but apparently we persuaded our class to pour all of our break-time milk into the teacher's bag as a present for her. That was probably the first and last time Tegan did anything really naughty. Out of everyone I knew, she had life figured out. Which is why I turned to her for advice on anything, and everything. And why she was going to be the one to make me feel better.

Rach popped her head over Tegan's locker door, her perfect hair in those waves you only see on magazine covers. How do people know how to do these things? I have zero hair skills, so had guilt-tripped Jo into helping me put my short hair up this morning to try and look a bit more mature and fearsome just in case I did see Luke, but I'd just achieved Swiss goat herder instead. Still, goat herders must be scary to goats at least.

I beamed at Rach.

"Hey, good lock-ing. Fancy seeing you here."

She jumped round the door and gave us both a big hug. I already feel short enough compared to Tegan, but Rachel is proper model tall. I really should have chosen friends more wisely. "So, Tegan was just explaining why one week away made her think it was fine to cut me out..."

"Errrr, no. I was about to explain the practical logistics of what happens when your battery runs out, and then your phone falls through a tiny hole in your gym bag meaning you think you've lost it, until you're nagged into emptying it just before you set off for school on Monday morning, and then voila, there it is, full of slightly deranged messages." She raised her eyebrows. "So then you message your friends asking if they want to walk in together, but they both ignore you."

Rach and I simultaneously looked at our phones. A group message from Tegan asking if we wanted to walk in with her. Ooops.

"Well, for that I can only apologetic-face emoji at you, so let's call it quits." Tegan shook her head despairingly. We were chalk and cheese. If chalk liked sitting on sofas and cheese liked spending every hour achieving something useful. "So, while I've got you, all that's left is to find out what you know about *this*."

I scrolled to the pic that Luke sent. Her brown eyes hardened.

"Any idea why he'd send this to me and say it was you? We're like a fallen tree here. Totally stumped."

Tegan took it out of my hands and zoomed right in. Did she shoot Rach a look? I looked back. Nah, she was staring at the screen. Damn loser Luke, he was even making me paranoid with the two people I trust most in the world.

"So weird. TBH the whole night was a bit of a blur. So unlike me." Completely unlike her; she was always the sensible one. But I knew her well enough to recognize the signs that she might have something more to say if gently prodded.

"So you've got no idea *at all*?"

She sighed as if not sure whether to answer. "Well, there's *one* thing I can think of."

I KNEW it. Tegan lowered her voice to a semi-whisper.

"Since Rach showed me the message at the party, I've been going over it trying to figure it out. See if we'd missed anything."

I knew Tegan would be able to clear this up. She always did. She's basically like a TV detective, but in real life, and without the murders.

"The only thing I can come up with is that earlier in the night we'd been bigging up Black Bay. Majorly." Rach nodded. It's what she was saying yesterday. Tegan carried on. "Puke was sitting on the floor behind the armchair we were on. We *knew* he could hear everything we said. So we sort-of made out your holiday was wall-to-wall hot boys. And that they were

97

all well into you. That at one point you were physically fighting them off with a stick. And . . . and that you said it had made you realize what losers you'd dated before. . ." She winced. "And what terrible kissers they'd been. . . With questionable breath. . . And terrible choice in slogan T-shirts." She winced even more. "And that you couldn't believe you'd ever gone out with someone who had an Il Divo single." She bit her lip and winced. "I SWEAR we thought we were doing a good job for you, but looking back we *might* have got a teeny bit carried away."

They sure had. But . . . I kind of liked it. The Luke bits were all true, and the way we'd split up meant I'd never been able to say any of it to him. Even though he'd gone out of his way to tell everyone I was a loser that he'd never cared about me in the first place. It was clear to me that all he ever cared about was his reputation (and weirdly his World Cup 2014 sticker album).

I pulled my best Sherlock face and flicked up an imaginary collar.

"So . . . based on what I've heard today, I put it to you that Luke thought we'd invited him to the party to laugh at him? And sending me that pic was his weird attempt at revenge."

Tegan jumped in. She flicked her imaginary collar back up at me.

"Exacto. And a pic of him snogging a randomer wasn't enough. He knew he'd have to involve one of us to make you waste any time thinking about it!"

In Luke's nonsensical mind, this was *exactly* the kind of thing that would make sense. I felt actual relief at us figuring out the missing piece in the puzzle. Now I could stop obsessing over Luke's weird messages, and get back to concentrating on important things. Like dreaming about Zac and scrolling hopefully through *PSSSST*.

With Luke's weirdness solved, our convo soon moved on to the other party gossip and we unpacked our books for first period. (I never understood why we need books for geography, surely you just need a map?) Just as I managed to fish out my long forgotten textbook, one of the sixth formers shoved a wodge of printed paper into my locker.

"These were meant to go in your lockers. But I forgot. Hand them out will you?"

Without waiting for an answer, she walked off. I picked them out – flyers for the end-of-term prom. It was a perk of being Year 10 or above, as we each got our own party. This would be our first-ever one – and the biggest thing to happen all year. The three of us had been looking forward to it since we started St Mary's.

"I'll be having one of those." My least favourite hand in the whole school grabbed one out of my pile. Talk of the devil. And his hands. "If you're lucky, I might even invite one of you ladies. Probably Rach, as you're the fittest."

His idiot mates laughed. I crossed a mental line through my 'especially, definitely not seeing Luke' goal for the day. Was it fair to have this much bad luck before nine a.m.? Sensible people aren't even awake then.

Tegan grabbed the paper back.

"Did you not see the small print?" she asked. "It says no pets, parents or massive losers. Soooo, you should probably start making other plans. Got some stickers to collect?"

He shot me a look. I shot one back. Yes, I had told my friends, and no, I didn't care how much he hated me for it.

"Girls, please. It's getting embarrassing. First Saturday, now this. Surely you can find someone else to spend your time talking about?" He put his hand on Tegan's arm. She jerked it away. "Oh, and Tegan. Has no one told you a sharp tongue doesn't suit you? It was much softer on Saturday – when you had it in my mouth."

Rage rushed through me, like a human radiator that had been turned up to 'very hot' or whatever they get set too. That boy had SUCH a nerve. Lying in a message was one thing, trying to get away with it to our faces was another matter. Who did he think he was?!

But Tegan snapped first.

"The only thing YOU have in your mouth is a bunch of lies. So jog on and leave us alone." She slammed her locker door shut, barging him into the middle of the corridor with her body. I friend swooned. I was so proud of how brave she always was, standing up for what's right, even in front of all his mean mates. The most I was managing was furious looks, and they sometimes got confused with the sort of face you might pull if you have trapped wind.

But Luke didn't get the hint (although is it a hint when you spell it out and shout it in someone's face?). He stepped back into my path and looked me straight in the eye.

"Look, Bella, as a *friend*, I'm just looking out for you. No one wants mates they can't trust. Do they, Tegan? Fit Rach? I'm sure you'll thank me one day." He grabbed a flyer out of my hand and winked. "Even if I have to wait till prom to hear it. You know where I am if you need me."

His uber-smarm burst my mouth open. How dare he patronize me? He wasn't my mother, or a teacher! Or even my sister on a bad day. I felt like the Incredible Hulk, just less green, and more cross.

"Well, as a *friend* let me tell you THIS. It's true. You WERE a TERRIBLE kisser, so *whoever* was in that pic, I feel nothing but sorry for them." Gulp. Did I just say that out loud? I felt more shocked than Luke looked. People were staring. But my mouth was on a mission.

"Tegan would never snog you in a *million* years." Hello, out of body experience. I swear I was hearing the words at the same time as everyone else, like it wasn't *my* brain making them. Auto-mouth continued.

"In fact, she calls you Puke."

Luke bristled. One of his mates sniggered before getting elbowed in the ribs. But this time I didn't care. Messing with me was one thing, messing with my mates was another. "And if you think I'd believe YOU over HER, you're even more of an idiot than I thought."

Had I finished? Mouth, tell me we've finished. But no. It had other ideas.

"And, and . . . and as for prom, the only thing I'll be saying to you is, 'Have you met the fittest man in the world?' who incidentally, will be *my* date. That won't be you. Obviously."

Luke was frozen to the spot. Guess he'd never seen this side of me before. And neither had I.

A cough came from behind me. I turned and realized we were now surrounded by a crowd. Luke noticed the same and instantly jerked back into jerk mode. Being yelled at by me was not a good look for anyone. I'm sure it even cringed-out Mumbles.

"As if *you* of all people will have a date. Have you seen yourself recently? Unless he has a thing for –" he stared at my head – "goat herders."

Well at least I'd guessed the right insult for today's hair. Always one step ahead.

"Well, I do. And he's called Zac." I turned to face everyone as if doing a tour in a museum, but the exhibit was my love life. Well, my hypothetical love life, but now wasn't the time for disclaimers. "I met him on holiday. He's six foot and he's in a band and we're seeing each other, and he may or may not like goat herders, I don't even know, and he's going to be at prom. With me. And he's the world's biggest FITTIE. And he smells great."

Not the big finish I was hoping for, but oh well. But before anyone could react, a voice boomed through the hall, bouncing off the walls.

"WHAT ON EARRRRTH IS GOING ON HERE?"

If I didn't want one teacher to hear me yelling about fitties, our art teacher Mr Lutas was it. He was the antithesis of anything fit. Except for his trousers, which were way-too-tight fit. But it was Mr Lutas that was now looming over both Luke and me, and he was fuming.

"Congrrratulations on prrroving you can't even manage adult behaviour for twenty minutes of a new terrrm."

I threw Luke my best dirty look. This was all his fault. Typical.

"How verrry disappointing that you all just continue to live up to my verry low expectations." Mr Lutas clicked his fingers. "Now get to class immediately. THE LOT OF YOU."

I mumbled sorry, closing up my locker as the crowd disappeared even quicker than it had arrived. The last thing I wanted was trouble in prom term. You had to have enough prom points to be allowed to go and I didn't want Mr Lutas taking that away from me. Although at least then I wouldn't have to work out how on earth I was going to achieve the impossible: getting my big foot out of my mouth and proving Luke wrong by getting someone who had disappeared from my life to reappear at prom. As my date.

CHAPTER

TEN

The combo of Luke and Mr Lutas (do all evil things begin with L? No, lemurs) meant that we were so late for morning classes that we got held in over break. So not only did that mean no checking *PSSSST* for signs of Zac, it also meant my first chance to properly debrief with Tegan was over lunch.

Lunch was the same old routine: pick up Rach, pick up Tegan, get lunchboxes, secure decent lunch seat, chow down. I opened my lunchbox and was relieved that today's box of delights was cheddar, not lady-cheese sandwiches. We were going through a phase of bringing in kids' lunchboxes. Mine's a Peppa Pig one, which gives me major guilt whenever it contains a Peperami.

Tegan was deep in thought, chewing on something healthy and weird like celery. "I was thinking – should the three of us go back to Black Bay? Do you reckon our mums would let us?"

I'd obviously sold it better than I should have done.

"Ueermmmm. . ." It was the best yes/no/not sure noise I could muster through sandwich munching.

"We might get some clues on Zac and be a bit nearer to getting him to prom?"

I love how me getting Zac to prom was now a team effort. But I didn't think heading back to Black Bay could be worth it if he wasn't there. He'd said he only went for his gran's birthday.

"Er . . . yeah . . . (chew) . . . maybe . . . (swallow) . . . Sorry, big bit of cheese there." I swallowed again. "I guess we *could* look into it? Maybe a weekend? Next year? We could explain my future husband is on the line. . .?"

"Marriage isn't love, Bells. How many times do I have to tell you? OTPs are about the soul, not the surname." Tegan was right, but her surname didn't create a lifetime of jokes about mackerel.

"Yeah, sorry, and I guess we are only one semi-snog into our relationship right now." I slurped my Ribena wondering if there would ever be a time when we would have a more extensive relationship, like one full snog or above.

"So were Jay and Bey at one point and look where they are now." Good old optimistic Rach. "We've all got to start somewhere." She stared into the distance. "Although it probably helps if that start isn't exercising alone dressed as a cereal box."

I shook my head in despair but cheered up as I spotted a friendly face walking into the canteen.

"Oi, Mikey!" I waved my arms big style, like I was bringing a plane into land. He grinned and walked over. "Long time no speak."

"Got to keep myself in demand." His hair had grown since I last saw him, mainly outwards. I looked at it curiously.

"So the rumours are true – you really are trying to grow the first ever in-built hair-helmet?" I sometimes wonder if he takes hairdressers an emoji as his inspo pic.

"Well, isn't that what girls are completely mad for these days? Safety *and* style?"

He ran his fingers through his thick black hair, like he was in a hair advert, but gave up as he realized he was rubbing finger crisp debris into his hair, creating salt and vinegar potato dandruff.

Tegan politely pretended not to notice the falling morsels.

"If we can possibly hold ourselves back, might you be joining us for lunch?" She pulled out the spare stool beside her.

"Can't, I'm afraid. I've got a full week of homework to do, and thirty-seven minutes to do it."

And he was still prioritizing lunch. I loved this guy. Although it was unlike him to turn down some Tegan time.

"Oh well, tomorrow? Same place, same time?"

"Sure – I could do with people seeing me hang out with the most badass girls at St Mary's. In fact –" he did a full 360 degree turn – "do you think they're seeing me now?"

Wow. I have never been called a badass before. Laughing, I pulled his jumper.

"Siddown. And tell us *exactly* what you've heard. . ."

"Only that between the three of you, you totally annihilated Luke in front of all of his mates? *Everyone* is talking about it."

My stomach knotted. As much as I was glad we'd done it, I didn't love the idea of everyone chatting about it.

Tegan looked disapproving.

"Well, everyone needs to stop talking about it, and get on with their own lives."

But the hint went over Rachel's head — funny, considering she was so tall.

"It *was* amazing, though. I wish you'd been there Mikey! Srsly. Tegan and Bells were *on fire!*"

I jumped in.

"Not literally. You would have heard the alarms. And our jumpers would have melted."

"Thanks for clearing that up, Bells." Mikey laughed. "But melted jumpers or not, I wish I'd been there. It's about time that douche got a taste of his own medicine."

I never understood that phrase. Surely the only medicine we taste is our own, or we'd all be stealing strangers' medicine, which sounded very risky. Mikey stood back up.

"Tomorrow you can tell me *all* about it. Just not loud enough for Tegan to hear, cos we don't want to be on the wrong side of Ms Power Woman!" He winked at her. "So I will love you and leave you as I've got a geography essay due in on South America and all I've got so far is — 'it's like America, but lower'."

Mikey was not like most of the other boys I knew. He was sort of, well, nice. I didn't have a brother, but if

I did, and it was OK to have once fancied him for 0.5 days, then I imagine he'd be a bit like him. He'd been the honorary boy in our group ever since four years ago when he'd asked Tegan if she wanted to join their kick about on the playing field in our village. What started off with needing someone for a five-a-side, had developed into him being hopelessly and utterly in love with her. Not that Tegan could see it – or would believe it even if she could.

As soon as he was out of earshot, Rach gave me a cheeky eyebrow raise and I knew we were in for a classic instalment of BUM-ing. A pact we'd secretly made with each other to Big Up Mikey (BUM) to Tegan until she realized that he was a boy and not an inanimate object.

"Is it just me, or is Mikey looking all kinds of cute these days?"

Helmet hair aside, he *was* looking good. But Tegan didn't react one way or the other, and soon we got back to chatting about this morning and how we'd have to stay below the radar to make sure we didn't drop any prom points. Everyone started the year with twenty, and you needed ten to go to prom, so normally it's only the total troublemakers and jokers that are in real danger of not going. But Mr Lutas's bad side is a dangerous place to be. The only fun he has is when he's stopping other people's. That and painting bowls of fruit. Why can't he just take a picture of them instead, it's much quicker?

Mr Lutas had already docked me six prom points this year for being too engrossed in an article about the true meaning of your crush's messages, and accidentally switching off a freezer instead of a camera charger. I'd melted the entire Year 7 first-ever attempt at ice sculpture. On the plus side, I did learn when someone messages you with 'See you later', it 'ninety per cent might mean that they'll see you later'.

The bell rang, shattering our prom plotting, and Tegan and I reluctantly headed to double physics. As if that should be allowed on a Monday. Our surnames meant the two of us were in the same class for all of our lessons (top set, but on average our year thinks Macbeth is a type of sandwich, so it's nothing to be too smug about). The one good thing about physics was that it was so boring, it gave me plenty of time for thinking about more useful things. As Mrs Scuse droned on, I wondered whether, since she was so good at physics, she could explain why in her lab sixty seconds seemed to take six hundred. Or how my life could get so messy in 48 hours. In just two days, I'd landed myself with the problems of figuring out how to avoid Luke AND Mr Lutas for a whole term, and how to make a boy, who probably isn't speaking to me, doesn't go to school any more, and is wandering around Wolverhampton totally unaware, be my date for prom.

Mrs Scuse caught my eye and I did a fake-interested smile. Seriously, lady, as if I have any time to care about the heat generated by burning a peanut when all this is going on. The only thing I need to know about Kcals is that it's the bit of a crisp packet I don't look at.

As soon as the bell rang, Tegan and I scrambled towards the door, our bags already packed up as of five minutes ago. Rachel met us at our usual spot – by the tree with the enormous nobble, AKA Bum Tree – so we could walk back together. But someone I only half recognized was heading our way. She looked like one of the girls from JOGS.

"Hey, Teeg!" she shouted in our direction.

Tegan gave a tiny wave back, but her normally friendly face was lacking its usual smile. And so was Rachel's. The girl marched over, unaware.

"Hi, Rachel, great party, thanks. Bella, shame you couldn't make it."

Was the atmosphere weird, or was it just me? I half-smiled, not wanting to be rude. But now she was closer, maybe I *did* recognize her after all. And she knew me. Wasn't she one of Tegan's gymnastics friends? She rummaged in her bag. Yeah. It was definitely her.

The weird tension suddenly made sense as gymnastics friend pulled something out of the bag. A wide-brimmed purple hat. THE wide-brimmed purple hat. She pulled it over her long brown hair, as if it wasn't the most vital clue in a snog-mystery ever produced. It should be in a museum, not on a head! As the hat weight went on to her shoulders, it instantly came off mine. Hurrah! Hat-rah! So SHE snogged Luke! Mystery solved!

I prodded the other two, but they hadn't twigged as quickly as me. Maybe I could get a selfie with us and The Hat, and send it to little liar Luke to show him he'd been caught out?

Hat girl registered the awkwardness. All three of us were acting oddly, but in very different ways.

"Sorry, have I interrupted something?"

The only thing she'd interrupted was us solving the final mystery. I wasn't cross with her. I was delighted! I leapt in to answer slightly too enthusiastically for someone she's only met once.

"You're not interrupting, it's GREAT to see you. Honestly. Really great, hatually, sorry, actually."

Did she look relieved or unnerved? My manic smile must have struck again.

"Well, it was just a quickie. For Tegan really." Tegan was slowly shaking her head. Hat girl looked confused.

Hat girl looked back at me. I gave her a reassuring nod to carry on. She didn't need to explain herself. It was Luke who had caused all the problems.

"I just wanted to say *thanks*. For putting my hat back in my locker. Seriously, Tegan, I knew you'd take care of it. And you looked HA-MAY-ZING in it. You can borrow it again any time you like."

I didn't hear any other words.

The hat wasn't a hat after all. It was a bomb. That Tegan and Rachel clearly thought they'd diffused. But they hadn't. And it had just exploded my world apart.

CHAPTER

ELEVEN

Plus side: at the age of fifteen years and one hundred and twenty-seven days I'd already achieved the worst day of my life. Opposite of plus side: my life was ruined and I could never go back to school again. And last year when I'd asked Mum about home-schooling, she'd suggested learning the Karma Sutra instead of biology, which meant that option was out too.

I couldn't figure out what was worse.

Having two ex-best friends.

Having the whole school see me shout at my ex for being a liar.

Having the whole school knowing all along he was actually the true-er.

Having a person I don't really know forever thinking

of me as 'that girl who had the most extreme reaction to a hat, ever'.

Being called a goat herder.

I *should* be cringing so hard right now, but luckily/unluckily my cringe muscles are fully occupied with feeling one hundred per cent gutted instead. How *could* Tegan and Rachel do this to me? HOW? And *why*?! Why couldn't they have just told me? It was the lying that twisted my insides way more than the kissing.

I'd been walking, going nowhere, since it happened, hoping that being alone could help me work it all out. But all I'd worked out was how to get really sore feet, and that I should definitely de-junk my school bag more often. (Note to self, no one person needs to carry around seven half-used lipbalms. Unless they have multiple mouths. Which they won't.) My eyes ached with the feeling of tears pushing to come out. *Well, water blobules, you can stay right where you are. You're not deserting me too, not like everyone else.* I pushed myself upwards on the swing, the rush of air helping to seal them in. If there's one way to claw back some dignity after the most humiliating day of your life, it's by spending the evening solo-swinging in a children's playground. At least MIAGTM wasn't here to witness the tragedy of my life. Although he'd probably heard about what happened, and was laughing at me along with the rest of the world. I'd achieved the kind of humiliation that spreads all-years, all-school. Probably all-countries. People in Papua New Guinea were likely laughing at me right now. Eurgh. I was a human embarrassment epidemic.

I felt sick. Like that time I had to take two days off school after accidentally eating some potpourri thinking it was Bombay mix. It was obvious now. *SO* obvious. How stupid could I be?! Silly me for thinking that being a friend meant 'always offering to share clothes or nail varnish or deodorant (even if it's roll-on) and being an OK person', not 'being a total lying, scheming, ex-boyf-snogging, two-faced betrayal machine'. It made me so cross I actually 'bleurghed' out loud, causing a pigeon to throw shade at me. After all the things I've done for them over the last fifteen years. The list was endless.

- I've *never* told a soul that it was Rachel who set off the school fire alarm last year when she was trying to hair-straighten her maths homework.

- I've pretended Tegan's evil cat, Mr Nibbles, is cute on a daily, even hourly, basis. I hate cats. I hate Mr Nibbles even more. In fact, I'd go so far as to say he is my nemesis and gives me evil looks when the others aren't looking.
- I must have watched Hunger Games with them at least one hundred times – with added horror of Mr Nibbles glaring at me from behind a curtain – although SHOCKER I prefer the books.
- For eight years I've kept my promise to Tegan about not saying anything about her hide and seek 'problem'.

My swing jolted, almost throwing me off. In my rage I'd almost gone vertical. I didn't want a broken face to add to my list of woes. *Why was everything so rubbish?!* How could someone whose initials were BF be so BF-less?

If only I could snap my fingers and be magically transported to under my duvet with the base of my bed transformed into a giant fridge so I could exist there happily for ever after. But as I can't teleport, or even click my fingers, I guess I'm stuck here.

"Bella, thank goodness I found you. I am SO SO SO SO sorry."

So Tegan had figured out where I was. And the girl who never showed a chink in her armour was crying so hard she could hardly speak. I swung myself up higher.

"I didn't mean for any of this to happen. I SWEAR." STAY WHERE YOU ARE, TEARS. Don't you dare let her see how much she's upset us.

"It was when I saw that pic. I freaked out. It was just a game – you know?" She gulped in breaths between tears. I concentrated on trying to make hanging on for dear life to some children's playground equipment look aloof. "I have no idea WHAT was going through my head. As if I ever play snog and nom?!" Classy. "I swear I said I wasn't playing a zillion times, but something made me cave in. I'm so annoyed with myself." She kicked at the floor. "SO annoyed!"

Great. The one time she gives in to peer pressure, and it's caught on camera. How brilliant for us both.

Tegan carried on, her normally calm voice bouncing all over the place.

"Then just as we started, Luke appeared out of nowhere. Seconds later he got snogged and had to nominate. He chose me. You should have seen his smirk. I didn't know he'd get someone to take a photo.

I didn't even know he was still at the party till it was too late. And I thought if I made a scene and said no it would look like it was a thing. Like you were still into him. I SWEAR I was thinking of you." She paused. "And now look what's happened." She glugged a breath in. "And it's all my stupid fault."

So it was a game snog then? Not a party snog? If that was true surely she could have just 'fessed up on Saturday? I could have dealt with the news, then laughed with her about how furry Luke's tongue is.

She let out a loud sob. It felt so awkward. This wasn't the Tegan I knew, but then maybe I'd never known her all along. In a matter of hours, I'd gone from trusting everything she said to not believing a word.

"I thought you'd be so mad at me. When I saw that picture I knew how bad it looked. I just couldn't face it... I talked Rachel into going along with it. I just..." She paused to blow her nose. She was the kind of person that always had a clean tissue folded away for emergencies. I was the kind of person who used my sleeve. "I just can't say sorry enough."

Understatement.

The old me would have felt bad at seeing her bawl her eyes out. The new me reckoned she deserved it. Game or not, she'd made the decision not to tell me.

Between them they'd chosen to make the three of us become the two of them – and me. Tegan carried on apologizing for the next ten minutes. I carried on pretending I couldn't hear the apologizing. Hard when you're in a field that's totally silent except for some loud apologizing.

"Bella – please? Are you even listening?" I'd continued my extreme-swinging. "Won't you say *something*?!"

"Something."

What did she want me to say? 'Oh, it's totally cool that you lied about snogging my ex and schemed behind my back and shall we go make Oreo milkshakes?' We'd only invited Luke to show him I didn't care, and instead she'd helped him hit the humiliation jackpot.

"Are you going to hate me for ever?"

Good question. My gran always says, "Better an empty house than a bad tenant." I think it's something to do with farting, but it probably applies to ditching terrible friends too. I spat my answer back.

"Probs."

A bit of me felt good at sticking to my guns. The rest of me felt horrified at hearing me confirm I officially now had no one to hang out with. LOL – Loser Out Loud. Uh-oh. Major tear prickle. Dangerzone. Time to get of here. This conversation was only heading downwards (although physically I was still going down and up and down and up). I jumped off the swing. Tegan looked panicked.

"Don't go! I want to make it up to you."

I nose-snorted. Although I don't know where else you can snort from.

"What? Instead of just making things up *for* me?"

Tegan had known me long enough to know that if there's one thing I hate as much omelettes, it's conflict.

I turned to leave, but had to swallow down the instinctive feeling of guilt, at seeing her so upset. But she *should* be sad – this *was* all her fault. I needed a big finish. But I only had three metres of path to figure out what it could be. I strode towards the gate.

Think of something Bella. Quick. Think of something, anything, to make her realize how much they've broken every rule of friend-dom. I breathed deeply and forced out my best adult voice.

"Tegan. Time can heal but this won't, so, so . . . if you come in my way just . . . just DON'T."

Man. Sadness was obviously good for my dramatic endings. I slammed the gate shut and stomped across the field.

It was only when I was fishing out the key for my

front door that it hit me. I wasn't a creative genius. I was someone who in crisis accidentally yelled Taylor Swift lyrics thinking they were my own. Shame on me now.

I opened the door to find Mum in the hallway. She took one look at my face, put down her cup of green tea that smelt of socks, and stretched out her arms. She was ready to absorb me, and all my problems, like a human cushion. Despite technically still being in a mood with her, I let myself be bundled up into her arms.

"Come on, tell me. How are you feeling? *How are your feelings?*" she pecked my hair with kisses. Without waiting for any answer she continued. "Do you want a choc-ice?"

Her answer to everything. World peace? Have a frozen dairy desert. I grunted a no-word-needed response, wriggled away towards the lounge, and sprawled lengthways on the sofa, ignoring Mumbles as she licked at my face. I also ignored that my sister was curled up by the radiator reading a book that looked bigger than the dictionary. And probably had more words. It was her favourite spot in the house, and so ever since Dad left, it meant I could have a whole sofa to myself. A more than worthwhile swop. Crap dad for cushions.

Mum plonked herself next to me, trying to wedge herself on the spare bit of seat, but actually sitting very much on me.

"Come on then, buggerlugs. Tell your mum what's really up. Remember, I've been there, seen it, done it all – many times over."

I very much doubted that, unless she too once knocked over her school's 'Pupil of The Year' trophy and had to glue the handle back on with bits of chewed up Chomp (and are still panicking someone will notice and run DNA tests).

"It's nothing. Just friend stuff."

She looked positively relieved.

"Oh well then, that's fine! I thought you were going to say you were with child."

Jo snorted. I didn't blame her.

"Pregnant? How?!"

"Well, Bella, when two people. . ."

"MUM! My day's been bad enough already without you being completely gross. And also, I'm not seven."

"There's nothing 'gross' –" she did rabbit-ear fingers around it as if it was a novel new word – "about two people loving each other, darling. Or would you rather you'd never been born because conception isn't to your liking?"

124

She had it in one. Jo looked up from her dictionary novel.

"Mum. Please. Bells is clearly not in a good place right now. Talking about your bedroom habits is not what *anyone* needs."

Wow. Jo on my side for once. She *must* be feeling guilty.

"It wasn't in the bedroom actually. It was right here in this lounge."

Jo and I made simultaneous spew noises and shifted in our places, neither of us keen on sitting on a bona fide mum mating spot. Still, at least cushion covers were washable; I couldn't say the same about the carpet.

Mum shook her head, as if us not wanting to hear about her boinking with Dad was entirely ludicrous, and returned to her own armchair to get back to enjoying reading the obituaries in the local paper. Jo bum shuffled – buffled – across the floor and lent on the arm of my sofa. Maybe she'd had the same carpet conclusion as me? She lowered her voice and put her hand on my arm.

"Has it got something to do with the party drama?"

I nodded – which is hard to do when your chin is resting on something solid.

"You want to talk about it?"

"Not really."

"Furry muff." She always said that when she meant 'fair enough'. "Well, if there's anything I *can* help with. . .?"

I kept my voice low.

"Can you drive me to Wales slash Wolverhampton and try and find that boy from Saturday, apologize for you being a maniac in front of him, and persuade him to come to my prom? And get me some new friends on the way? Oh and also sort out a way to make an entire school forget an entire day?"

She smiled. Maybe having an older sister wasn't all bad.

"Wow. You really have messed up, haven't you? I mean, that sounds bleak, even by your standards?!"

Nope. It was all-bad after all.

I quietly hit my fists together and made my left hand into an 'L' shape, which is British Sign Language for 'G' and 'L'. Get lost. We'd been finding ways to annoy each other in silence for years.

She made an 'S' and an 'up' and buffled back to her radiator spot, soon lost again in her book.

I zoned out, letting the soothing sounds of a man stuffing a turkey on TV slow drown my thoughts. As he pulled out something from the turkey that looked like tonsils, but clearly wasn't, unless you also have them up your bum, I had an idea.

It wouldn't help, but it would make me feel better. I got my phone out.

HIDE AND LEAK
MY FRIEND TEGAN USED TO GET SO
HYPED PLAYING HIDE AND SEEK THAT
WHENEVER SHE HID, SHE GOT SO EXCITED
SHE WEED HERSELF. TO THIS DAY, HER
MUM STILL BLAMES MY DOG FOR THE
SMELL IN THEIR WARDROBE.

I hovered my finger over the upload button, fighting off a pang of guilt. But sharing a silly story with a bunch of people who don't even know who I am was nothing on what Tegan had done to me. Still, I went back and changed 'Tegan' to 'Tee' to make myself feel better, before pressing upload, and watching it fly into the stream. I shouldn't have worried so much. Seconds later it was already old news. I scrolled through everything else that had been shared since I last looked but didn't spot anything Zac-ish, so went on a follow spree to widen the net. But just after I turned it off, my screen flashed. Gulp.

NEW MESSAGE.

A number I didn't recognize. My stomach sank. If this was Luke and another one of his games, I didn't want to be part of it. Maybe I should delete it?

My phone flashed again, cross at being ignored. Where were you when I *wanted* messages, hey? Stupid two-faced phone. Phoney phone.

Cross, I picked it up ready to delete whatever it had to say. But my middle left finger is more nosey than my brain, and before I could stop it, it pressed 'read'.

The words on screen made me sit bolt upright. The words on screen made me hold my phone above me like I'd just won the World Cup but then simultaneously developed a metal allergy. The words on screen were so life changing I had to check the room to confirm they hadn't been accompanied by a low to medium earthquake.

The words on screen meant my life might not be over after all.

They meant it was about to get all kinds of awesome.

CHAPTER

TWELVE

I hadn't stopped staring at it since I got it yesterday. This must be what it's like for art people who stand and look at the Mona Lisa for hours, hoping to spot a hidden meaning. Except I didn't have a grinning lady to obsess over, I had tiny little letters. The alphabet was a wondrous invention.

Once we turned off the road and on to the playing field, I let Mumbles off the lead and looked again.

Hi Bella, thanks for a great night/black eye.
Guess you had to take off. Or had second
thoughts?! Be cool to stay in touch. Z

Officially the dreamiest one hundred and one characters ever written. And yes, I'd counted (one hundred and twenty-five with spaces). Be *cool* to stay in touch? Cool?! It would be so cool that J-Law could segway past it and she'd still think 'Woah, I wish one day I could be that cool'.

These twenty-nine words (plus one initial) had made today bearable. Who needs friends to sit by at lunch, or someone to reassure you that everyone wasn't giving you sympathetic looks (they were), or even just point out I'd accidentally biro-ed myself in the face, when you had a message from the boy of your dreams? Except he wasn't dreams any more – he was living, breathing pixels on my phone. If pixels breathed.

When it arrived last night, it had made no sense. I remembered every blink Zac had made – how had I forgotten giving him my number?! But before I could prod him for details he'd followed up:

PS – surprise! Hope it's OK but my gran talked
Black Bay into handing over your number.

JOYBALLS! He'd gone on a covert mission to get my number, which involved an elderly lady AND probably breaking a low-level law. *Surely* this meant we now had to become life partners?! I was SO happy I'd registered for Black Bay's stupid text mailing list. Now I literally loved their terribly spelled spam messages!

I stared at the message for the one hundred and twelfth time. On the one hand, it was the best thing in the world that could ever happen to me, beating my previous dream of being appointed 5SOS tour masseuse. On the other hand, it's turned me into a nervous wreck. I'm now at risk of sending Zac a crazy message at ANY GIVEN MOMENT. That's like a 24/7 pressure. For the rest of my life.

I thought of Mum's advice and breathed in the evening air to try and stop my brain freaking out. I didn't need meditation though. I needed normalization, because it is NOT normal to be constantly on the verge of typing OMGILOVEYOUCOMETOPROMPSMARRYME. In fact I've thought about it so much that I'm worried my phone knows and wouldn't even try and autocorrect it into something less insane. I rooted around in my bag and pulled out my woolly winter gloves that I never bothered to clear out. Desperate times called for desperate knitted measures. I tugged the gloves on to my hands. If my mind couldn't be trusted, at least my fingers now had a physical barrier to prevent out-of-control messaging. Still, I already looked bad enough in Jo's running hoodie that I'd pulled on at the last minute when I'd panicked it would rain but didn't want to get any of my own stuff muddy. It had actual reflective bits on it, like I was some sort of child's bike.

I had managed one normalish – emphasis on 'ish' – reply though. In the absence of best friends/any friends for advice, I'd Googled 'funny replies to messages'. But seeing as I didn't want to send him a picture of a cat with a beanbag on its head, I'd had to figure it out on my own. In school they should ditch teaching how rivers are made (we don't need to know, as the whole point is, they make themselves) and teach dealing with blank messages instead. A couple of badly chosen words and I could ruin everything. I shuddered at the memory of when my mum started saying 'WTF' to everyone, thinking it meant 'Way Too Fantastic!' Anything could happen.

After practising for over half an hour, this is what I'd managed:

Hi Zac, I had a great time too. Hope your eye's OK. OOPS. Family emergency meant I left first thing. Sorry! Deffo stay in touch. Bx

I'd removed a smiley face to appear more seventeen-y, but still panicked as soon as I'd pressed send. Did I sound like a loser? Did I sound too casual? Too formal? Too weird? Was the kiss too much?! Would he still like me enough to reply? Would he... And then my heart had stopped. Would he notice that I'd accidentally written POOPS in giant capital letters?!

I'd swallowed my last crumbs of pride, and decided not to try and explain in case I sent something even worse. He hasn't replied since.

Mumbles barked, dragging me out of Zac daydreaming and into real life. She only barks at people or balloons, and seeing as we were in a field, and not at a children's party, she must have heard voices. I called her back and clipped on her lead.

The voices got louder as a group of lads walked through the gap in the hedge twenty metres away from where I was standing. I was in a wide, open space, covered in shiny reflective material. Hiding was not an option. I pretended to pat Mumbles, using my peripheral perving skills to work out who they were, watching as they walked towards the centre of the football pitch. I didn't recognize any of them – any of them except one. MIAGTM/MIAGTM (UIMZA) – (Unless I Meet Zac Again). Great – the one day I finally stop thinking about someone and leave the house looking like a sporty scarecrow, they appear.

"Come on, kiddo, time to get outta this joint." I pulled at Mumbles' lead. Yes, that's right, lads, I *do* talk to my dog like she's in a crime drama. Mumbles trotted at my heels, a stick in her mouth that was ten times wider than her body. Shouts drifted across from where the boys had started to warm up. Mumbles whipped her head around, almost taking me out with the stick. Were they shouting in our direction? No way I was going to check and look like an uber-keeno. Although, what if they're shouting 'heads' and I'm about to get knocked out by a low-flying football? I tugged at Mumbles' lead and hissed, "Come on", trying to get to the road before any drama occurred. But the shouting got louder, and as it did, in an act of total disloyalty, Mumbles rooted herself to the spot like she'd been turned into a doggie statue. TRAITOR.

She wouldn't budge. She was ruining my 'pretend not to notice they're there' strategy. I had no option. I turned round.

Worst fear confirmed. They WERE all staring at me and/or my statue dog. Except one: MIAGTM. And he was walking right towards us. SHUDDERBALLS.

What if he was coming to verify that I was the

person at the centre of the 'no friends scandal'? Or was he about to yell at me for the time Mumbles ran into their end-of-season game and ate their football? Or had he noticed my stalking and was about to issue a restraining order? Whatever I do, I *mustn't* take any paperwork from him. I must also shut my jaw, which had fallen open as a result of my first full-on, full-frontal MIAGTM perv. How can someone get fitter when they're closer? Doesn't that defy all rules of seeing-ness?

He was wearing a grey hoodie with the hood up (and nothing reflective on it). For me, that's the girl equivalent of boys liking sexy underwear. And now he was only seconds away, pushing his brown hair back off his face as he approached. He smiled. I never knew he had braces, and they made him even cuter. *Please God/ God-Like Thing, whatever is about to happen, if you do one thing for me ever – other than making Zac fall in love with me and mending my entire life – please don't let my maniac dog spring back into life and dive head first into a stranger's crotch.*

Now, I'm not saying this is conclusive proof that there isn't a God/God-Like Thing, but if there is one, he/she's clearly got more pressing things to attend to than my groin-sniffing woes. Mumbles burst towards

MIAGTM's dangle region, dropping her stick and sniffing his jeans wildly, like a police dog who'd found an industrial stash of extra-strength drugs nestled in his pants. MIAGTM stopped still, his hoodied-gloriousness making me wish a sinkhole could appear, just big enough to swallow one person. After all the years of watching him from afar, I was not equipped to have an impromptu conversation from a-near, right here, right now.

His blue eyes looked at me like I was in some way responsible for my dog being a sex pest. I looked at him wondering if my sinkhole could be big enough for Mumbles as well. And also, wondering exactly what a sinkhole was.

"So *you're* the owner of the world's first football-eating dog?"

OH MY MIAGTM. We Were In Conversation. But he was distracted trying to bat away the football-eating-dog-head that was firmly lodged between his legs. His trousers must smell intense. Hope he doesn't have hygiene issues. As casual wafting wasn't doing the trick, he crouched down to Mumbles' eye level, cutting off her groin-access. He grabbed her collar, flicking out her tag that had got stuck, and ruffled her ears. This just got her even more excited, and I swear she tried to mount him. It was like she was acting out my inner thoughts.

I garbled, "Sorryabouthershe'sjustabitweird" and pulled so hard on her lead she glided backwards without any of her legs actually moving. Ignoring the sound of dog strangulation coming from around our knees, he carried on.

"Ah, I think she's pretty cool." Swoon! He thinks Mumbles is cool! She's totally getting extra Marmite on her toast tonight. "Anyway, me and the lads have seen you walking her down to the football pitch a couple of times. . ."

He'd noticed my stalking! Result two! Of sorts.

". . . and we noticed that today you're in your kit, and . . . we're a player down, so wondered if you wanted to help out with our team? We're always on the look out for a keeper."

"A keeper?! As in a GOAL keeper? A keeper of goals?"

I couldn't disguise my surprise. What was he on about? I can't even catch a netball when it's deliberately thrown towards me by someone shouting, "Bella, catch!"

"Well, yeah. I know we've never seen you in action, but you've got all your football stuff on –" he nodded towards my giant, Zac-message-preventing woolly gloves – "so we figured it was worth an ask."

Hold up. The big 'L' and 'R' on my gloves were adorbs, weren't they? Not sporty? I looked down. Jo's top shone back. And he DID know that the massive 'Worcester Ladies XI' on my back was about my sister's running club. Surely? I mean do I *look* like someone who enjoys competitive sport?! The earnest look on his face suggested I might. Cringe cringe crange.

"We have some other girls that play with us sometimes, if that helps?"

Bella, DO NOT snigger that he just said 'girls that play with us'. Think! He was waiting for an answer. I'd only managed to say eleven words so far, and now the rest were going to be confessing to him that I need gloves in the summer just to stop me sending messages to fit boys. First impression – goalkeeper. Second – loon.

"Er, yeah, I just sometimes, erm, help out at the, erm, with my mum's . . . with the . . . with the local, erm, youth team, Ladies X I, or erm. . ." I scrabbled in my head. It wasn't X and I, it was a number, wasn't it!? ". . . twelve, no eleven. YES! But I'm not that great, so should, probably, er, say no. You know. Goal keeping – goal-giving-away? That's me! But, thanks. I think?"

The lie couldn't have been more obvious than if I'd had a giant perm fashioned into the words 'I'm telling you a massive lie, right now'. Even Mumbles looked embarrassed and she sniffs bums for fun.

MIAGTM didn't seem phased.

"Sounds cool. What league do they play in? We might have them on our fixtures list?"

Why could he not just end this torture humanely?! Must say something he definitely won't have heard of.

"It's the, er, Church and, erm, Orchestra's League Of ... Newbies?" It would have sounded more convincing if I hadn't said it like a question. He looked unconvinced. I needed to make it sound more of a thing. I thought back. "We call it ... COLON."

Oh goodness. Did I just shout 'colon' at MIAGTM?! The fact his eyes were almost popping out suggested I did. I had to leave. Immediately.

"Anyway, what's the time, I better be heading off." I pulled out my phone to fake check the time, but because of my big, goalkeeping-gloved fingers I instead proceeded to flash him a picture of me and my ex-friend Rachel that I'd just been about to delete. It was the one where we'd sellotaped up our faces to look like pig-people. I was on fire today.

"Weird. Someone must have just sent me that. I

have no idea what it is. Other than a picture. Of some
people. Who I do. Not. Know." I stuffed my phone
away. "So, I should probably go and find out who. Or
practise goalkeeping, and kicking. And throwing. And
all the other football things that I definitely do. That's
football!" MIAGTM looked baffled. "So that's what
I'm going to do. Now. As in now. So bye. C'MON,
MUMBLES."

I fled, not risking waiting for a response, or worse,
me saying anything, ever again. His last impression was
just going to have to be the sight of me sliding Mumbles
along the whole length of the playing field, her legs like
rigid lolly sticks, while she stared longingly back at his
crotch. I made it to the safety of the road then ducked
down behind the hedge so the lads couldn't see me any
more.

Thank goodness I'd met Zac. Because now, in
under two minutes, I'd guaranteed MIAGTM was
now more likely Man Who Would Never Ever Marry
Me Not Even If The Human Race Depended On It.
MWWNEMMNEITHRDOI.

Why was I so bad at life?! But as I crouch-walked
along the never-ending hedge, it hit me. I didn't *have*
to be this way. I HAD to start turning my life around.
Messaging Zac wasn't enough. He was the one ticket I

had to proving to the world I was normal. He was the one thing that could shut Luke up, and at the same time, prove to Tegan and Rachel that my life was just fine without them. I had to step my game up and get him here. And I had to do it by prom.

CHAPTER

THIRTEEN

Hiding behind the hedge would have been a lot more successful if a car hadn't sped round the corner, its lights turning me and my reflective top into a human-outdoor-disco-ball. It swerved behind me, and Jo lent across to shout out of the passenger window.

"Want a life? Sorry, lift?"

She was clocking up more miles than Lewis Hamilton since she passed her test. First time, of course. I swear she only did it to make me feel worse about being stuck at home and a million years from having a car of my own.

"I have a *life* thank you very much." Complete lie.

"Oh yeah – sorry to interrupt your lovely walk for one bent double behind a hawthorn." She revved the engine, challenging me to put stubbornness before laziness. "Nice top, BTdubs."

I pretended she hadn't just said that.

"Fine. I'll have a lift then." She took her foot off the accelerator.

"What's the magic word?"

Jo was so annoying.

"Please?"

"No, it's put-that-smelly-dog-in-the-back." I rolled my eyes and got Mumbles to jump on the back seat. She loved looking out of the window as we drove – like she was some sort of royalty-dog looking at lesser animals that had to degrade themselves by using their actual legs as a mode of transport.

I jumped in the passenger seat, slamming the door loudly so that the lads could hear me. See, I *might* have a complete absence of conversational skills, but I *do* know someone with a car. Although I guess so does everyone, if you include parents. Oh no, I hope they didn't think my mum had come to pick me up. Why did I slam the door?!

"Not on boy-spotting duties tonight then?"

"As if."

"No, of course, that's why you only ever offer to walk the dog when it's not raining, it's not too dark, and you've spent hours staring in the mirror first?"

"Whatever." I *should* have stared in the mirror after putting this ridic top on.

"You only hate me cos you know I nailed it."

"The only thing you nail is being the most annoying person ever invented."

But Jo didn't have time to reply as out of nowhere she had to slam on the breaks. My body jolted forward against my seatbelt. A car had screeched out of a driveway in front of us, not bothering to check that we weren't right in its path. Jo swore under her breath and flashed her lights, before quickly composing herself again, letting the other car hurry away.

"Sorry about that. You can tell Mum he didn't even look."

If there was one thing my sister was, it wasn't careless. I was both careless and carless.

"Don't worry, I saw – what an idiot. Wonder why he was in such a rush?"

"You spotted who it was, right?"

I hadn't. Although I did know the house – everyone did. It belonged to my headmistress, Mrs Hitchman.

"It was Mr Lutas, the art teacher – well, he was mine anyway."

Sadly, he was still mine too. But what reason did he

144

have to be at Mrs Hitchman's house – and to be leaving it in such a hurry? Was she an underground chalk smuggler? Did she have the most exceptional bowls of fruit to paint?

"You *sure* it was him?"

"I'd recognize that grey caveman-vibe hair anywhere. And he's still got the same car he had back in the day. He didn't notice us, though."

Phew. I'm already in his bad books without him knowing we'd caught him on some dodgy late visit. "He's such a weirdo."

"You don't need to tell *me* that. I was in the year where he went on that legendary school trip – to the arrrrrrrt gallery. This old guy who ran it ended up showing us this massive drawer full of work Mr Lutas had done. Honestly, it was *packed* with all these naked self portraits. Him stepping up on to a chair, him crouching at an oven, oh God, even him doing a press up. Naked. It still gives me nightmares now."

Thanks for sharing, sis. Now I was going to have to attempt a life without sleep to avoid the risk of mentally-seeing the same terrifying night vision.

"That's REVOLT. Why would *anyone* do that?!"

"Well, in fairness to him, he didn't *mean* for us to see them, and they *were* kind of arty . . . but once you've seen it, trust me, it cannot be unseen. I reckon that's why all our year got decent art marks."

Wow – guilty secrets for good grades. I'd never thought Jo would admit to being caught up in anything dodgy?!

"*How* have you not told me this before?! The others would have LOVED it." My heart lurched as I remembered just how much things had changed between us. "Oh well, guess they'll just have to keep on not knowing. Their loss."

"Have you still not sorted things out?" Last night I'd filled her in on the mess of my life in a fleeting moment of forgetting how annoying she was.

"Still? It's only been a day and a half! And there's nothing to sort out. It's un-sortable."

Jo flicked the indicator to turn into our little drive. The light was on in the kitchen and Mum was dancing as she stirred a pan.

"Look, I'm not telling you what to do." Jo always said that when she told me what to do. "And it was really crappy what they did. But *try* and have a think whether it's worth losing your two best mates over one mistake."

"I have thought. And it is. Cos it wasn't one mistake – it was one big massive plot. They snoozed, they lose-d."

She shrugged and got out of the car. If perfect Jo didn't have any advice then I really was in trouble.

By the time we got into the kitchen Mum had already served up her interpretation of vegetarian toad in the hole – basically sticking random vegetables vertically into batter. I chewed through semi-raw carrot, fielding parent questions on my sorry excuse of a life. How could she grill *me* if she couldn't even grill cheese on toast? *How were Tegan and Rachel?* (no comment). *Had I seen Luke this term?* (way more than I'd wanted). *Was Mikey still holding out hope for courting Tegan?* (no one says courting any more). *Did I need any mother-daughter exam-meditation?* (no, because I can't get exam stress if I pretend they're not happening). I completed the required amount of small talk for happy family-ness and ran up to my room. Normally I'd flop on the sofa and read whatever book Rachel had lent me. Or laugh about the TV on our group messages. Or spend the evening scouring YouTube for some throwback links. We'd customized loads of stuff in our rooms thanks to some craft vids from Tegan, and Rachel had got me into some really funny book vloggers. Still, that was *then*, and having zero friends freed up my time to concentrate on mission Life Reinvention. I pulled out my lucky pencil (it once impaled my hand when I was searching in my bag and thus got me out of a gym lesson) and drew up a list.

1) I need to make sure I can get to prom, so NO MORE drama is allowed. Except in drama lessons, where I need to be really good.

2) I need to somehow convince Zac that I am alluring enough to want to see again. And at least seventeen.

I looked at my leg-forest which was peeping out from under my jeans. This was going to be hard.

3) (toughest one yet) I need to get Zac to be my date to a Year 10 prom – my Year 10 prom – even though he thinks I'm at college.

Still, even if he just walks in, realizes it's a school prom, and walks out, that's technically 'attending' so Luke would have to say sorry, and Rachel and Tegan would be totally gutted that they hadn't been more supportive.

4) Become amazing, so even after potential prom disaster Zac realizes that I am the only person who can ever make him truly happy, and suggests buying a caravan and moving to Wales to spend our lives eating Nutella sandwiches and talking about art (extra note to self: need to learn about art).

I looked at the list. When I broke it down, it seemed *slightly* more doable. Plus, now I had his number I didn't need to waste any time searching and posting on *PSSSST* any more. I opened up the app to delete it. But what I saw made me change my mind. I'd got over 200 likes on the post about Tegan's Hide and Leak. Wow. As my real life was getting dangerously friendless, my non-real life was suddenly popular with total strangers. Or as Mum would say, 'friends you just haven't met yet', which is the opposite of every other mum's advice, ever. They say 'stranger danger' – my mum says, "Hello stranger, have you met my daughters, here's a cup of tea." Maybe I shouldn't delete the app just yet? It *was* nice to be appreciated. Maybe I could just post one more and see how it goes? I needed to pull out a big gun.

I racked my brain. Could someone please hurry up and invent Google search for heads? Burrowing past song lyrics to access actual memories was way too tough. Although ... something did pop up. Something that would probably get quite a few likes.

I went to type, but stopped as I remembered the pact Tegan, Rachel and I had made to never breathe a word of this to anyone. But in the very same convo we'd made the same pact to never lie to each other. If they could break the rules, so could I. And if they hadn't broken the pact in the first place, then I wouldn't be spending my time trying to fill my friend-hole with internet likes. It was the least they could do.

MENS-UN-TRUE-ATION

MY FRIEND R CAUSED A MASSIVE MIX-UP ONE GAMES LESSON WHEN SHE YELLED, "CAN I BORROW A TOWEL?" EVERYONE FREAKED OUT THINKING SHE'D JUST BECOME THE FIRST TO START HER PERIOD. SO, FOR THE NEXT TWO YEARS, INSTEAD OF 'FESS UP, WE HAD TO HELP HER FAKE THEM – COMPLETE WITH MONTHLY MADE-UP MOODY MOODS.

I smiled remembering what lengths we'd had to go to. We even staged buying some tampons so Lou would see us, but had to return them later when we realized we needed the money for emergency potato wedges.

But they were the old days.

I double-checked that I hadn't used any incriminating details and pressed post. *PSSSST* might be anonymous, but I wanted to be extra sure it stayed that way.

I wasted the next ten minutes doing an internet quiz to find out what flavour chewing gum I'd be (Sugar-Free Cinnamon) and tried to not pay attention to the fact that no one was paying my *PSSSST* any attention. But as I started a fifty questions quiz on what dog was my destiny, my phone beeped. Could this be the start of my internet-sensation-ing?

Oh no. Oh yes! It was way better. It was a message from Zac. I sat down on my bed, needing cushioning around me in case my bones jellified on reading.

Hey Bella/Bells for short. I'm in Worcester for a college thing on Fri, isn't that your area? Wanna meet Sat morn? Z

Thank goodness I had 360-degree mattress cushioning. Every bone, muscle and nerve failed me. I splodged on to the bed, not even able to coordinate bodily functions enough to blink. Zac, of being half kissed by me fame, was coming to visit no-friends-and-no-goalkeeping-skills me. This was major. This was happening. IN FOUR DAYS.

I threw the rule of waiting the obligatory seventy-five minutes or more to reply out of the window. Every second was a second he might change his mind.

Sure! What time? Be good to catch up.

'Sure' – how funny am I?! As if I didn't mean 'OF COURSE THIS IS THE BEST THING THAT WILL EVER HAPPEN IN MY LIFE (AND ALSO THE MOST TERRIFYING BUT YOU DON'T NEED TO KNOW THAT)'.

I grabbed my laptop and started a search-athon in case Zac was about to ask me for suggestions of what to do, seeing as it was me who lived here. I looked up 'most romantic places in Worcester', 'things to do on a first date', and also 'Zac Black Bay photo' in case anyone had put anything up in the 24 hours since I'd last checked. As I waited for a reply, I also checked, 'how to look fierce in the morning'.

Cool, 10am. By the Helga Statue? Though it's meant to be crazy stormy this weekend – lemme know if you want to rain check.

Ten a.m.? What was he? A parent? Did he know Saturday firmly occurred in the period of time known as a 'weekend'? In which plans should not be made before eleven a.m.?! I looked up the weather report. As if I cared about rain?! It was just like a shower, but outside. But the BBC brought joy to my heart. It didn't look stormy at all. I screengrabbed the evidence.

If you mean Elgar Statue, yup I'm in. And look – weather's fine. Unless I'm talking hot air. . .

I attached the pic of my laptop screen. He wasn't using rain to, er, rain on my parade. I buried my head into my pillow. Am I on fire right now or what? Have I, Bella Fisher, become the kind of person who someone actually arranges to date? Well, at least meet up with someone for a period of time when they're in an area where they don't know anyone?

See you then. I will try to look fierce.

How did he know?! Great minds think alike. My stomach plummeted. Or maybe they don't. Maybe minds-which-you-send-a-picture-of-your-laptop-complete-with-completely-embarassing-search-terms-about-fierceness-and-looking-for-photos-of-himself-and-being-destined-to-be-a-Bulldog-in-your-tabs think alike. How could I be such a massive moron?! I can never message him again. I need to superglue my goalkeeping gloves on.

I flopped back and stared at the ceiling. The next 4.2 days were now project PFSZ. Preparing For Seeing Zac. Must make a list of all the slight exaggerations I've told him, to keep on top of them . . . and places to avoid. And people. And how to make sure Jo is NOWHERE near town to repeat sabotage.

I sat bolt upright as the reality of seeing him hit me. What on earth can I wear? Can I grow my hair the two inches I really want in sixty-six hours? Should I write a list of conversations I can start, so I come across as interesting and mature? Should I revise anything? I opened up a tab to stream BBC News. Watching the news is what Jo does – and programmes about bands in black and white on BBC Four. That must be what seventeen-year-olds do too. What else does she do? Wear actual perfume, be put up a year a school, and be on time for stuff. I can do that, easy. From now on she could be my muse. Although I mustn't let myself get brainwashed by how dull she can be.

Wowsers. What a day – maybe things were shaping

up to be less than terrible. I may be two bessies down, but now I'm one huge, big, fat, massively exciting, real-life date up.

CHAPTER

FOURTEEN

I, Bella Fisher, am officially a lone wolf. But it doesn't bother me as much now I'm a lone wolf with a big woolfy date on the horizon. Ow-wooooo. Between chews on my gherkin sandwich, I glanced over at Rachel and Tegan. I'd like to say they were using their lunch to huddle round an effigy of me, sacrificing Year 7s in an attempt to show their repentance, but in reality they were just eating some Mini Cheddars. Gawd, I hated them (Rachel and Tegan, not Mini Cheddars). It's *so* unfair that I'm the innocent one here, yet I'm the one who's sitting with my B-list friends, watching *them* just eating crisps like nothing's happened. Well, I hope they get soggy globules stuck in their teeth and no one tells them for the entire afternoon.

Still, B-list friends beat fake friends. I smiled up at Sarah. I'd spent every lunchtime with her since Hat-Gate. She hadn't mentioned the drama once, despite all the looks and whispers rippling around me wherever I went. She'd been nothing but nice to me, although in fairness I've never met a mean Sarah, ever. But somewhere deep down, hanging out just didn't feel right. I nodded my head along with the others at the table, channelling my efforts on smiling at the right points in her netball story. It was normally Tegan who dealt with sports chat that came our way, and I was out of my depth.

My pocket buzzed. It was another message from her.

Come over? We've got a sorry Babybel for you.
R&T 🧂 ☺ 👀 🌙

One for the bin. With huge hand actions I pressed delete, like my phone had big imaginary buttons. *Look! I don't want to be around your digital communications, let alone actual you.* They could stick their Babybel up their bum.

I SOL-ed (snorted out loud) at mental images of Bumbybel, but got weird looks, so tried to weave the laughter into whatever it was that Sarah was saying. I realized too late she'd moved on to talking about her cat dying. I shut up.

"You like quizzes. What's five letters and begins with S?"

EURGH. That smug voice made me want to spit out my sandwich. I spun round. Why had *Luke* come to speak to me? What did he want *this* time? Oh well, there was nowhere to run (plus running is forbidden in the canteen, plus plus I have a really embarrassing run). I plonked my gherkin sandwich aggressively back in my Peppa Pig lunchbox. Intimidating.

"Don't know. Don't care. So how about you leave me alone?" But Luke dug his hands further into his pockets. He wasn't going anywhere.

"Wrong answer. It was 'sorry'. But I'll accept your apology however you want to give it to me."

As if.

"Get lost. If I wanted to speak to you, I would have come over to douchebag corner, or wherever it is that you hang out these day."

He grinned patronizingly. I swear even his nose was condescending. How could I have ever thought he was anything other than vom-inducing?

"You can always ask your *best mate* Tegan. She's

often aware of my personal movements, if you know what I mean?"

He was trying to wind me up about the kissing, but he didn't know that 'personal movements' was the exact phrase my mum used for having a poo. 1–0 to me. I matched his condescending smile, hoping my nose also joined in.

People were looking over at us, excited at the prospect of another shouting match. I caught Tegan and Rachel staring, concerned. Please tell me there were no more revelations? All I wanted was to be left alone.

"Look, I'm not in the mood for this. Just go away."

I turned back to the table and took a big gherkin-y bite. *Can't you see I'm chewing here?* This whole situation bummed me out so much that it almost – but not quite – put me off my sandwich. It wasn't just everything that had gone down. Or being the centre of all the unwanted attention. It was the humiliation of everyone knowing there was a time when I *liked* Luke. I could kick myself at being sucked in by his fakery. I should have known we had, we *have*, nothing in common. He likes blonde girls that wear black bras under their school shirts; I like going to fancy dress parties in a sleeping bag and pretending I'm a caterpillar. He likes girls on bikes; I like boys with guitars. He likes making ramps; I like trying to recreate album covers with nail varnish on my toenails. Everyone knows who he is; a lot of people still think my name is Tina (always Tina, I have no idea why).

A battered rucksack slammed down next to my Peppa flask (note to self, must work harder on intimidating Tupperware).

"She doesn't want to talk, all right? So if you could do one, that'd be great."

Mikey plonked himself on to the stool next to me. I hadn't seen him since Tegan, Rachel and I had fallen out – it was good to know he hadn't switched to the dark side too.

Luke slapped his hand on Mikey's shoulder as his mates bunched up around him. Did they ever speak, or just spend their spare time choreographing 'threatening lad' moves.

"If I wanted the opinion of a nobody, I would have asked a Year 7."

Mikey stood up again, and drew his shoulders back. I swear he was a foot taller than normal.

"Well if *we* wanted the company of the biggest jerk in school, we would have asked that loser who once put the wrong answer when an exam paper asked for his own name. Oh sorry. THAT'S YOU."

160

Luke pushed at Mikey's shoulder.

"If you've got a problem with me, mate, just come out and say it."

Mikey smiled warmly.

"I am saying it, *mate*. I've got quite an epic problem with you."

Wow. I'd never seen Mikey have a problem with *anyone* or *anything*. Was it wrong that my main thought was that it was kind of hot? But when I looked back at him, I realized this wasn't about me. Because despite Luke being all up in his face, Mikey was distracted, staring across the canteen, the anger gone from his face. He wasn't just protecting me, he was protecting the person he couldn't help but watch to make sure she was OK. Tegan. And she was oblivious, whispering to Rachel. With all her As and full marks, she could sometimes be so clueless.

My heart sank for Mikey. He'd give anything to kiss Tegan, and Luke had done it just for laughs. No wonder he was so angry.

"BOYS."

I looked up. A furious looking teacher was striding towards us, his face wrinkled with the strain of not smiling for at least fifty years. I tugged at Mikey's jumper.

"BOYS, ENOUGH!"

Why was it *always* Mr Lutas that arrived at the wrong second? Maybe his jangly pockets were stuffed with misery magnets that automatically dragged him to our worst moments.

Mikey murmured a sorry. Luke thought he was far too cool to actually say anything and swung his shoulders instead.

"You do not need me to rrremind you that aggrrressive behaviourrr is not tolerated at this school. So unless you want to lose YET MORRRREE prom points, I suggest you put this petty feud to one side and start behaving a little less like children. Understood?"

Mikey nodded. Luke still did nothing. Mr Lutas jangled his keys/coins/magnets in his pocket. I didn't try to work out what – no one wants to see teacher groin jiggle, whatever the mechanism. Instead I smiled at Mr Lutas, trying to distance myself from the drama. But a cold-as-ice stare met my gaze.

"And that goes for you too, young lady."

Oh excellent. He hated me enough *before* this term.

"One morrre wrrrrrrrrrong move from ANY of you and it's a one-way ticket to detention."

It was the worst timing ever, but my face went rogue and looked inappropriately impressed at his monumental tongue roll. Mr Lutas totally noticed. I tried to regain control. "NOW GET GOING!"

Luke stormed out of the canteen. Mikey sat back down beside me. The rest of the room switched back from gawping to gulping. My shell-shocked lunch crew looked horrified. The most drama they'd ever had at their table was when Sarah's best mate Pam discovered her Oxtail soup was actually made of an ox's tail, and it wasn't just a posh name for a vegetable. I hoped they knew this was kind of high-visibility new to me too. But, quickly, kindly, they got back to lifting the mood with chat about how OMG, they just realized they'd all visited the same cat crematorium. Mikey didn't even pretend to listen and turned to talk to me.

"Sorry about that. I didn't know Mr Lutas was around." He reached out and stole a crisp. "Luke winds me up something chronic."

"You and me both." I picked my packet of crisps up off the table. "Thanks for helping me out. Him *and* Mr Lutas seem on the warpath for me this term. It sucks."

"Tottalius suckius muchius." He stole another crisp. "Well, guess I just wanted to say 'hi'."

I put my crisps into the safety of my lunchbox.

"Hi?"

He waved before swooping his hand down to nabble

the last crisp in the packet. I shut my box lid on his fingers. He pretended nothing had happened. "Now we've both said hi."

"Sure have, a 'hi' point of my day."

We laughed, but his face flushed at me catching him shooting yet another look at Tegan. I couldn't think of what to say. All I had was, 'Isn't the girl you are in love with a total and utter cowbag, so how about stop looking at her?', and I didn't think that was a dead cert to help the conversation flow. Mikey sensed my awkwardness (yet again proving he is the most un-boy boy I know).

"OK – well, cool. I don't want to disturb you and your friends any longer." He stressed the words *friends* as if to say, 'Who are these people that I had no idea you even knew, but whatever that's fine'. "And thanks for the crisps." He winked, and waving goodbye, walked out of the canteen in the opposite direction to Luke.

I wanted to make a move too, so stuffed my mum-made vegan, dairy-free, no-chocolate brownie (with added bits of Chomp in) back into my lunchbox. I still had fifteen minutes of break to kill, which meant fifteen minutes to head to the library to locate a book on Modern Art, for Zac-date revision purposes. Annoying I couldn't just borrow one of Rachel's, but I wasn't about to ask *her* for favours. Zac said he was in to a man who painted soup cans, which sounded like the kind of art I'd like. Wonder if he painted beans and sausage cans too? I waved goodbye to Sarah and the others.

"Bye, Bella – see you same place tomorrow?"

"Totally." Well, it sure beat any other option I had.

"Don't forget to let me know how it goes with netball today? The team's going up any minute?" Oh yeah, *that*. Sarah is also one of the sporties in our year. The reason we first got talking is because, in the nicest way possible, she'd asked me why I'd suddenly got off my arse in games lessons and had started joining in. Games lessons had previously been an opportunity to gossip with Rachel, keeping one eye on our overenthusiastic games teacher, so we could break into action if she looked over. Tegan achieved enough for the three of us anyway. Now, it was a whole other ball game. Literally. This week, taking part meant avoiding unwanted convos, and winning the tiniest chance of finally getting into a team. And teams meant points. And points meant prom. I only had fourteen – four more than I needed to go, and with Mr Lutas already unimpressed with me, I wanted more spares in the bank.

I walked the long way out of the canteen, strategically avoiding any places I could bump into Tegan and Rachel, past the team noticeboard – that didn't have my name on – and underneath the menacing picture of Mr Lutas on the wall. Even his fake eyes on me made me shudder. His only happiness seemed to come from making others massively unhappy. Although . . . maybe two could play that game?

I swung by my locker to grab my phone. We were only meant to use them for emergencies, but this kind of was one.

NAKED AMBITION
WHAT KIND OF A PERSON LIKES TO
DRAW THEMSELVES NAKED? OUR ARRRRT
TEACHERRR, THAT'S WHO. AND FROM
WHAT I'VE HEARD, HIS BIG PERSONALITY
MAKES UP FOR SOMETHING ELSE
NOT SO BIG. IN HIS PANTS.

I mean, Jo hadn't *technically* said that, but I'm sure she would have done if she hadn't been trying not to think of the detail.

I pressed send. I didn't need to be on *PSSSST* any more, but I was kind of enjoying it. Now I had someone/something I could tell my secrets to, who was actually going to keep them safe.

I made my way into the library and began revising. I felt like an intellectual being here on my own, as normally I'd only come here with the others to whisper-gossip.

But as I flicked through the art books I recognized from Rachel's room (must remember, the bigger the artist's hair, the more 'influential' they are), practised imaginary chat about my college, and made playlists of bands Zac would approve of, I neglected the one thing I should have been reading up on.

If only I'd hunted for the book on, 'Ten Top Tips On How Not To Make A Massive Dork Of Yourself In Front Of The World's Hottest Man. Twice.'

FİFTEEN

Why does my face always know when there's a crucial Bella life event and develop a strategically placed comedy spot? I gave myself – and the massive spot between my eyebrows – evils in the mirror. I hope my face knows I am cross with it.

I looked out of my bedroom window. Everything looked normal considering it was a totally un-normal day. Today was Z-day. And Z-time was only thirty-five minutes away. I wouldn't get up pre eight a.m. on a Saturday for anything else. Probably not even a house fire.

Today was the day I had to try and make Zac like me again. As in, *like* like. I'd planned to messy-style my bob, paint my nails (the advanced polka dot look I've been working on), shave my legs, pluck my eyebrows and clean some of the grime off my shoes. However, even though I'd geared my entire week around today, I was totally behind schedule, and only had time for emergency plucking of my hedge-esque brows (avoiding spot of doom). I also had to abandon nail painting too, meaning only two out of five on each hand have got gold dots on. I'm going to have to pretend it's a *thing* here.

I'd almost suffered a physical meltdown too, as I tried on over thirty outfit combinations in under fifteen minutes. Skinny jeans are basically a workout. Someone should make a fitness DVD out of it.

I shouted downstairs.

"Mum – can we go PLEASE? I don't want to be late." There was no way Zac could see me cadging a lift off my mum, especially not in the brown Mini of shame. My rare attempt at not being late triggered the Mum-suspicion-alarm.

"Just need a wee. Who are you meeting again darling?" Classic mum move – interrogation disguised as casual concern.

"Just my new netball friends." I'm *sure* Zac could love netball, so this wasn't technically a lie until he said otherwise.

"I thought they stopped speaking to you yesterday when you fractured the captain's wrist in PE?"

Correct. In real life they probably *were* never going to speak to me again. But this was made-up life.

"That was *yesterday* Mum; this is *today*. We've all moved on. Accidents happen."

"If you say so. . ."

We both knew she wasn't convinced, but we both also knew that if she carried on the questioning, there might be an unwanted bladder-based carpet puddle situation.

As we drove, I did what I'd been doing since Zac had first arranged meeting up. Running through what would happen at 10.01. The first sighting since Black Bay. How would we greet each other? My usual awkward wave? No, shameful. A handshake? Too parental. A kiss on the cheek? Too forward? Argh?! What were the rules here? It was times like this I really could have done with some advice from Tegan. Although she would have probably suggested a massive stab in the back.

Mum pulled up at the bus stop. I opened the car door.

"Thanks for the lift. See you later."

"When can I expect you back?"

Why couldn't she have asked me all this before I was halfway out of the car and at risk of being spotted mid mum-lift?

"Dunno, seven. Ish. Eight?"

"Well, let me know. I'll be at a goat-milk-soap-making workshop until four but can pick up messages." Fingers crossed none of that soap ever makes it home.

"Cool, good luck. Soap it goes well." I smiled at her. See – happy Bella! Nothing-to-worry-about Bella! So-you-can-leave-me-alone-now Bella.

"Oooh, is that them over there?" She pointed to the alley by Sainsbury's.

"No, Mum, I think they're homeless people."

"Oh right, I can never tell these days. I thought that sort of hair was fashionable again. It's so wild, I love it!"

The give-away clue should have been that wild hair or not, keen players of netball probably don't sleep outside TK Maxx. Unless there's a mega sale on. Oh well. I waved her off and sat on the bench. Ten minutes. Tick tock. Please don't let him be early. That would be unfair.

Do I look relaxed enough? Got to stop tapping my foot. Do I look OK? Did I check for any foundation lines? Or Cheerios stuck in my teeth? My spot feels bigger than when I left. Has the cover-up made it go flaky and more noticeable than if I'd just left it alone?

I looked at my watch. Eight minutes. This is torture. I'm never being early/on-time for anything again. Is he here? Still no. Got to stop looking up every five seconds. I rummaged in my bag and tapped at my phone like I was reading an imaginary message. What a very funny imaginary message it was. Hahahaha. Imaginary thinking face for an equally hilarious response. Pretend typing. Pretend send. Pretend satisfied face. Phone back in bag.

Seven minutes.

What am I going to say to him when he actually gets here? *If* he gets here. I looked back at my revision notes: some sort of weird political scandal about mortgages, what mortgages actually are, the Brontë sisters (who I'm imaginary-college studying, along with my imaginary art course, and whatever imaginary option pops out of my mouth), Alex Turner songs past and present (Zac mentioned he 'quite liked' the Arctic Monkeys), Andy Warhol (big hair, paints soup), and towns in the UK (that I may or may not be hypothetically going to for Uni). Must remember Leeds is in the north, but Leeds Castle is south. Why do map people try and confuse me so?! I put my phone away, all the info instantly disappearing with it.

Five minutes.

I reapplied my free magazine lipgloss even though I'd applied ten layers in the last two minutes. Stop putting more on, moron.

Four minutes.

What if my mind goes blank and I can't think of anything at all to talk about and we have the world's longest ever awkward silence? Oh crapballs, it might never end. It could be a record breaker. Night could fall and everything and we'd still be here on this bench, in silence, me looking at my feet and sporadically replying to imaginary messages.

"Boo!"

Aaaaaargh! I threw my lipgloss on the floor. Zac! The Zacman! He's here! And I'm totally unprepared!

"Zaaaaaaaaaaaaaaaaaac!" I screeched back, sounding more like small bat than alluring female. Interesting technique – avoid awkward silence by being awkward loud instead. I leapt up from the bench. Wowsers, even in full daylight he was still the most gorgeous boy I'd ever seen – and I like to think the internet has enabled me to see at least ninety per cent of all boys.

"Well, are you going to give me a hug hello?"

"Er, yeah?! Huggalo, here I come!" Oh dear. That was meant to be a brain-thought, not a mouth-shout. He stretched out his arms and I flung mine around him brushing my hand against some sort of actual six-pack action. My knee buckled with the intense swooningness of this contact, resulting in me then pretending I had a small bit of grit in my shoe. It could only get better if an open-top bus tour of Worcester (which doesn't exist as there's nothing to see) pulled up alongside us and pointed out, using a loud hailer AND laser pointer, to the tourists on-board (which would include Tegan, Rachel AND Luke) that I, Bella Fisher, was currently in a full-body embrace with a totally hot older boy.

Zac stepped back and smiled. His grinning, cheek-dimpled face and deep brown eyes seemed genuinely happy to see me. The fact that I was trying not to dribble on myself proved I felt the same.

He broke the conversation ice.

"Sooooo ... long time no see. What's been happening in your world?"

"Er, you know. Things." I thought back to my notes. "Just working on some art projects, getting pretty caught up in it all, you know how it is. You?"

He nodded, not picking up on my shaky delivery. "Sort of similar. Although, long story, I might have to finish my last few weeks of term up in Birmingham. That's why I'm here, checking out colleges, so thought I'd jump on the train and see you before I went back. It's only an hour away."

I'm so glad chins were invented or my jaw would have dropped off. Was Zac, Black Bay Zac, telling me he was going to moving within train-able distance from me?! I put my hand on a bin to steady myself. Serious plus point to mission get-Zac-to-prom. And to my entire life. I couldn't *wait* to hear the long story. Every detail.

Where was he going to live?

Why was he moving here?

Would he mind if I licked his face?

Which college had he looked at?

Would he life-partner me?

But all I could do was blink. Lucky he was still good at saying words.

"Which college did you say you were at again?"

My jaw un-fell. Reality struck. Long stories meant details. And questions. And detailed questions about details. There was *no way* I could pull off convincing college lying if he'd been doing research into the area.

I had to change the subject, and quick. The long story could wait till he was thirty-two and I was thirty, and then the age difference wouldn't seem so bad.

"Well, that'd be telling, wouldn't it?!" I tried to look mysterious, even though it made no sense, as that whole point of asking a question is for someone to reply with some telling. "Let me know if I can help though..." Vague, good. Now what?! Think of the notes, quick?! I shuffled awkwardly on to fake-grit foot. "So, er, pretty crazy news this week, huh? With the, er, mortgage scandal and stuff?"

His forehead scrunched.

"Really? Is something kicking off?" Uh-oh he was meant to be the one that knew this sort of stuff.

"Yeah, it's just been pretty big news, in the, news." Not a strong start. "That's what the newsreader said?" I thought back to one of the assemblies from last week. "I mean Emmeline Pankhurst didn't die so people like me couldn't keep up with politics and vote."

"But we *can't* vote yet. We're not old enough."

Must pay more attention in assembly.

"Well no, of course. But metaphorically?"

This was something Jo said when she talked to people about intelligent things and no one ever seemed to reply, but in a good way. It did the trick. He smiled, although potentially more in confusion than agreement. I needed safe ground.

"Anyway, I can't believe I got dragged away from Black Bay. How was it after we left?"

I outwardly sighed with relief as he threw himself into holiday chat, launching into a story about his trip to the beach with Keith the dog – who ate a stranger's picnic. I wanted to smile, but could only manically grin, lips stuck together, as I was painfully aware that I never got to do my final check for any teeth nuggets. But, just like before, he wasn't phased by my total weirdness.

Thanks to my terrible planning, we ambled round nowhere in particular, him politely not pointing out we'd walked in at least twelve circles. On our second walk down the alley that smelt of fish, he asked me what had happened with Jo and the whole Luke drama. My insides buzzed with happiness at him remembering life details about me – even though technically he thought they were about my shouty sis. This was a good sign, right? But as I reeled off the edited highlights, he looked puzzled. And sort of revolted (although still fit-revolted). Had I been rumbled? Did they even have canteens at college?! What had I done?!

"Are you OK, Zac?"

His wrinkled nose fell back into position.

"Oh, sorry! Yes. I could just smell . . . well it just smells, well . . . really fishy."

RELIEF. It was mackerel, not me that was freaking him out.

"Oh – *that*! The massive fish smell. I guess I'm used to it." That came out wrong. "Not as in *I* smell of fish, as in, this part of town does. Smell of fish." Still wrong. "It's just right next to the indoor fish market, you see. So it's nothing fishy. Well it is, but as in, nothing dodgy. I mean, I'm literally called Fisher, if *anyone* knows about fish it's me. But not because I smell of it." Great, if there's one word to repeat on a date, it's 'fish'. I shut up for a bit.

We didn't walk past the fish market again.

Since we last (and first) saw each other, Zac hadn't had any dramas like me – but he had been up to loads. He was major buzzed that he'd done so well on his course that he'd been shortlisted for the most amazing sounding summer tour round Italy, to work with all their top art colleges (personally I was more vibed by the thought of a holiday that guaranteed daily lasagne, but either way I could share his excitement). As part of his application he'd even made a new music video for Velvet Badger. I tried to ask as many questions about it as possible, so he didn't suss that the best evening

I'd had recently was solo-re-watching my old *Pitch Perfect* DVDs, complete with karaoke sing-a-long. So much of the stuff he'd been up to sounded so cool that I was running out of responses, other than just repeating 'Wow', 'Awesome' 'Amazing', 'OMG' and 'wowawesomeamazingomg'. He was like the inverse of me, chatting away as if making conversation was a normal thing to do.

After loop fifteen, I suggested heading to the river. I really should have spent more time planning the day, rather than not learning about house buying. We carried on chatting and ambling – chambling – and slowly meandered down to the quiet towpath. It was one hundred per cent dreamy. Maybe this was how Jane Eyre felt? I'm not sure who she actually was, but she definitely sounds like the sort of person that would go for walks along rivers with boys.

"OK then, seeing as you've taken the time out to show me around your town" – he politely didn't add 'FIFTEEN TIMES ON ROTATION LIKE SOME WEIRD GROUNDHOG DATE' – "I thought I could return the favour and take us to see a film later? My last train back's about tenish. . . So, have you got plans or can I steal you till then?"

WHAT THE WHAT?! He wanted to evening-hang

too?! He could steal me, squash me into a suitcase, take me to Yemen and I'd still be happy.

"Yeah. That sounds cool. I've got nothing on that I can't cancel." I had nothing on at all, and that's really easy to cancel. I messaged Mum, telling her I was going bowling with my netball buddies. It was harder for her to say no if I didn't give her a choice.

"There's a film that looks awesome, *Count to Trois*. Sort of French cinema meets Saw. Can you imagine?"

I could, and it was terrifying. Who knew we'd have such different taste in films?! I'm such a wimp that I keep my eyes closed in anything that's a 12+, so reading the subtitles was going to be logistically impossible. So unless all they do is ask for cheese baguettes, the way to the swimming pool, or any of the other nine French GCSE sentences I can remember, I wasn't going to understand a word. Although, GULP – an even more terrible thought hit me. Zac could easily pass as eighteen. What if I got ID-ed in front of him?

Agreeing to this film was the worst idea ever?! Could I backtrack?!

"Well, why don't we just see what's on when we get there?"

His cute face fell at my lack of enthusiasm.

"But it's meant to be ace. Honestly. It's a gore

thriller – the first one was amazing. It'll be fun, I PROMISE. And it's proper scary so it won't be packed with kids either."

Kids like *me*. But his 'please' face so was damn sexy, it dissolved my logic and resistance.

"Fine. Fine. You're the guest. It'd be rude not to." It'll be ruder if I run out of the cinema screaming – either from getting IDed or from seeing someone get decapitated – but I'd cross that bridge when I came to it.

He ran his hand through his hair, making him look even taller than his six-footness. "Merci beaucooup. I owe you one. And if the film gets too scary, we could . . . we could always do something to take our minds off it?"

Did he share my favourite cinema pastime? Extreme popcorn eating. I once did a large bucket by the end of the third pre-film advert – I threw up into said bucket before the film started.

But his eyes had a cheeky glint in them. And his dimples had reappeared. And his tiny scar was doing its excited wobbly thing.

UH and OH. DID HE MEAN PICKING UP WHERE WE LEFT OFF AT BLACK BAY?! Was he actually suggesting we attempt a non-interrupted snog? Had I really not ruined everything?!

He was still smiling.

I looked for another bin to steady myself on, but in the absence of anything almost leant on a small child.

This. Was. Terrifying.

I'd spent so long figuring out how to make Zac not hate me that I hadn't given a second's thought to what if he actually liked me?! I wasn't mentally, physically or lipbalm-ily prepared to re-snog this wonder specimen.

MAJOR GULP ALERT.

What if I'd forgotten how to kiss? What if I couldn't manage anything more than a half-snog because he was so fit I exploded? What if he tried to do it in a scary-film bit when my eyes were closed and I headbutted him causing a second black eye?

I smiled back at Zac and tried to hide my sheer panic.

Forget *Count to Trois*, today was now *Count to Argh*.

CHAPTER

SiXTEEN

As if spending the day pretending to be an older-better-funnier-better-at-geography-er me wasn't tricky enough, having the possibility of my first ever Zac full-snog hanging over my head made me totally lose the plot. How could something so brilliant in principle be so utterly terrifying in practice? Although I wish it *was* a practice. Just a casual five mins to get in the zone with a Zac lookalike.

I really hoped that ever since Zac had dropped the 'do something else to take our minds off it' bombshell he hadn't noticed I'd become a worried mess, even tripping over a dog at one point. We'd spent the afternoon in the park, picking at a picnic, as my nerves (and over-elasticated mum tights under my jeans) made me completely unhungry. However, it *was* a highlight realizing I was hanging out with someone who could make eating a Scotch egg look sexy.

But after what felt like only a few minutes, the light began to fade. Damn the passing of time. If they could invent freeze-dried ice cream for space people, why couldn't they invent a time freezer for normal people?

I rubbed my arms to get a bit warmer. Zac noticed.

"Shall we head off? I'd forgotten you had the body temperature of a Cornetto."

I shuddered at the thought of heading to the SOS. Scene of snog. The MOT. Moment of truth. I stood up, dusting the grass off my clothes, as he watched. Could I stall for time? I rummaged in my bag for inspo and spotted the perfect thing. My pride and joy. My camera. It might be cringe asking, but a photo of Zac AND time wasted was too good to not try for. I tried to sound as casual and college-studenty as I could.

"Before we go, while you, er –" DON'T SAY LOOK PARTICULARLY FIT – "have such, er, good light, could I grab a photo of us?"

I pulled it out of my bag before he could say no.

"Wow, that's some serious kit."

I nodded proudly.

The one thing I owned that wasn't broken – or

borrowed from Jo. I'd won it in a school comp last year and since then I'd taken it everywhere with me. The photos from it – of Mumbles, and feet in sand, and early morning sunrises on the playing field, and a really great sandwich I once made – were strung up all over my room (with spaces where the ones of Tegan and Rachel had been). Still, a pic of us could fill the space way better than their faces ever had done. Although, so could another sandwich.

Zac polite-coughed, reminding me I'd got distracted. Better hurry before he changes his mind. I fiddled with the F-stop, set the focus and in a move I'd practised to perfection, swivelled the camera round and stretched my arm out. Zac leaned in, but the shock of him putting his arm round me made my finger snap down, unprepared. We looked at the picture. Him grinning, me blinking. Lucky SD cards don't melt, because he looked all kinds of hot, whereas people like me are why cropping was invented. Hello, new phone background/pillow case/duvet set/ bedroom wallpaper.

Zac looked pleased. I felt like I'd just created a Picasso.

"Approve?" I could only nod back. The photo was so good it'd rendered me temporarily mute. Zac reached out towards my camera to get a closer look. In a panic I yanked it away from him. He looked a bit put out but one wrong left click and he'd get an eyeful of my earlier bum selfies, from when I was checking out today's outfit choice.

"Got any college work on there I could look at?"

"NO!" I didn't mean to shout. He looked scared. I looked happy my mute-ness wasn't permanent after all. "As in, *yes* I have. But *no* you can't see them. You know how it is? Creative control. Art. Want to edit them before I share."

Truth was I couldn't swipe right either, as it was the photoshoot Rachel and I had done last month of our upside-down heads with faces drawn on our chins. And chin-face probably isn't the challenging new college art concept Zac has in mind.

"Wow, you take it seriously, don't you?" He seemed impressed. Had I finally carried off something vaguely cool? He took his phone out. "Your turn then." My nostrils flared, like an inbuilt facial panic alarm. Taking photos, I love. Having a photo taken, I hate. I can never make my face look right. That's why selfies were invented, not you-lfies.

"Do you *have* to? I look like Mr Potato Head in photos. Well, Mrs. But only just."

He pointed to my camera.

"Fair's fair. I get something to remember today by too."

I couldn't think of anything worse, but the fact that he wanted a memento made me feel a bit fuzzy inside, like someone was running a warm bath in my vital organs.

"Well, OK, but if I say delete, you delete."

"OK, OK, diva! Next you'll be telling me you have a best side?!"

I do. It's my left side, but now I totally couldn't tell him that. I'd just have to manoeuvre it so it worked out that way. I took a sly glance at my reflection on the back of my phone. Great, I'd laugh-cried all my mascara off and I had at least twelve twigs lodged in my hair. Unless Zac had a thing for goth scarecrows, this photo was already doomed.

He held up his phone. Breathe in, Bella, shoulders back, smooth hair, tilt chin down, smile with your eyes. He pressed the button and . . . laughed.

He literally creased up with laughter.

"Zac, show it to me. What's so funny?!"

I grabbed at his phone, but he'd clutched it to his chest. Had he only just realized the true extent of my nostrils? They *are* exceptionally uneven.

He fanned his face with his other hand like you do when your laughing overrides your breathing.

"Look whatever it is, you're deleting it, OK? You promised."

"L-l-llll —" he was trying, and failing, to speak between laughs — "loo. . ." gasp, fan, bit of breath, ". . . ooook!"

He held out the screen. There I was, standing awkwardly, my smiling eyes looking more like squinting. Sure, it wasn't my *best* photo, but was I really *that* gross? He jabbed his finger above my head. There was a weird black streak above it. I looked up at the tree — nothing there now. He zoomed in. What was it? All there was above me was just branches. Branches with birds. . . Oh no, am I *really* this unlucky?

I put my hand on the back of my head. Affirmative. Wet and slimy. The one photo Lord Swooningham of Swoonshire owned of me and I was mid being bird-pooed on.

Zac was crying with laughter. I too was almost crying, but for totally different reasons.

"I'm sorry, Bells. But it's SO funny. You can actually see . . . see. . ." more laughing, ". . . you can see the poo!"

Mortifying. I stop fancying boys when I see them eating crisps in a funny way — how on earth was I going to get through this!? Should I style it out? Run off and cry? Should I hold a bird at ransom until it poos on Zac's head? Should I poo on a bird's head, so it could see how unfunny it was?

I tried to dab the evidence off, but this was no ordinary fly-by-pooing.

"OH MY GOD. IT MUST HAVE BEEN SOME SORT OF DINOSAUR. HELP ME, ZAC. HELP ME. IT'S GOING DOWN MY NECK!" I started running in tiny circles, flapping my arms as if moving would help me get further away from the thing on my head.

"CALM DOWN." He tried to regain some composure. "A bit of poo never killed anyone... Well, other than millions through the spread of disease and bacteria."

AND POTENTIALLY ME – I was at serious risk of dying of shame. I grabbed a handful of grass to scrape it off, but just gave myself bird poo lowlights.

"DELETE THAT PICTURE NOW."

If only I'd been born before technology existed. Before being born existed.

Zac opened up his bag.

"Here, have my top – put the hood up. No one will ever know."

"But I don't want to poo-up your hood." When I'd

planned what I was going to talk about with Zac, I can safely say this wasn't on my list of alluring phrases. Oh well.

I pulled on his top, ignoring my hair, which had now started to crust. It smelled amazing (his top, not the hardened poo). I stood patiently as it took another couple of minutes before Zac had stopped laughing enough to form whole sentences.

"Sorry. I think I'm OK now." He took a deep breath in and said "Woooooo" as if breathing out the last of his laugh. "Bright side? We've definitely missed *Count to Trois*, so we can go sit in a dark, low-bird-poo-visibility room, and watch your choice of film instead."

This *was* a glimmer of good news in all the crap. Literally. With my camera safely back in my bag, and the photos synced to my phone in case of mugging/ falling in river, we walk-jogged to the cinema. By the time we got there, the only film that had tickets left had just started. Zac bought the last two, grabbed my hand and marched us in. It was packed. As in, you'd think this was the X-Factor-final-featuring-a-naked-One-Direction-reunion-special packed. I pulled his hoodie up further to hide my face as he pulled me towards the only empty seats. The snog-repellent second row. Maybe I would be spared finding out if I could actually kiss any more? Although then I might never get to snog Zac ever again. Argh! Why was life so complicated? Why was snogging so terrifying? Surely it's just like chewing – but with another person attached?

As the film blared out I tried to relax and stop thinking about crusty poo hair, attempted snogging or lack of attempted snogging. The plot was so painfully unfunny the cinema was entirely silent, all except one person who explosively laughed like a horse every 2.5 minutes. And that one person was Zac. So much for loving foreign cinema.

"Oi," Zac prodded me in the leg. I stared straight ahead, didn't want him thinking he was more important than the film, even though he was x one million.

"Bellllaaaaa," He prodded again.

"Oh . . . yeah?" You said something? Why, I'd been so wrapped up in the *hilarious* scene with a cat having its hair crimped that I hadn't noticed.

"Just wanted to say thanks for today."

Wow. My first genuine smile of the whole film. As they started to straighten the hair of a hamster, I felt something. Something on my actual knee. He'd only put his hand right there. On MY leg – like a COUPLE! Alert people! *Life-altering moment happening in seat 2F right now.* What should I do? Put my hand on his hand?

Put a hand on his knee? Put my other knee on his hand?! Help! Why does no one teach you these things?!

He gently pulled my leg towards his. Uh-oh. Was I mistaken or was this going to be an SOS after all!? What could I do? I scanned left and right. BUMBALLS. I can't even dash off for a fake loo trip without tripping over at least ten people. *C'mon, Bella.* Just sit, breathe and pretend there aren't about two hundred people about to see you not able to deal with whatever is about to happen. But I didn't have much time to compose myself. Slowly, calmly, Zac leaned in. And he kissed me. And I kissed him back.

Oh boy. Oh boy, oh boy. It felt nice. Even nicer than hand on knee. Nice enough to decide that I didn't care what anyone else thought, or what anyone else saw. Here I was with the most amazing boy in the UK/probably world and we were kissing. He was kissing me!

Even though my lips felt dry on his, my head was swivelled round like some sort of human-owl and I was getting cramp in my right shoulder, this was, without doubt, the hottest moment of my life. Take that, rules of cinema dating – you thought snogging was all about the back row, well guess what? Bella and Zac are in town, and tonight it's all about row two.

My stomach felt like it had been replaced with helium. Here I was watching a romantic comedy, and my actual real life was one billion times more happy-ending-y. We carried on half-film-watching/half-kissing until the overly loud exit music shook us back into the real world.

Zac switched on his phone. And as it came to life he shot out of his seat.

"Crap. I've got to run. Like *run* run. My train's in ten."

Thank goodness I've already been initiated into the cinema fire-exit-exit. It's one of those rights of passage that once you know, makes everyone leaving the normal way less cool. Older people would argue it's pointless walking down dimly lit stairs and dark alleyways, but that's why they're wrong. And that's why they're old.

I dragged Zac double-speed along the row, out the door, and across the road to the station. We dashed up the stairs, getting to the platform just as his train pulled in. 'Yay' for him not missing the train, 'Aaaaaargghrubbish' for this being the end of the evening – and him noticing that I gave myself a hiccup trying to hold in my out-of-breath-puffing.

Without time for a proper goodbye he jumped on-board. "I'm so sorry to run off like this. It's been great seeing. . ."

The beeping of the train doors drowned out his words, so instead he waved and walked down the carriage. He sat as near to where I was standing as he could, settling in beside an old lady who seemed to be reading a tutorial on knitted seagulls. I threw her a look to say 'hands off he's mine', with a bit of 'and also I didn't know you could knit a bird, that's quite impressive'.

Seconds later the train roared into action, and with no words left to be said, Zac smiled and waved. So did the old lady. Probably trying to get him on her good side before she made her move. I used both hands to wave them both off, and carried on waving until the lights of the train disappeared into the distance. I felt as empty as the platform.

I stomped back down the steps feeling sorry for myself. Everything here already seemed so boring without him, and he'd only been gone seventeen seconds. I wished he hadn't gone, but stealing people isn't legal. And I'm not good at carrying.

My phone buzzed – probs Mum wondering where I am. *Open message*.

There it was. Me all in all my pre-bird-poo glory.

Hey Poohead. My new fave pic. Z x

And this was now my new fave message. I wandered to the bus stop, thinking of how to reply. But despite missing him already, I couldn't help but smile. Against all odds, had I managed to undo my cereal-box/Jo damage and make Zac like me? I'd even trebled my TSS (time spent snogging). Maybe something more *could* happen between us? Maybe he *might* want to see me again? Maybe getting him to prom *wasn't* such a crazy idea?

A light flashed in my face as a car screeched into the bus stop. It was Mum and Jo. Good timing. I jumped in the back.

"Darling. What are you doing?! You know I don't like you hanging round bus stops late at night."

"Maybe you could increase my allowance so I don't have to?"

"Maybe you could come home earlier so it's not an issue?"

I quickly moved the convo on. I didn't want to dwell on the details of this evening.

"So, er, how was soap making?

"Oh, Bella – it was excellent. Which was just as well, as we've had the most dreadful evening. Jo and I went to see a truly terrible film. Not only was it really unfunny. . ."

Jo interrupted.

"As in, a-hamster-going-to-a-hairdresser-unfunny."

Wait. As in — the-exact-same-film-as-me-unfunny?!
Where was this going?!

Mum carried on.

"... but there was this couple in the second row
who spent the whole film kissing."

What the what the WHAT?! Seeing as Zac and I
were sitting beside a Scout trip, SHE COULD ONLY
MEAN US. How could this be happening?! Had we
really been that noticeable?! Actual inward spew. I
spluttered some words out.

"That. Sounds. Awful." Not a lie. It was *entirely*
awful that the two people I was most closely related
to had been less than two metres away from the most
romantic encounter of my life. Thank goodness I'd had
that hoodie up, if they worked out it was me, I'd be in
deeper poo than I had been earlier.

Jo twisted round in her seat and peered through the
headrest.

"Srsly. Mum's not even being mum-ish. They
slurped the entire way through the film." I felt dizzy
with bad luck. Had we really been 'slurping'? This
could not be happening. Did Zac think I was a 'slurper'?

"Jo's right. The only good thing was that when the

boy's mouth was covered it stopped his horsey laughing. It was positively a bray. I mean, who finds a cat falling into a bin funny?"

Should I set a phone reminder of 'Never let Zac meet and/or laugh/bray in front of my family'? Thank goodness there had been nothing funny when Jo kind of met him, so she didn't recognize his unique sound.

"Still, we did treat ourselves to a pizza before. I can't believe they now do ones with hamburgers in the crust! What's next, fish fingers instead of straws?"

That made no sense, but relieved that the conversation had moved on, I let Mum chat away, as I zoned out, staring out of the window and thinking about Zac. Maybe he could be the one thing in my life that could finally go right? The one plan that goes to plan. All I had to do was not mess it up – and stay away from all birds. And somehow get a second opinion on my 'slurping'.

But my plan had forgotten the one thing that could derail it most of all. Luke. And in less than two weeks I was going to find out just how much damage a loser ex-boyfriend could do.

CHAPTER

SEVENTEEN

It turns out that a substantial part of the fun of a date is the telling other people every sordid detail (date-tail?). So, in the days after what I now refer to as 'Love Zactually', in the absence of best mates, I told pretty much everyone else. Including a girl who I only knew because I once got my fringe caught in her rucksack buckle.

Zac had mentioned he didn't use *PSSSST* any more, so I'd even been sharing details on there. Seven posts later and my likes were still going up. WORLD BE ON ALERT. One of the basic laws of existence was turning on its head. I, Bella Fisher, might potentially be rebranding as a fit-boy-snogger, normal-life-haver and internet-sensation. Hold on to your hats. Gravity will be the next thing to go.

I leaned against my locker and scanned the corridor for teacher danger. All clear. Perfect for a check on this morning's Zac date post – it was on track to break my PB with 250 likes.

WHEN IS A DATE NOT A DATE? WHEN IT'S A
RAISIN.SRSLY, THOUGH. HAVE YOU NEEDED
TO PLAY IT EXTRA COOL ON A DATE WITH A
MEGA HOTTIE? WHEN YOU'RE NOT EVEN SURE
IS TECHNICALLY A DATE? WELL, IMAGINE THAT.
THEN IMAGINE SHOWING THE MEGA HOTTIE THE
TIME ON YOUR PHONE – JUST AS A MESSAGE
POPS-UP SAYING 'HOW'S YOUR DATE WITH THE
WORLD'S FITTEST MAN????'
WELCOME TO MY LIFE.

I cringed at the memory. I should never have given Sarah my number. Zac had been sweet about it, though, and pretended not to notice.

I scrolled down. Better than I'd even hoped. 400 likes. And quite a few comments.

LILDRUMMERBOY: I CAN GO ONE BETTER.
IMAGINE BEING ON AN 'IS THIS A DATE' DATE,
WHEN YOUR EX COMES OVER TO THE TWO OF

I nose-snorted. How reassuring that other people were also a danger to society. And a boy too.

"Ms Fisher. Is there a rrreason you think you're exempt from the rrrrule of not using phones? Or is 'chatting with online friends' now an emergency?"

Wow. Misery magnet strikes again. Could my timing be any worse?

"Sorry." I stuffed my phone back in my bag. "It won't happen again." Well, it definitely would, I'd just be more careful not to do it in plain sight.

"Glad to hear it. And to help you rrrremember, I am taking away two prom points."

As if! Then I'd only have twelve left. And that was only two away from prom exile.

"But, Mr Lutas. I *swear* it was an emergency."

Mr Lutas flashed his coffee-stained teeth at me. I only ever see his smile when he's ruining someone's day. Although recently I had witnessed one extra-curricular smile – when he saw Mrs Hitchman. What *was* the deal with those two? Last I heard she was happily married – and Mr Lutas was happily totally alone.

"Swearing is also not allowed. So let's make it three. Now, I suggest you move along."

Eurgh. How dare he! Eleven points was major danger zone, I could not risk losing a single point more, so I moved along. There was no way *I* wasn't going to prom when I'd made such good progress on getting Zac there. It's been four days since the date, 15.8 (he pressed send too soon on one) messages, one photo of his dog, Keith, and I *still* seem to not have put him off. This is extra remarkable as one of my replies was meant to be a picture of Mumbles, but ended up being an accidental under-the-chin selfie. I'd even plucked up the courage to ask where he was going to college, but he'd turned the tables and told me it was my turn to wait and see. And that he'd tell me on our THIRD DATE?! I'd rolled off my bed and plopped on to the floor with uncontainable glee.

Smiling to myself, I rubbed the large bruise I'd got on my elbow as a result and headed towards my only school safe haven – the library. There was something comforting about being in a place where people were actively forbidden from talking to me. But when I got there, there was no one on duty, meaning everyone was chatting at full volume, so instead of a library it was just a normal room, but with a lot of shelves.

I searched the rows looking for books on French cinema but couldn't tell if I was having any luck as the titles were all in French.

CRUNCH.

I stomped on something that wasn't carpet. It made the same crunching noise as when I'd once stepped on a dead pigeon in the dark. I looked at what I'd just crushed. A pile of books on a bag.

"Sorry – I totally didn't see your bag LYING IN THE MIDDLE OF THE FLOOR." I hoped the owner would pick up on my sorry-not-sorry subtlety. But it wasn't a regulation school bag. It was the really expensive leather version that nobody had. Nobody, that is, except Rachel. Who on cue appeared from around the corner.

"Don't worry about it. It's full of junk anyway." She swung it off the floor and on to her shoulder. She smiled. I didn't. "I shouldn't have left it there."

I'd been trying so hard to not care about my ex-friends any more I was surprised how much hurt flooded back at seeing her.

"You're getting pretty good at bad decisions lately, aren't you?"

She flinched. But what she did expect? I didn't want to speak to her. Not now. Not here. Not ever. Over the last few weeks I'd proved to everyone – not least of all me – that even after all these years, I didn't need them. I didn't need to be in a group any more. I could make it through the day without them. What they'd done was unforgiveable, and it didn't matter how much they begged me to accept their apologies or promised to make it up. Which they'd done on a daily basis.

I grabbed a book dramatically, and stormed off to my table-for-one where I'd spent most of my recent breaktimes. I stared out of the window that overlooked the playground. Some Year 8 girls were walking towards the wall that Rachel, Tegan and I used to sit on. The place we'd claimed since we'd first arrived at St Mary's. The placed we'd talked through every detail of Rachel's first kiss like it was our own, cried together when Tegan's dad got ill and a year later cried with laughter when Mikey debuted his first Taylor Swift routine. And as the Year 8s sat in the exact spot, something nagged at me. Something I'd been trying to pretend I wasn't thinking. But it was sometimes hard to ignore myself, as I spend a lot of time with me.

I was so *sure* of how cross I felt with Rachel and Tegan that I'd been ignoring how I felt about *me*. I took a deep breath and faced up to the thing I'd been trying to bury. As I'd settled into my new routines, my new places to sit and my new people to speak to, I'd started to feel unsettled about something else. Was pushing the others away actually making me any happier?

"Room for another?"

Without looking away from the window I shook my head at Rachel.

Being an independent woman was tiring. Beyoncé doesn't mention that in any of her songs, does she? Or maybe that's just like how no one ever has a wee in *EastEnders*.

Rachel ignored me, and crouched down resting her hands and chin on my table. She looked like a very odd table ornament.

"Can we talk?" She glanced at the teacher who had just walked in and lowered her voice. "Well, whisper. Please?"

"I've got nothing to say slash whisper to you."

"Well, I've got loads I want to say slash whisper to you. So maybe instead of talking, you'd be up for listening instead? I'll only be a min."

I thought about doing what I normally did. Walking off. But something made me stay where I was. The nagging feeling I'd been trying to ignore.

I stayed because, however mad I was, and however much I'd found new routines, I missed her. I missed my friend. I missed having someone in the world who knows what is happening in your every day. Who knows that you cross the street to avoid cats (that you have identified as having an attitude problem). Who knows that you wear an extra pair of knickers over your tights ever since they once fell down when you were walking up the stairs to a history lesson. Who knows that you when you're feeling happy, or sad, or poo-ed on by a pigeon, or like your heart has exploded on the second row of Screen One, you need someone to share it with. Who knows how you feel when Mr Lutas docks you three points.

"OK, here goes. . ." She paused, bracing herself for me to listen. "We're sorry. So, so, so sorry. We made the WORST decision ever. Sure it *was* Tegan's idea, but I went along with it, and that's no better."

Figured. Rachel can't even follow the plot of Disney movies without asking what's going on, so I didn't ever consider she'd orchestrated the deception. That's probably why I still felt the maddest at Tegan.

"We just knew how rubbish you'd been feeling about Luke, and how hurt you'd been about the whole Blobfish thing."

Oh yes. When we came back to school in January, Luke had got his techy friend to change my name to

Blob Fisher on the internal email system.

"So we didn't want him having any more ammo on you. On us. It was meant to prove how little we all cared, not create the world's worst pic of him and Tegan. They really did only kiss for like two seconds. And when she realized what she'd done, she was mortified. You know when Tegan gets a fright and loses her voice? Well that happened." I did know it. I'd seen it once before when her mum had been using her dad to help her pin a dress she was sewing, but Tegan had walked in and thought he was a secret cross-dresser.

"It was a total accident, but she felt like she'd let you down. Like she'd let the three of us down. You know how good at life she *normally* is?!"

Well I knew how pretty excellent at life she *was*. The person that always sorted out *our* dramas, not made her own. Which is why this had hurt even more.

"I know it doesn't help, but it was just a massive wrong place, wrong time, bad decision. So she figured pretending it never happened – and I KNOW how crazy that sounds now – but she really did think it would make Luke look even more pathetic . . . and be the best thing for us."

I waved an instant goodbye to my mouth-staying-out-of-it rule.

"THE BEST THING?! What planet were you on?"

"Planet Total Idiot? Honestly, if there was *anything* we could do to take it back, or to put it right, we'd do it. In a second. . . We miss you."

She smiled softly. Hopefully. Like her words could be the superglue we needed to stick our friendship back together.

"And I want to hear the details about Zac. The gossip's going crazy. Someone said you're moving in together?"

I couldn't help but laugh. If only.

But Rachel's face fell.

What had she seen? I turned to where she was squinting. Through a stack of books on yeast and fermentation, I spotted The Grossness. Luke. Too bad he saw me too. And he wasted no time in coming over.

"Wow, Rach. So the technique does work then. Standing next to an ugger does make you look even hotter?" He didn't even bother whispering. What. A. Rebel.

"She's *crouching*, actually."

"Whatever. Crouching fittie, hidden minger."

It didn't even make any sense.

SSSHHHHHH.

First official shush. But Luke didn't care and carried on talking like we were outside. He'd probably never been in a library before.

"So, B. I heard you've got even more carried away with your imaginary boyf?"

I hated how he always used nicknames, like he was our friend.

"So, *L*. He's not imaginary. Or my boyf." I annoyed myself with the speed I snapped back. "Yet."

"So even an imaginary dude won't go out with you? That's next-level tragic."

SHHHHHHH.

Rachel stood up, eye to eye with Luke, leaving me staring up at them both like a naughty child. Her voice was at a whisper, but she sounded fierce.

"You don't know what you're talking about."

"Oh, don't I? Do you not think it's completely blates that Blobfish here has made the whole *boyf* thing up to make herself look popular? It's so embarrassing, and *everyone* thinks it."

Correction, everyone only thought it now he'd gone out of his way to make sure they did. Sarah let it slip. Man, he made my blood boil. Deep breath, Bella. He's just trying to wind you up. I picked up my bag and

208

stood up. If you can't beat them, flee.

"Look, Luke." It kind of rhymed. "When is it finally going to go in? Leave. Me. Alone."

He nodded.

"Will do. When I get an apology. For saying *I* was the liar when *your* bessie snogged me." Rachel shook her head, disgusted, but Luke wasn't stopping. "And for not admitting that, just like your mates, you can't seem to tell the truth either. Unless of course you want to come clean and admit you made this whole 'Zac' thing up?"

How DARE he threaten me?

"Why is it ANY business of yours who I see – and what I say about it?!"

Luke's face hardened. I'd riled him. Good.

"Well *you're* the one who got all up in my face about how you were going to bring this hot new kid to prom. This new boyfriend – sorry not-yet-boyfriend – who literally *no one* has even seen. It's time to grow up, Blob. Time to accept that no one wants you – and we all know it."

"HE DOES EXIST, YOU MORON."

Erk. My crossness broke the shouting rule. I COULD NOT get into any more trouble today.

SHHHHHHHHHHHHHHHH.

But maybe there *was* a way I could shut Luke up

once and for all? Make the rumours stop. That's the thing with Luke. That's how he functions. Makes me do things sane me would never do.

"And I don't need to wait for prom to prove it."

I took out my phone. All I had to do was share the one thing I'd been keeping private. Keeping special. Vacuum packed in happy memories. The pic of Zac and I together. I closed down *PSSSST* and opened up my camera roll.

But as I scrolled down through my post-date smiling selfies, feeling Luke's breath on my hair as he watched over my shoulder, smirking under his breath, I thought of how brilliant that day with Zac had been. And how it had been so brilliant because it was real. So what was more important to me? Shutting Luke up, or keeping Zac out of his stupid games? I stared at my screen wishing I knew what to do.

"PHONE AWAY, MS FISHER."

The library plunged into total silence as the teacher on duty shouted across the room. He was giving me serious evils from behind his desk. Just my luck to get spotted. I mouthed 'sorry' and stuffed my phone out of sight. The picture could wait. I couldn't risk a single prom point just to shut Luke up, as much as I'd love to wipe that stupid smug grin off his face.

I waited till the teacher had got back to marking papers before I dared to risk whispering again. I stood up so I could hiss straight into Luke's ear.

"Guess you'll have to wait for prom after all."

He smirked.

"Guess I will. And let me tell you, I am literally counting down the days till I see you turn up dateless. Can. Not. Wait." He turned to leave. "And enjoy that book. You've got a lot to learn."

He held up his hand like a phone, mouthed 'call me' at Rachel, and walked off. What book was he talking about? I looked at the table and registered what I'd dramatically grabbed earlier – *From Erections, to Earlobes: The Truth About Boys' Bodies.* Classy choice, Bella.

I was shaking with rage. There are only two things in life I want to take back. One is last year when my bikini top snapped whilst on a zip wire at a water park in Stafford. The other is ever going out with Luke.

Rachel put her arm around me and guided me back into sitting.

"I know you hate me, and I get it. But how about you let me make it up to you? We could start by sitting by each other in PSHE later – and figuring out what to do about Puke. Maybe you could fill me in on all the non-imaginary-Zac deets?"

But for a change I wasn't thinking about Zac. I was thinking about me. Rachel was right. I needed a plan to deal with Luke, cos avoiding him wasn't getting me anywhere. And his hate campaign wasn't doing me any favours when it came to getting back into the teachers' good books. I needed every prom point I could get, and right now I was dateless, inviteless and planless.

Fixing everything was going to be tough.

I could do it alone. Or. . . I looked at Rachel. Or . . . or I could have someone there with me.

"How about I see you in PSHE then?"

She smiled. And for the first time in weeks I smiled back.

But I wasn't as happy as I looked. There was one more big thing I needed to sort out. Figuring out what to do about Tegan. As scary as it was to face up to, if Rachel and I were going to try and be friends, then it was going to be harder than ever to ignore her. Sooner or later we were going to have to talk. But was I going to be able to let her back, or would I have to push her away for ever?

CHAPTER

EIGHTEEN

'I, Bella Fisher, take you Zac Whose Last Name I've Still Forgotten To Ask, to be my lawful life partner.' Wowee, imaginary Zac looked good in an imaginary suit. And that imaginary chocolate life-partnering cake tasted good too.

I threw my chocolate wrapper in the bin outside the art classroom. If I hid the evidence, it was like it never happened. Still, I was celebrating. Not only had I just imaginarily pledged my allegiance to Zac, not only was it almost the week anniversary of being friends again with Rachel, not only had I not seen Luke since the library, but today was also the day that for the first time ever my name had gone up on the netball team noticeboard. Sure, I think it was because

I'd accidentally caused physical injury to three of the regular team, and Sarah had no other options as it was the same night as craft club. But that aside, I, someone who sometimes got out of breath putting my hair up, would officially be representing St Mary's this week as goalkeeper when we took on JOGS. One small step for netballing teams, one giant leap towards me having spare prom points. Although I have very limited leaping skills. Now all I had to do was get through this week, starting with a mega-long art session.

Which didn't seem that big a deal.

Oh boy. Could I have been more wrong?

CHAPTER

EIGHTEEN B

I switched off my phone. I never want to think about what happened earlier ever again in my whole life. Surely Mondays aren't legally allowed to be this dramatic?

If I close my eyes and wish hard enough, can I magic myself somewhere else when I open them? Maybe Australia – no, not far enough. Weren't they looking for people to move to Mars?

I opened my eyes. Still in my room, and even worse, my bedside mirror confirms I'm still blushing four hours after the incident. After all we'd been through, couldn't it be kind and lie to me?!

Ow. My phone vibrated next to my head. Who now?

My name's not Bella, it's Bell-errrr-ina?!!! Classic!

lololololol xxx

Thanks, Mikey. So he'd heard too. Glad someone's finding this funny.

I cranked up my music to try and drown out Mum and Jo watching re-runs of *Countdown*. I HAVE to distract myself. I absently opened *PSSSST*. I'd posted this time yesterday, when Tegan was playing on my mind, and I'd remembered one of our first-ever big secrets.

ONE OF MY FRIENDS KNOWS EVERYTHING
ABOUT EVERYTHING.BUT WHEN SHE WAS LITTLE
SHE DIDN'T USED TO UNDERSTAND KISSING – ALL
SHE KNEW WAS SHE HAD TO BE GOOD AT IT. SO
AT A SLEEPOVER SHE CALMLY ASKED HER MUM IF
WE COULD PRACTISE ON HER. EWWW!
(FYI OBVS HER MUM SAID NO. BUT STILL!!)

Seeing as it was all on the d-low, I didn't think it mattered that the other secret was that it was actually me who had suggested parent pashing. It was totally innocent, and only Rachel and Tegan had witnessed it, but asking to snog your mum, whatever the circumstances, is probably some form of criminal offence. I checked the post. Wow. It already had 300 likes. My highest yet.

Any other day and I'd be buzzing, but right now I felt like my body and mind were on power-saving mode and all I could manage was blinking. And breathing. And feeling sorry for myself. *Eurgh*. This time yesterday I'd just got back from a great day. I'd spent the afternoon at Rachel's house doing some YouTube tutorials on how to tone eyebrow muscles (I'd put my foot down at inviting Tegan), had an excellent MIAGTM sighting, got another funny comment on *PSSSST* from LilDrummerBoy, found some hilare pictures of Jo with a haircut that looked like a penis, and was about to eat a shepherd's pie. Now? Now everything had changed.

I flung back the covers, pulling on my horse slippers for the three-second journey to my crisis area. The floor by my radiator.

Dear World, I, Bella Fisher have decided to never leave my house again and resign as a member of the human race. I am no good at it, and every day gives me more opportunities to entertain all other humans with my misfortune. Please consider this my resignation following today's pivotal events. Au revoir.

Using French made it seem more dramatic. More 'romantic' tragedy, than 'I'm a massive tragedy'. Must write it down and post a copy to everyone, like a bad news Father Christmas. Yes. I felt a bit better already.

The scene of the shame was the art room. Mr Lutas's domain. Last lesson of the day. A totally average occurrence, where totally average things should happen.

The room had been noisier than normal as for the first time, we were going to be joined by some of our sixth formers, including some newbies. Teaching support was part of one of their modules and they'd been assigned our class to help out with until the end of term. But what was causing the chatter was that apparently one of the boys was hotter than the sun. I was obvs avoiding eye contact with Tegan, but my side-eye had spotted that even *she* had applied clear (school regulation) lipgloss awaiting their arrival.

I was sitting in my usual place, all of my work on this month's project in trays in front of me. I was happy, I was laughing, I was totally unaware of what was about to happen.

Earlier this year, Mr Lutas had set us the title of 'Trilogy of Emotion' and my project had been going surprisingly well. I think it was because it was the kind of art that didn't actually need to look like anything, so if you went wrong, no one could tell, and you could just say, 'Oh, well that *is* art'. For 'Hate' I was originally going to make a photography project, with loads of pictures of conceptual toilet-door gender signs. It drives me mad – how am I meant to know if I'm a mermaid or a seahorse, or an elephant with or without a tusk, or a cake or a biscuit? I just need to wee. However, I thought taking pictures outside toilet doors might get me A-rrested rather than an 'A', so instead I'd done a clay sculpture of a chunk of Stilton, with a whole pineapple on top. Cheese + pineapple = true crime against food. Sculpting cheese was also mega easy. I just had to make one big shape, because cheese can be any shape. Cheesey-peasy.

My second completed one was for 'Fear'. I'd tried to appeal to Mr Lutas, by making a piece that represented being 'Born to Succeed?' (the question mark was very important, so I'd outlined that bit in Tippex). I'd made a dangling baby mobile made up of pictures of things that are intimidatingly successful. It had gone quite well, Mr Lutas nodding with approval as Emma Watson's, Beyoncé's, Anna Kendrick's, Steve Jobs' and Michelle Obama's faces drifted round.

After seeing my clay cheese creation, Mr Lutas had advised me to really 'concentrate on conceptualizing a strong creative vision'. I think he'd meant, 'don't make something so awful ever again'. So I knew I had to nail it with my final piece, 'Love'. My work on it already took up most of the space on my table. I'd started it a couple of weeks ago, when my vision for it had been totally clear. There was only one love in my life – apart from my music collection, aye-ayes, anything with marshmallow in, my camera, Chomps, sleeping, beluga whales, all other whales, Mumbles, MIAGTM and lasagne – and that was Zac.

Mr Lutas wanted effort, and that's what I'd given him. I'd told him it wasn't inspired by a real person, but was a representation of how a person can embody all the feelings of 'love'.

To call what I had created 'art' would be a gross underestimation. It was a multi-layered, schizophrenic, 3D tribute to Zac and my obsession with him. Pictures of caravans, a doll's shoe, a lock of my sister's hair (well a clump I stole from her hairbrush), a badger dressed as an arrow. I'd even recently added a secondary layer of varnished popcorn and a pigeon's footprint. With each new addition it became more of a monstrosity, and the more Mr Lutas couldn't decide if it was insanity or genius. I couldn't tell either. I'd called it 'Lights Camera Zaction'. Last lesson Mr Lutas had called it a 'deeply troubled creative vision'.

Either way, award-winning or alarming, today was the day I was going to finally complete it with its crowning glory, AND get back in Mr Lutas's good books. So, as soon as he gave us the nod, I was off. Within the first ten minutes I'd got to where I wanted to be – placing on the giant letters – Z, A and C – all made up of messages that the two of us had sent. Mr Lutas congratulated me on my use of 'découpage', and said it might help me get full marks. I'd nodded thoughtfully, said 'thank you' and decided not to admit that I had no idea what découpage was.

I tried not to look at the other end of my table, and compare my project to Rachel's, which was probably going to be exhibited in the Tate. Maybe painting triangles is the way to making millions.

Just as I stuck the Z down, Mr Lutas announced he had to leave us alone for five minutes, and strode out of the room. The noise exploded up like when you accidentally sit on the TV remote and almost shatter your windows with the *Coronation Street* theme tune. But when he strode back in, the chat stopped even more quickly than it had started.

"Everyone, settle down. I'd like to intrrrroduce you to our teaching assistants."

The girls exchanged looks. It was their time to shine. I carried on gluing down the letter C.

"As you should know, some of our specially selected sixth formers will be joining this class between now and the end of the terrrrm. It's part of their course to explore the worrrrld of teaching, so please consider them as extra teachers and treat them accordingly." He'd turned towards the door. "Come on in, lads, ladies."

I'd grossed out at Mr Lutas saying 'lads'. The rest of the room rippled with excitement. Arrival of fresh, older eye candy. In they walked.

You know in cartoons when someone's jaw hits the floor? Well my jaw fell so hard it dented the extra popcorn I'd just glued on. There were indeed some hotties – as well as some bored-looking cool girls. And one of the boys was indeed the hottest person I'd ever seen. No wonder everyone had been so excited to meet him. Tall, dark, smart yet scruffy hair, gorgeous eyes.

But hand on heart, he wasn't hotter than Zac. Oh no, it was way worse than that.

He *was* Zac.

HELLO, WORST MOMENT OF MY LIFE.

Luckily Zac didn't spot me in the sea of drooling faces.

If I threw up on my artwork, would Mr Lutas grade it higher for 'creative concept'?

I rubbed my ankles together as fast as I could in an attempt to spontaneously combust my socks, or at least set off the fire alarm. But with no flames emerging, Mr Lutas started introducing the students. All I could hear was my head screaming, 'WHAT AM I GOING TO DO?!!!'.

"Err, hello, everyone. I'm new here, so bear with me." Zac coughed to try and clear a path for his words through the stifled giggles. "So, any questions, please ask, and I'll do my best to figure out the answer."

I had a question – what the hell was Zac doing in *my* classroom?! He said he was going to BIRMINGHAM?

It all rushed through my head – the holiday, the date, the lying about my age, the fact that that I'd now half-snogged (hogged?) one of our sixth formers through deceit and treachery. Was that even legal?! There was no way he could see me. Or my artwork. WITH HIS ACTUAL NAME ON.

In a puff of madness I'd dived under my table, timing it perfectly, as at the front of the room Lou caused a distraction by putting her hand up. She's one of those girls who doesn't care about marks, as long as she's the centre of attention. Fine by me, I was hiding on the floor. We had very different agendas.

"Hello, sir, great to meet you." She'd used her most suck-up voice. "I was wondering, could you come and help me make 'love' on my canvas?"

Mr Lutas spluttered, the class erupted. I contemplated a daring, under-desk crawling escape.

"Oi, Rachel. Oi!" I'd tugged at her skirt. She'd waited till the coast was clear and hissed down.

"What on earth are you doing??"

"Ineedtogetoutofhere. NOW."

But it was too late. Four feet, with two people attached were walking towards us.

"Bella, what arrrrre you doing down there?" Mr Lutas seemed personally offended by me being under a desk.

"BELLA!" Chalk dust from his groin rained past my head as he stamped his foot.

Escape options flashed through my head like a DVD fast forwarding.

"BELLA get up here NOW! Unless you want to give up on the hope of holding on to any of your prrrrrom points?"

But I couldn't move one single muscle.

Mr Lutas cleared his throat. "Be clear, you *can* consider this yourrrr FINAL WARNING."

I only had one option. And even I was ashamed to try it.

"My name's not Bella —" yes, I'd attempted disguise — "it's, er, Bell-errr..." THINK! "...ina?"

I swallowed.

"BELLERINA?!" Mr Lutas bellowed so hard one of his spit globules hit my left foot.

"Er, yes?"

Cringecringecrange.

"WHATEVER YOU ARE CALLED." I figured when someone is apoplectic with rage is probably not the time to tell them you'd actually been aiming for Belinda but only just remembered it. "I don't know what you'rrre playing at, but get up off that floor. NOW."

I, Bellerina, had embarrassed Mr Lutas in front of his hotshot college students and I was going to have pay. To say things were not going to plan would be like saying Louis Tomlinson can afford to buy a single Chomp.

I'd buried my head in my hands, trying to hide both my face and my intense shame. But hands weren't enough, so I'd pulled my jumper up and over my head, cocooning myself in a beige cavern. Classy. But Zac not recognizing me was bigger than what Mr Lutas, or any of the thirty people clearly staring at me, thought.

Under the table a hand thrust towards me.

"Er, hello, Bella. Nice to meet you. I really hope it's not me that's made you sit under a table with a jumper on your head."

Zac clearly thought I was the class weirdo, and used an extra supportive 'I'm on your side' voice. I know Zac had told me he liked unpredictable girls, but surely this overstepped the line. And then circumnavigated the globe and then re-stepped over it again.

"No, no, I'm fine. I'm just, er, having an allergic reaction to some paint."

But would he give up? Of course not. He was Zac. Caring. Persistent. Calm. Totally annoying.

He did exactly what I hoped he wouldn't do. He bent down to my level. I was face to face with him. Just he didn't know as there was a layer of wool between us.

"Can I do anything to help?"

Mr Lutas's aftershave wafted in the air as he bent down too.

"I said. Get. Up. Off. The. Floor. And take that jumper off your head."

There was no way out.

I slowly pulled my jumper down, my horrified face revealing itself millimetre by painful millimetre. Zac did the world's biggest double-double-take. Maybe even a double-double-double-take, which is like eight takes.

"What the hell?!" He'd recoiled back so hard he whacked his head on the desk. Without another word – other than 'ow' – he made his way back to standing, pretending that he'd slipped.

In that one second, under that one desk, I, Bella Fisher, had officially ruined my life. How was I going to ever be able to explain *any* of this to Zac? I'd crawled back up and slumped into my chair, pretending not to hear the whispers.

Rachel looked concerned.

"Are you OK?" she'd mouthed. But the worst was yet to come. Mr Lutas wanted to reassure the placement students that I wasn't a danger to the teaching profession, and *normally* functioned as a *normal* student.

"When this young lady is not hiding under tables for no explicable reason, she can be found working on quite an interrrresting interrrpretation for her 'love' piece. Isn't that right?" Mr Lutas grabbed

227

my work and held it up proudly. "Just look at that découpage!"

Maybe, if I was beyond lucky, Zac could be perfect in every way except for lacking the ability to read his own name.

But I was anti-lucky. A black hole of luck.

Mr Lutas pointed to the messages I'd just stuck on.

"See how Bella has made up some messages that only someone in the complete throws of a teenage crush would send? Great creativity. See?" He pointed to the exact messages that I'd sent to Rachel that morning. "If Z was a country, he'd be Fitaly – national dish Spag-hottie." He pointed at another. "He's so hot that if we put bread on his head it would turn to toast." And also, "Even his wrists are fanciable." Mr Lutas did an actual chortle. "I mean she's really captured the mind-set of somebody out of control with young love! Really on the brink of madness."

If Zac wasn't already speechless, standing beside a 3D (4D if you counted the smell of popcorn) shrine to himself achieved it. I couldn't look at his face. Or his wrists. I was numb with embarrassment. The class must have thought Zac was overcome with my art. I knew he was probably wondering whether to call the police.

228

I fixed my eyes on my feet as if I'd just discovered tiny Borrowers doing a Mexican wave on my toes.

"And *what* a coincidence that she chose your name. Maybe you can give her some extra guidance?"

Rachel's eyes widened. The penny dropped. Along with the bottom out of my world. Thank goodness Mr Lutas whisked Zac back to the other sixth formers to show-off far more impressive/not-hiding-under-a-table students.

I was so cross with myself I wanted to screw up my whole art project, throw it in the bin, then jump in after it, but I knew I couldn't risk any more drama around Mr Lutas. And I'd probably get stuck in the bin.

Once the hysteria of having real-life fit people in the room had died down, everyone got back to their work. My progress was severely stunted as I was so scared of locking eyes with Zac, I couldn't walk to get any of the stuff I needed, so had to fake paint with a pencil for forty-five minutes, occasionally stepping back and looking at it knowingly. When I finally confirmed to Rachel that Zac was THE Zac, and yes, he *was* even better looking IRL than in the photos I'd shown her on almost an hourly basis, she had to physically sit down and fan herself. When she recovered, she reasoned I shouldn't be so miserable, as I now had living proof of the world's best-ever pull.

In one lesson I'd gone from wanting to see Zac every day, to having the possibility of it – and wishing I didn't. WHY had I lied about my age? WHY OH WHY did I say I was at college? Oh yeah – to kiss him. But was it worth it? Er, yes, but that's not the point. I'd ruined EVERYTHING. He was never going to talk to me now, let alone go on date number three. And if he wasn't speaking to me, it was going to be hard for me to speak at him to explain myself. Or suggest a life of happiness together.

I don't know how I made it through the rest of that lesson. Through the end of the day. Through the walk home. Through Jo giving me a hug on my bed as I spilled the full Zac story from standing-him up, to seeing him in Worcester (minus cinema trip), to revealing my accidental art shrine to him. I never thought I'd be grateful that she was home for exam leave.

As I lay in bed trying to figure out what to do next, my phone lit up. New message. Probably more abuse.

Well that was awkward.

ARGH! As if Zac needed to remind me. I stared at the full stop. He'd never just full stopped me at the end of a message before. But then he'd never known that I was a fake-art-college-student-called-Bellerina until today.

I panic messaged back before I could overthink it.

> I'm SO sorry. None of this was meant to
> happen. OBVS.

I followed up with one of the many things that had been on my mind ever since it happened.

> How come you didn't tell me you'd already
> moved?

I didn't mean to sound moody, but I couldn't work out how he was here. In my town, at my school, and I'd had no idea. No warning. No time to even make sure I wasn't wearing my school jumper with the brown sauce stain on it.

> I was going to give it a week to settle in and
> surprise you. Didn't see your name on the college
> list, so didn't think we'd run into each other there.
> Guess you're the one full of surprises ☹

Mortification. He'd been trying to be extra nice, and I'd been an extra-massive disappointment. If only there was a 'Please forgive me, I'm a total idiot, and I make terrible decisions when around insanely perfect people' emoji.

Was there anything I could do to convince him to give me a second chance? Try and remind him how much fun we had before all this? I HAD to go all out. I HAD to get him to hear me out.

I'm not. I swear. I'm sorry x 1 million. Can we talk? Tomorrow at first break?

My life hung in the balance of his reply. 'Typing'. TYPE FASTER!

Y'know my Italy trip? Well, it's a yes IF I get full marks for this placement. So I can't risk any drama, or anyone finding out we've got history. I was getting in touch to say we should probably give each other some space... Hope you understand.

I stared numbly at the screen. His one-hundred-and-ninety-eight-character way of saying 'no'. He'd been so excited about trying to get on that Italy/Fitaly art trip – and I'd been so excited for him. I never guessed I'd end up being the one thing putting it at risk.

Another message popped up.

Look, I'll know about the trip by that end of term party. How about we speak then? I'll be supervising.

Eurgh. He meant prom and that was almost two weeks away. So much for him being my date to it – now he was going to be the one telling me off for walking on the wrong side of the corridor.

I picked a pin up off my desk and prodded it into my leg. Ow. This wasn't all just an elaborate nightmare. Zac was the one thing that had been making my life amazing. But now pretending each other didn't exist was the one thing standing between him and the trip of a lifetime.

Can you emigrate when you're fifteen? Or become a hermit? Or both? Hermitigrate? It was all so grim. I stared at my stupid phone, wishing it to change. Wishing everything to change.

I messaged a final 'sure/sorry' and turned my

bedside light off. Tonight was a no-teeth-brushing-sleeping-in-bra kind of a night.

My mind raced, playing out every scenario, hunting for a needle of hope in my haystack of hopelessness. But there was *something* – something Jo had said. Zac was probably as shocked as me. Maybe even more. So maybe, just maybe, if I did what he said, gave him the time he wanted, stayed out of his way between now and prom, then I *could* talk him round?

YES.

All might not be lost! But if I had *any* hope of a second chance, Zac had to get on his art tour, and I had to be at the prom so he could hear me out. So what should be first on my list of turning my life from chaos to fully in control? From problems to prom points?

One thing was certain – I *had* to let Luke carry on thinking Zac didn't exist. There was no way he could connect the dots between my date-bragging and me hiding in art. Luke would make sure the whole school knew I'd been obsessing over the new sixth former and it could land both Zac and I in a whole heap of unwanted attention. And trouble.

Plus, it wasn't going to help my 'I'm actually not totally lame so pleeeease give me a second chance' campaign if Zac knew I'd already told the whole school (and even the goal shooter from a visiting netball team) the minute details of both our semi and full snogs.

EURGH. How does Luke even manage to mess up the bits of my life he doesn't even know about?! Still he did have his uses. I opened up *PSSSST*. I was still getting new followers every day. I was up to 323 and had over 900 likes on my posts. I sass-waved my nails to my invisible fans. Bella, you got this.

A GUY I KNOW (BUT WISH I DIDN'T)
USED TO REALLY LOOK UP TO HIS BIG SISTERS.
SO MUCH SO THAT HE USED THEIR NORMAL
EXCUSE TO TRY AND BLAG HIS DAD TO BUY
HIM SOME CRISPS. SHAME HE'D NEVER
ASKED WHAT IT MEANT. APPARENTLY THE
WHOLE SUPERMARKET WENT SILENT WHEN
A TEN-YEAR-OLD BOY YELLED 'BUT DAD,
IT'S MY TIME OF THE MONTH!'

I couldn't help but smile for the first time since Art, remembering how Luke's mum had almost cried with laughter when she'd told me that. Luke had gone redder than he probably did when it actually happened. And *that* is why parents should never meet people you fancy. Unless the parentals are asleep. Still, if I could get people to like me on *PSSSST*, maybe I *could* get Zac to re-like me in real life?

I closed the app and with a new sense of optimism, set my alarm for the next morning. The time had come to take control and mastermind the triumphant return of Bella and Zac.

CHAPTER

NİNETEEN

6:07. I hit my alarm clock like it had wronged me. Poor alarms, it must be rubbish knowing your entire purpose in life is to make people miserable. Still, why *had* I actively chosen to wake myself up at this hour? Oh yes, to prepare for Traumatic Tuesday. With in-control-ness to aim for, prom points to win back, and a threat of a Zac sighting around every corner, I needed more than my usual sixteen minute routine of shower/tinted moisturiser/run out the door with wet hair.

Well, that was the idea, but an hour later I had to face up to the fact that I'd used my extra morning time to progress four levels on Puppy Dash Saga and make a pie chart that had worked out that my biggest hitters on *PSSSST* all seemed to feature Luke.

I *had* managed to solve one problem though. Step two of my cunning plan was to sneak into art at lunchtime and de-Zacify my art. *Obviously* what they'd seen was a work in progress; the end product would be about a niche Chinese philosophy called 'Zao'. It was so niche, that it only had one follower. Me. I wonder if I can get Jo to set up a Wikipedia entry on it later?

As if summoned by my thought process, she poked her head around the door, annoyingly catching me mid-steal of her 'fresh glow' cheek highlighter. Personally I think it should be rebranded as 'makes you look shiny in a perspiring way' highlighter, but the damage was done.

"Oi, sweaty, want a lift? I've got a meet, so am going your way."

Jo often had meets – they were day-long athletic sessions that seemed to consist of running all over the place in tiny shorts while people shouted at you. I still cannot believe that this is something anyone would do voluntarily. She'd been having loads recently as her county athletics club were off on another tour.

Jo looked at her watch. She had her special one on that recorded things like split times.

"You've got three minutes. So get a move on. I can't be late or I'll miss the coach."

Before I could reply, she dashed back downstairs, probably setting a new PB.

I tried to un-sweat my face, but mainly just smeared my blusher. Wearing make-up for school was tough, as you had to make it look to teachers like you weren't wearing any, but still appear flawless to the rest of the world.

I heard the engine starting, so grabbed my stuff, ran downstairs and jumped into Jo's car. But I'd forgotten the downside of getting a lift. Being locked in a small space with my sister. It wasn't a risk at home, as even bathroom locks were against Mum's 'freedom principles'. But in the car meant I had nowhere to run, and nowhere to hide. Jo went straight for the jugular.

"So, what are you going to do about today's big decision?"

"I thought you said I wasn't old enough to resign from school?"

"No, doof. Is today going to be the day you speak to Tegan?"

BLEURGH. She made it sound so simple. But with all the Zac drama I didn't have the time or energy to deal with any more problems. Maybe I *was* better off without her? Rachel would just have to be like a child that we time-shared.

"Bells, I've been thinking it about after our chat last night... If you want my advice."

"I don't." Annoyingly I did, but I didn't want her to know that I did. Luckily she ignored me. She'd had 15.5 years of practice at doing that.

"Well, you're in my car, so you've got no choice but to get it. Plus, it's an older sister's prerogative." She smiled smugly. "So, I was thinking, what do you want Zac to do after yesterday's run-in?"

Run away and start a new life with me in Wales and/or California?

"Hmm, I'd take anything at this point ... anything from not hating upwards."

"OK, and *then* what? If you got everything your way?"

Good question.

"I guess he'd hear me out at prom, realize that I'd only done it so he would give me a chance in the first place, forgive me ... and then start a new life with me in Wales making fancy-dress outfits for puppies?"

"I see..." She sounded unconvinced. "So, dog costumes aside, if you're so desperate for him to give you a second chance –" she paused, letting me fill in the answer in my head, before she said it out loud – "maybe you should think about doing the same for

Tegan? Seems to me you could do with an extra friend right now?"

Argh. Why was she always so wise?! Like an owl, but with less head movement. And feathers (I hope). How come it felt so much less reasonable to forgive and forget, than to ask for it? EURGH.

For the rest of the morning I skulked around, my brain carrying out only two functions (well, three if you counted sustaining vital organ function, but that was way down on my priority list) – bouncing Jo's words back and forth in my head, and helping me stealth-avoid Zac, Mr Lutas, Luke and Tegan. I really was collecting people to hide from.

When I finally plucked up the courage to dash through the corridors of doom to get to the canteen, Rachel and Mikey were already at a table, and they'd saved me a seat. Rachel had her head in a book and Mikey was staring across to the table where Tegan was. She was talking to some of the girls from Tailor Swiftly, her after-school sewing club. Earlier this term, she'd helped them rebrand from Mend It Like Beckham, and they'd been pretty tight ever since. She looked deep in chat, probably working out some more designs. Good. This seemed very undramatic.

I opened up Peppa – what delights did today have

in store? Last night's meatless-meatballs and cauli-rice (which Mum had added ham to). But as I tucked in, I felt like I was being watched.

I was. It was Luke – but as soon as I turned towards him, he flicked his eyes back to his mates. Still, he was a safe non-prom-point-losing three-table distance away. Seconds later, the room shushed, signalling teacher arrival. Mrs Hitchman strutted in behind me, in full-on professional teacher mode.

"And for those that don't know, this is where the younger years have lunch. It's a multi-use space, for supervised activities like bake sales and any entrepreneurial projects they come up with."

I choked on my ham. As if anyone had ever done anything off their own back?! (Except that time that Lou attempted to sell five minute massages, but got busted for charging extra for additional snogging services.)

Rachel kicked me under the table and mouthed, "Sheila's sack."

'What?' I mouthed back.

She pointed her fork behind me to where Mrs Hitchman was getting ever closer. She mouthed more slowly this time.

"She's. With. Zac."

I re-choked on my ham. This was meant to be a safe zone! I dropped my fork so I could hide my head in my hands and hang my hair forward like a privacy curtain. Maybe this is how Cousin It got started. Pleeeease don't let them notice me. Pleeease don't let Luke notice me noticing them. Pleeease don't let Luke notice them either noticing or not noticing me. Please just walk on by.

But the clack of Mrs Hitchman's heels came to a stop. Along with the sixth formers who she was briefing on their teaching assistant duties.

"And don't panic. Supervision's not a big job. Especially at lunchtime – all the students seem to be well behaved when they've got food in front of them! Isn't that right ... Bella – I know you love a good meal?"

Argh! Why had I just stuffed a second meatless-meatball in my mouth, so I looked like a human hamster? As much as I'd rather do *anything* else in the world, including being photographed in a beige unitard while eating an egg sandwich, I looked up. Zac didn't react. Everything about him was icy cold. Even his hands looked less friendly. He was blanking me harder than if I was in an invisibility cloak. I gulped so hard both meatless-meatballs disappeared. Please let them have gone into my stomach and not my lungs. Mrs Hitchman ignored me ignoring her.

"Great, great... Any questions before we move on?" No one said a word. "Excellent, well let's go and have a quick chat with today's lunch attendant."

Mrs Hitchman power-marched them to the corner of the room, stopping to chat to the head girl. The sixth formers waited beside her, being all, 'Let's act like we don't think we're being watched, while being all brooding cos we totally know everyone's staring at us.' But something made my insides twist like when Mum rings out my swimming costume. Why was Lou slinking her way over to Zac? Why had SHE stopped beside him way too close for (my) comfort?? Why was she batting her eyelashes and fiddling with her frayed jumper cuff at *my* OTP? Why wasn't I allowed to speak to him, but *she* was getting away with oozing her extreme-girl-ness all over him?! I clutched Rachel's leg like it could whack out a Stupefy across the room. Or at least a Deflirtify.

I. Could. Not. Watch.

"You alright, B?" Mikey looked genuinely concerned. "Do you need me to Heimlich? I watched it on *Casualty* once." He pushed his stool out to stand up.

But like an angel in a tweed two-piece, Mrs

Hitchman came to my rescue, breaking up the conversation by summoning the group out. Lou tossed her hair over her shoulder and wiggle-walked her way back towards her friends looking pleased with herself. I harrumphed. Mikey looked disappointed he wasn't going to put his dubious medical skills into practice. Rachel rubbed her hand on my mine and gave me a supportive smile.

"BREATHE, Bells. Just because you and Zac are on a blip right now..."

I spluttered cauli-rice in her face.

"BLIP?! As in, he won't talk to me, thinks I'm an idiot and is now realizing that everyone else in the school – who isn't an idiot – wants to snog his face off?"

"Well, yes, that little blip. But it doesn't mean he's had a total brain transplant and is suddenly going to go for girls like Lou-ser. She knows even less about French films and art and stuff than you." Was this meant to be reassuring? "She probably doesn't even know who Munch was?!" I didn't point out I thought he/she/it was a type of crisp. Rachel grabbed my shoulders and gave me a firm shake. "Be strong, B. He liked you before. And no one except Tegan and I know what really went down, so let's make sure it stays that way and then work your magic at prom. Simplington."

Rachel made the plan sound way more doable than it felt. Especially when the only prom magic I had up my sleeve was knowing the full rap to 'Drunk in Love'. Although thanks to Tegan's patient tutorials I could also do a pretty good Stanky Leg.

I stabbed at a piece of ham like it was to blame. In fairness, the pig should have a lot more beef (well, pork) with me than I did with it.

"Long time no see."

GULP. Why was Luke here? And why had he brought Lou?

"Mind if we join you ladies?" Luke looked at Mikey. "I include you as one of those."

Mikey spoke for the three of us.

"We do actually."

But Luke slid on to the stool next to me, Lou draping herself forward over his shoulder, knowing full well Mikey could see right down her shirt. Note to self, stop sitting at tables that have spare seats. In fact, stop sitting – moving targets are harder to converse with.

"It'll only take a sec. I'm just a bit confused about something. Well, we both are. Because yesterday Lou had a chat with me. Didn't you?"

They were probably arguing over which one of them did the best duckface selfies.

"Sure did." Lou smiled sweetly. This was obviously something they'd rehearsed. "I was telling Luke about our art lesson, when that new sixth former turned up." I stopped mid-chew, like I'd chomped on a piece of concrete. What did this have to do with anything?! "The really fit one? The one I was just chatting to?"

Oh flapballs. I HAD to make sure they didn't make a connection between Zac and me. I forced myself to chew and tried to channel all kinds of nonchalance.

"I didn't see, soz – *were* you speaking to someone?"

Mikey looked baffled. Seconds ago he'd almost had to medically intervene to help me get over the exact thing I was now pretending hadn't happened.

Lou lent up on to her elbows.

"Don't act stupid. I KNOW you were watching."

I pretended to think so hard I must have looked like I was recalling an event from ten centuries ago, not ten seconds ago.

"Hmmmm. I was probably just staring and thinking. Stinking?" That didn't work. "Or not. You know, like when you stare at a teacher, but you're thinking about who on *Hollyoaks* you'd most like to date."

"No. I don't do that."

Of course she didn't. She probably just dated them in real life.

Rachel loudly snapped her lunchbox shut and cleared her throat.

"Look – is there a point to this, or can you leave us in peace?"

Luke grinned. "Rach, can I just say how especially fit you're looking today."

Rachel tucked her hair behind her ears and tried her hardest to look anything less than amazing. Although she just looked like an amazing person with hair tucked behind her ears. "No, you can't."

"Well, I just did. But that's not what I came over for. Lou was telling me what a massive scene you made –" Luke stared right at me – "when that kid walked in."

Lou nodded.

"Yeah, it was well embarrassing – even for you. And when you got up off the floor I *totally* heard you telling Rachel that he was the one you'd been snogging. The one you've been going on about all over school. I was *right* behind you."

OH SLOW-HAND CLAP ME. Why had I been so busy not looking at Zac that I'd forgotten to see if anyone else was around? Especially someone who spent their whole time sliming over Luke. I looked to Rachel for support, but she just mouthed 'gulp' which wasn't hugely reassuring.

Luke pulled his stool nearer.

"You see, Blobfish, that got me thinking. Why were you telling your bessie mate this kid was your imaginary boyfriend? That the guy in school that everyone is after and Fishy Balls had been the one to get him?" He laughed as if it was the funniest thing imaginable, rather than the exact thing that happened. "You really are TOO FUNNY."

But Puke and Lou were the only ones laughing.

Lou twirled her hair around her finger. "So I went to chat to him. Y'know, get to know him a bit better." She winked. I wanted to stab her in the eye with my fork. But then I'd have an eye on my fork, and that would probably put me off my lunch. "And I asked him if he was with anyone. . ."

My response came out too quickly. A bit too not-not-bothered.

"What did he say?"

"He said that he was completely single. New to the area, and didn't know anyone here. That he was 'open to offers'." Ouch. That stung. She winked again. I had to drop my fork on the table as I couldn't trust myself.

I did know deep down that, as normal, she *had* to be exaggerating – there's no way Zac would tell Lou he was on the lookout if he was trying to ace his placement – but it still wasn't a highlight to hear him act as if I didn't even exist.

Luke lent forward.

"Oh dear, oh dear. Has the time finally come to admit your lies are a bit out of hand? Just like when you tried to pretend you hadn't been massively binned off by me?"

ARGH! How could one person be so evil? Was it a class he took on Saturdays?

Mum always says the best thing to do when someone was winding you up is ignore them. But she wasn't here. And I couldn't keep calm any longer.

"When will you just SHUT UP?! I didn't pretend ANYTHING! We broke up. Who cares?! Seriously, if I could take back a SINGLE second I spent with you, I would."

"Oh, diddums, still not over me, are you?"

It took more restraint than I knew I had, not to run around the canteen waving my hands in the air, screaming 'SOMEBODY DROWN THAT BOY IN THE VAT OF SCHOOL BOLOGNESE'. But this wasn't the look I needed. I could NOT let this stupid game-playing loser push me over the edge and make a scene.

"AS IF. I've deleted the whole massive mistake from

my memory. And then deleted it from my brain deleted items just in case. So can you just do one? Both of you?" I shut my mouth, frustrated I was letting Luke see he was getting to me.

Luke didn't budge.

"Not until you admit you're lying."

Mikey stood up. I shook my head at him, willing him to stay back, keep quiet. I didn't want to make Luke more mad, attract any more attention. But oblivious, Mikey walked round to my side of the table and stopped right behind me.

"Mate, I haven't got a clue what's going on here." Luke muttered 'like normal'. But Mikey was better than his low blows. "But one thing I do know – none of Bella's business has got ANYTHING to do with you. So just leave her alone. Unless of course it's *you* that's not over *Bella*? Which is what it's starting to look like..."

GULP. This was *not* the definition of how to not make Luke more mad. Luke looked like he was one word away from punching Mikey on the nose. His jaw was clenched so hard his whole face had gone square.

I did a quick scan for any teachers looking our way, but we were still in the clear. I needed to keep it that way.

But Luke had other ideas. He was almost at a shout.

"Over her? OVER HER? I was never even 'on her', mate." He spat the words out, along with a small bit of his lunch. "She was just something to make me laugh. And now I want everyone else to see how tragic she is too."

Luke put his face up close to mine trying to intimidate me, but all it did was remind me he borrowed his aftershave from his dad.

"So if she's not going to make this easy for me, I'm going to have to prove it some other way. Wonder what that poor newbie's going to say when he finds out some loser Year 10's been making up fake dates with him? Poor little Blob's probably going to get in very big trouble."

Luke put his arm round me, giving me a fake supportive squeeze, making sure everyone could see. I wriggled free desperate to get his hands off me.

But as I opened my mouth, he jerked back, brushing at his hair, like an electrocuted caveman.

"Who threw that?" He stood up, his voice louder this time. "Who. Threw. That?"

Flakes of potato were raining down from his head like carbohydrate dandruff. Mikey and Rachel looked like OMG emojis (slash ones that were trying to not laugh). The entire canteen had shut up, like someone had pressed a real-life mute button. People love drama, especially when they're not involved.

"I said. Who. Was. That?" He was practically at a yell. Lucky the attendant was still outside with Mrs Hitchman.

A morsel of potato clung to the top of his spikey hair like a flag on the top of Mount Everest. I would have laughed if I wasn't so transfixed by its wobbling.

I looked around to figure out who it was that had thrown it. Who was brave enough to stand up to the one person who would now dedicate their life to making theirs a misery?

But the second I saw them I knew. It wasn't something everyone would notice, but behind that calm face, that neutral expression, I saw the glint of someone who had finally had enough.

THUD.

A lone baked bean joined its potato friend at the top of Luke's hair.

He span round to face Matt, one of the prefects in our year, who always has pink cheeks like he's accidentally just walked into the girls' changing room.

"Was it you, you . . . you red-faced . . . baboon?"

Matt shook his head, but he didn't look scared. He

looked like someone who wanted to point out baboons didn't have red faces. And I respected that.

"Wasn't me. I'm allergic to haricot beans."

Luke spluttered, as some bean juice dripped on to his nose.

"They're baked, not Harry Co."

The thrower stood up.

"Haricot beans ARE baked beans. Idiot."

OMG. Was I really in the middle of a fight about pulses?

Luke dug his hand into my meatless-meatballs. Next thing they were flying through the air. Why couldn't this be happening on a day when I had a rubbish sandwich instead? I guess the three-second rule doesn't apply to things that are on the canteen floor? The original thrower dodged out the way. They always were the most flexible person in our year.

Luke scooped up another handful, but just as he went to lob them, there was a loud splat, as some gloopy brie flew into his ear, cheesy globules flicking off on to Lou's face as it landed. There was only one person who brought posh cheese, not string cheese, to lunch. Mikey winked at me, and gave Rachel her lunch box back.

Half a second later, cauli-rice was showering across

the canteen, as Luke's friends joined in and a wave of Monster Munch and tiny tomatoes flew in our direction from their table. Lou crouched and fled the danger zone as tomatoes were joined by peas, unidentifiable brown crumbs and some Alphabites (our cheap canteen variety only has Os, Hs and Ns so it looks like 'OOOH NOOO') flying through the air. I ducked, trying to avoid the flying feast, grabbing the red and yellow bottles on our table and squirting them at Luke. As a fan of food, it was against my principles to throw it, but these sauces were technically so rank they were inedible, so were fair game.

Suddenly someone at the back of the room yelled.

"MRS HITCHMAN'S COMING."

Suddenly the prom-point-losing reality took grip of the room. And my don't-cause-any-drama mission sprang back into life. We shoved our food away, tried to de-crisp/cheese/bean ourselves and scrambled to appear as normal as possible, which is hard when there's a carpet of peas between three tables and one of you looks like a Jackson Pollock (an artist I'd learnt about during Zac revision, who basically threw paint everywhere, and then got people to think he was a genius for doing it, which is actually incredibly genius-ey of him) but with mustard and ketchup.

Mrs Hitchman looked like she was going to pop

with fury. I silently shouted at my face to not look guilty. Or have any pea on it. Zac and the rest of the sixth formers she'd dragged back looked mortified that they were soon going to be supervising people who didn't know the difference between a basketball and a baked bean. I couldn't even look in Zac's direction in case Lou or Luke were watching me.

With no obvious culprit (luckily Luke had the sense to take off his splattered blazer), there was no obvious person to blame, so the whole room got a group guilt-trip instead.

When Mrs Hitchman eventually finished yelling and left the room, the canteen returned to normal. Spitting insults at us (the potato and bean still clinging to his head like triumphant rodeo riders), Luke finally went back to his table.

But despite his threats, I was a little bit happy.

I waved the thrower over.

"What made you do that?"

"Well, words didn't seem to be getting through. And when he put his arm around you, I lost it. So, y'know . . . when all else fails, shot-put a potato."

I laughed. So did Rachel and Mikey.

"Shot-potato." I replied then stopped as I worked out what to say next.

A lot depended on it.

"Well, as much as I wanted to eat my meatless-meatballs, not use them as darts. . ." What decision was I going to make? ". . . Thank you."

Thrower smiled. The kind of smile that made having a chunk of omelette in my shoe OK.

We still had a lot of talking to do, but for now, it was good to have Tegan back.

CHAPTER

TWENTY

It was only thirteen days till term ended, but for the first time this year, maybe ever, I was looking forward to going to school. Now I had my friends back, everything felt more positive. With their help I could focus on the most important thing during these two weeks of exams. Keeping Luke away from Zac. And hanging on to every single prom point.

Tegan, Rachel and I arranged to meet in our usual before-school spot outside the post office – which doubled as supplier of emergency morning chocolate and/or crisps depending on how bad the morning was going/how dire Mum's cooking had been the night before. As yesterday's dinner had been Tuna and Natural Yogurt Surprise – and the not surprising surprise was that it was entirely unswallowable – I bought both.

I waited outside, chewing on my chocolate breakfast and checking *PSSSST*. What had started as something to fill my friendless moments was now making me feel more popular than ever. I had my real-life friends back to tell my real-life dramas to, so could keep *PSSSST* to share the things that made me laugh. The cheese-in-ear story had gone down a treat. One person's evil-ex is another's six-second internet LOL. As well as the followers, I'd also got more people commenting. LilDrummerBoy made me laugh so hard with a post about sniffing his sister's scented nail varnish, but getting too close and gluing glitter on to his nose for two days, that I was still chortling when Tegan bounced up. She had a massive smile plastered across her face. We'd spent most of last night on the phone, her talking, me listening, her apologizing, me slowly beginning to realize that forgiving her wasn't betraying me. In fact, it kind of made me happier – give or take the annoyingness I felt at Jo being sort of right. I'd had to keep checking she wasn't listening at the door, ready to say 'I told you so'.

Tegan hadn't said anything new, but the difference was I was finally ready to hear it. Plus, it's always nice to talk to someone who hates Luke as much as I do. We'd ended up catching up on everything – from Zac (who I sent photos of to Tegan, while on the phone, causing her to involuntarily gasp and say 'oh my' at his beauty, like she was in a black-and-white movie), to Luke making out I was a liar, through to my prom point problem – promlem – and even a new gymnastics student Tegan's teaching who's only five and keeps saying Tegan has a gentle face. Except he pronounces it 'genital'. Despite two threats from Mum to get off the phone, we ended up speaking right up until bed. Friendship Goals 1, German Homework 0. But, I'd woken up, bleary-eyed, to some picture messages from Tegan. Fact – there is no better way to glue a friendship back together than with the surprise gift of conjugated German verbs. I don't even know what 'conjugated' really means. I thought it was something that happens to your eye.

When Rachel finally turned up, we set off for school. She'd been held up by a manicurist her mum had booked to come to their house that morning. Her mum literally nails life.

The three of us linked arms and we set off as a six-legged mono-person. I didn't spoil the moment by mentioning a substantial bruise was forming where the corner of Rach's maths textbook was whacking into my ribs. Rachel squeezed on both of our arms, happy to be back in the middle of us, rather than stuck in the middle of our argument.

"Sorry to sound like a cheese, but it's so nice being back together. We thought we'd lost you to the netball crew for a while."

I couldn't help but laugh.

"Pah. As if. Did you not hear that I let in fourteen goals on my team debut?"

Tegan's bad attempt at a shocked 'no' clearly meant an unshocked 'yes'.

Rachel smiled supportively.

"Oh well. Who needs to stop balls being thrown into nets anyway? It's not like that's the one thing you need to become an internet squillionaire, or a music photographer," she looked at Tegan, "or a human writing lawyer."

Correcting her for the millionth time didn't even scratch the surface of Tegan's never-ending patience.

"It's human 'rights'. Still, you got the points for playing right?"I nodded.

"Yup, got the points, lost the respect of thirteen girls, two teachers and around ten parents. So, nothing new there."

Rachel laughed, but Tegan wasn't smiling.

"Seriously, you two. We need to focus. Rachel – you haven't lost any all term, right?"

She nodded. "Yup, still got all twenty."

"Good. I've got eighteen, as I lost a couple for having to wear my trainers after I forgot to put my shoes in my gymnastics bag. Bells – did you tell Rach where you were at?"

I rolled my eyes.

"It's not good." I cringed at how much I'd let my life slide. "Eleven. I lost three when Mr Lutas caught me on my phone again, but got one back for netball. Which I then lost the next day when Mr Lutas overheard me describe Zac as a 'sexicle'. He said it was derogatory, cos he doesn't get that being called 'sex on a stick' is a good thing."

Rachel OTT huffed.

"But that's not fair, because being a sexicle is just a factually accurate description for Zac. And that's not Bella's fault. Right, Tegan?"

Tegan nodded.

"Yup, definitely right. He's a bona fide hottie." I felt weirdly proud at this confirmation, as if I myself had birthed him. "BUT we do need to hang on to every single point. The three of us not going to our first prom together is NOT an option. Especially if it's Bella's chance to get Zac back."

She was right. Prom was exactly what the three of us needed to put this rubbish term behind us.

"Agreed." I nodded firmly. "Times one million. So I suggest we start off with totally avoiding Mr Lutas. He's the Death Eater of points."

Tegan had a determined look in her eye. When she put her mind to something, she made it happen.

"Totally. And do you reckon we could help get you any bonus ones to be on the safe side? We have –" she closed her eyes in concentration – "fifty-four school hours to get them."

I chipped in.

"And fifty-four school hours feels like at least one zillion normal life hours."

She smiled.

"Exactly. Plenty of time."

We carried on walking, racking our brains for inspiration. I was going to have to tread very carefully. And that was literal as well, as I once almost lost a point for accidentally stepping on a 'Mile of Maltesers' that the Year 8s had spent laying down in the corridors for charity. It really is surprising how far hundreds of malt balls can travel with one accidental step.

Tegan squeezed my hand.

"Look, B, we got this. It's only a few more days of keeping Luke away from Zac, and staying drama free, and we'll be there. It's all three of us going to prom, or none of us, OK?"

It's what she'd said on the phone last night and she wouldn't take no, or even a 'm-bee, let's see how it goes', for an answer. But before I could reply, Rachel dug her elbow into my side.

"Look!!" she hissed, pointing repeatedly at the other side of the road with a single finger, like she was doing hand aerobics.

There, just waiting for the bus, as if it was no big deal, was MIAGTM. Blast from the boy past. And what a cute blast it was. He'd been off-radar for a while, but seeing as Zac wanted me to pretend he didn't exist, I figured it was no longer morally questionable to appreciate how hot MIAGTM was looking. And by the look on Rachel's face, she wasn't having any issues about admiring the view either.

MIAGTM was laughing with his mates, trailing a football under his foot as he leant against the bus stop. Why do boys always take them to school like they aren't provided? It's not like you see me packing a netball and desk to be on the safe side.

I swear the point of school uniforms is to render us all unfanciable in an effort to keep teachers' lives simple. But I can confirm, looking at MIAGTM, he breaks that rule. (I can also confirm, having looked in the mirror this morning, that I don't.) He's so funny too. I mean, I can never hear what he's saying, but I can just *tell* it's hilarious. As he his mates laughed at (probably) his most hilarious joke yet, I swooned out loud, like I was deflating.

"Oi! We can *hear* that." Tegan jerked my arm, narrowly stopping me from striding into a hip-height bin, proving once again why I needed friends in my life. "Haven't you got enough boy probs in your life?"

"Surely looking can't hurt?"

"It can when you almost land head first in a bin, you nugget."

I laughed. And stopped gawping. And gave the bin a dirty look for leaping out on me.

We spent the rest of the journey talking about the fact we definitely didn't need to talk about boys any more. But when we arrived at school, there was one waiting for us. And he looked unhappy.

"I'm so glad you're here. Wow, you're *all* here." Mikey took a moment to register that it really was all three of us. "I wanted to give you a heads up."

Gulp. This didn't sound good.

"Mr Lutas is on the war path. Apparently – wait for this – Luke blabbed it was us that started the food fight."

INWARD SPEW. How could Luke do this to me? To us? Mikey must have read my mind. Or just seen my face.

"Apaz he thought he'd get away with it if he dobbed us in, but he ended up getting in trouble too. Word is we might be getting detention."

Oh great, I love it when bad gets worse. If I wasn't trying to hang on to the points I had left, I'd kill Luke right now. Although 'psychopathic murderer' probably isn't the one quality that's going to score me a prom invite.

How dare Luke drag the others down with me?! Tegan had never had a detention in her life, and Rachel normally managed to talk her way round anything.

But Tegan looked like she had more than bad marks on her mind.

"Look, there's NO WAY you lot are taking the blame for this. It was me who started it, and I'm just going to tell Mr Lutas that."

AS IF. If it was anyone's fault, it was mine for ever getting involved with Luke, not hers for sticking up for me. I corrected her.

"And it was *us* who backed *you* up, 'member? You didn't squirt those condiments unaided, so don't even *think* about it. We're in this together, that's what we just agreed, right, Rach?"

Rachel nodded.

"Ms Fisher. Ms Allen. Ms Waters. Mr Jackson."

CRAPFLAPS. Surname address meant one of two things. We'd time travelled to Victorian England, or Mr Lutas was at the front steps, and he was calling us, in front of everyone.

Sadly (not that sadly) my uniform hadn't turned into bloomers, so I had to concede to the latter. Mikey was scanning the scene, assessing who had heard. Luckily it was just the trickle of latecomers. He hated people being reminded he was called Michael Jackson.

We walked over to Mr Lutas.

"You may or may not know that I have news for you. Thanks to the stunt you pulled in the canteen yesterrrrday, Mrs Hitchman has decided that you are to spend thrrreee of yourrrr rrrremaining evenings this term in DETENTION. A letter will be sent out to your parents."

Thank goodness Mikey had warned us, or I'd be in serious danger of yelling 'AAAARRRGGGGHHH, YOU MANIAC GIBBON' in Mr Lutas's face and

267

spending every evening for the rest of my life in detention. Instead I shot Tegan a look that said 'don't you dare say anything', trying to reinforce our earlier agreement with a complicated combination of squinting and slo-mo nodding.

"Underrrstand?" Mr Lutas growled.

Relieved that Tegan stayed silent, we all nodded, unenthusiastically, ignoring the nosey looks of everyone walking past. Mum was going to FREAK (a zen freak is still a freak) when she finds out.

"However, after a long discussion with the headmistrrress I have a prrrroposal for you."

My brain accidentally pictured Mr Lutas proposing. *Shudder.*

"End of term prrrom is fast approaching. One week. Two days away. Correct?"

Thanks, Mr Lutas. As if we hadn't been counting down ever since term started.

"Ya, richtig."

As I realized what I was saying, my jaw sprung closed like a mousetrap. A mouth-trap. It really couldn't be trusted. This is what happens when you don't do your German homework. All the tiny bits of knowledge you have come popping out at the wrong times instead. It was the wurst.

"Parrrdon?"

"Sorry – yes. I meant, correct." First rule of Mr Lutas – do not deviate from the most standard and formal response possible. He glared at me.

"As I was saying. I need some help. Apparently everyone is more than happy to attend and enjoy the end of year parrrties, yet no one is willing to put any effort towards making it happen. And your prrrrom is in parrrticular perrril."

I had no idea where he was going with this. Although I couldn't help but be hopeful that he hadn't said anything about docking points.

"So I have asked that instead of doing detention, you could help me with the prreparrration for that instead. You may have not *rrrrrealized* it," he made an unnecessarily long r-roll, "but it's what my deparrrtment does, every year. With little to no thanks. From anyone."

What? Time spent slapping some paint on a banner instead of writing detention essays? Hello, gift horse, I am definitely not going to look in your mouth.

"Mr Lutas, that sounds great, thank you. Although –" I felt I should manage his expectations – "although you do know that we're, well, *I* am not exactly the world's greatest artist?"

"I am awarrre."

Quick, someone nominate him for Supportive Teacher of the Year.

Ever the reliable friend (except the one time she wasn't), Tegan came to my rescue and spoke up.

"What do you need us to do?"

"Well, there'll be three sessions. Two this week and one next week, starting tomorrow. You'll be in my arrrt room making and painting scenery. Ms Fisher, we'll need that camera you won to take photos as we go." I nodded, as I didn't really have a protesting-leg to stand on. "All of you will need to bring some good ideas, but don't brrring any of that attitude you had yesterrrday. Underrrstood?"

Nodding a lot more enthusiastically than last time, we looked around at each other, clearly thinking the same thing. Maybe, just maybe, this could turn out OK?

"Excellent." He turned to walk off. "Oh, one last thing. It goes without saying that Mrs Hitchman –" he smiled to himself at the mention of her name – "has also decided to dock you all your rrremaining behaviourrr points, so decorrrating for the prom is the closest any of you are going to come to it. So, make the most of it! Or you'll have the other students after you as well."

WHAT THE WHAT?! I looked up to see if I could spot any asteroids careering towards us. Surely this was the end of the world? But all I could see was a pigeon, and it didn't look like it was about to unleash fury on mankind.

Mr Lutas strode off. We stood in silence letting the news seep in. Our prom dream was over. Someone should email the Queen (or whoever it is that decides) to ask them to erect (note to self, must learn to use that word without laughing) a commemorative plaque where we were standing. 'Site Of Worst News Ever Delivered At St Mary's (Except When 1D's 'Hiatus' Was Announced In Geography).

As the others began to work out whether there was any way we could redeem ourselves, and how it was no one's fault (even though I felt like it was all mine), I could only picture one thing. Luke's smug face. Not helped by the fact that when I managed to yell at my brain enough to get rid of it, the real-life smug Luke face came round the corner, followed by his posse of pathetics. He barged his way past Mikey and walked right up to my face.

"Sorry, girls. I might have let slip to Mr Lutas about the food fight. Guess you've heard?"

I gritted my teeth. I couldn't risk a repeat of yesterday.

"Guess we have."

"Got to admit, I'm kind of looking forward to detention. More time to check out Rach."

Luke and the idiots (which would be a good band name, if it didn't make me want to hurl) burst out fake-laughing, and swarmed off into school. This detention proved he really would stop at nothing to ruin my life.

Moaning about what a crime against oxygen Luke was, the rest of us trudged off to lessons racking our brains for a way out of our predicament, and back into prom. Despite the three of us spending our entire lunch hour crouched in a human tower behind a leaflet stand, trying to catch a glimpse of Zac from afar, we still didn't come up with anything.

When I finally got home that night, I didn't breathe a word of any of it to Mum. That could wait until the letter arrived. Instead I headed straight to my room and begrudgingly packed up all my camera kit. I even included my brand-new lens I'd got for Christmas. Look, Mr Lutas, BONUS EFFORT!

But as well as being my pride and joy (everything else I owned was broken, or as I called it 'vintage'), my camera also dredged up another feeling. One I tried to ignore. Guilt. Maybe that's why, when I opened *PSSSST*, I decided to share a proper secret. About how I'd really

272

managed to win the camera that the whole school was after. It was something nobody knew. Well, no one except Luke, who was with me when I sent in my entry. It was the night he met my mum and she told him it was never too early to check for prostate problems. Probably the only time I've seen him speechless.

I took a deep breath, and confessed.

As I pressed post, I felt a tiny sense of relief, the guilt lifting a little. Was it weird to feel better now I'd told someone? Even though they were strangers, and no one could trace it back to me?

I skipped dinner – instantly alerting my fam that something major was up – and fell asleep messaging the others ridiculous ideas to help win back points. Day one of getting Zac back and going to prom hadn't gone exactly to plan. But I still had seven more school days and two awesome friends to try and turn things around. And with them on side, how bad could things be?

But the answer was 'very'.

Because I was about to discover a secret that was going to make my head explode.

TWENTY-ONE

EVER WONDERED WHY ONLY ONE OF MY
TEACHERRRS GETS TO TAKE HIS STUDENTS ON
FORRREIGN TRIPS? COULD IT HAVE ANYTHING
TO DO WITH HIM PAYING EXTRA CURRICULARRR
VISITS TO A PERSON WHO HELPS HIM GET
AHEAD? (COUGH, I MEAN, A HEAD)
(AS IN 'A HEAD MISTRESS*')
(AS IN I THINK THEY'RE SNOGGING)
(*INSERT GROSS TEACHER CRUSHING
ON EACH OTHER EMOJI*)

I looked at my phone. 3.34 p.m.. Crapballs. Detention started four minutes ago. How was I late for *everything*? Oh yeah, cos I'd been hiding in the loos posting the scandal the world needs to hear. But my *PSSSST* followers *had* loved the last Mr Lutas one. LilDrummerBoy said it made him 'crease like a T-shirt you've left in your bag for the entire summer'. Maybe it's because all art teachers are weird and it's part of the job description:

Can you draw a hedgehog? Tick.

Can you stare at a picture of dots for hours AND look interested? Tick.

Can you not laugh at statues with small man-dangles on? Tick.

Are you massively weird? TICK TICK TICK.

I pushed open the door to the art room. Voices were coming from the storeroom at the back – the others must already be here. Remembering that 'others' also meant Luke made my breath catch in my chest. Well, it was that or the smell of spray glue.

"Sorry I'm late, Mr Lutas – there was a queue for the toilet." Kind of true, as there was – once I'd finished getting reception, posting on *PSSSST*, reapplying deodorant and quickly squeezing a spot at the bottom of my neck that had been bothering me all day.

Mr Lutas didn't look impressed.

"I *will* expect you to make the rrrest of the sessions on time. . ."

He looked annoyed he had nothing else to threaten me with. But the only thing left now was being suspended, and that seemed like an excellent way of avoiding Zac-Luke-gate and all lessons. Plus, I'd get to eat loads of biscuits.

I slung my camera on the table in front of Mr Lutas to remind him I wasn't all bad. He peered at it, nodded an acknowledgement, and cleared this throat to address the group.

"The fate of this year's prrrom is in the hands of you. This sorry bunch." He pointed at us, just in case we weren't clear on what sorry bunch he meant. In fairness, we did look as unenthused as a bunch of people who had had to give up their evenings to decorate a prom that they couldn't go to would look. "So, it's going to be all hands on deck."

Tegan jumped in.

"Of COURSE, Mr Lutas – we can all work together really well, right guys?" She managed to simultaneously both smile at Mr Lutas and glare at us. I'd forgotten last night's agreement to play the extra-enthusiastic card in an effort to get him back on side. She probably wasn't delighted that I'd been late then. *Oops.* Rachel and Mikey twigged on to the plan at the same time, and we all made slightly too late 'deffos' and 'uh-huhs'. Luke just scowled. Guess being a bitter loner is to be expected when your evil plan backfires and you're made to spend your evening in a room full of people that want to impale you on paintbrushes.

"Excellent. Thank you, Ms Allen. So, first things first. You need to know the theme." Mr Lutas cleared his throat, as if it was a big reveal. "The theme this year is . . . YEARBOOK." He turned round a massive piece of card that had lots of scrappy bits of paper and bad school photos and pictures of yearbooks from the 90s stuck all over it. It was officially the world's most underwhelming mood board. More of a bored-mood. It really was baffling what teachers thought was cool. "As you can see, I've made a grrrreat start. But I'm looking for a big idea to tie it all together. A rrreal feature in the hall. Once we have that, you can get cracking."

The only thing I wanted to crack was Luke's annoying face. Into an easel.

We huddled round the big communal desk at the

back, Tegan doing the talking for everyone. The smell of sworn enemies was almost as suffocating as the paint fumes. Mikey occasionally said something to help her out but his body language screamed, 'Luke, this cooperation is not for you, and this time I'd throw an entire brie at you if I had one'.

Mr Lutas quickly got frustrated with the lack of input.

"Come on, please. You're intelligent people." He looked round with a fake smile. "Just."

I hope that one was aimed at Luke. I smiled straight at him to show I thought it was.

"We need some better ideas. . . Bella, Luke, that means you too."

Crapballs. I guess the one thing I can normally be relied on for is to talk, even if my ideas are terrible. But Luke beat me to it.

"I guess we could make it themed on sports year? Like alternative, you know. Fill the room with props and games?"

"What, like darts and curling?" Mikey deadpanned back, obvs not bothered about getting into more trouble.

"Mr Jackson – let him finish."

Luke smiled at Mr Lutas, loving Mikey being put in his place.

"As I was saying, I'm currently building some new ramps for the BMX trails, and Tegan's into gym or whatever. And Michael Jackson's probably into, I don't know, knitting." Mikey mouthed 'ha ha'. Mr Lutas ignored it and waved Luke to carry on.

"So we could have loads of different areas for what people are into? Recreate the highlights from this year?"

Mr Lutas looked vaguely impressed. "Well, that's certainly the best idea we've had so far."

Correction. It was the *only* idea. An evening of hanging out inside a room that had been made to look like the playing field we hang out at for the rest of the year – I don't think so?! Everyone would hate us. And the netball team already hated me, so they'd hate^2 me. I *had* to think of something.

"Erm, Mr Lutas. I do have *one* idea." C'mon, Bella, this could be your time to shine. "So you know we don't actually *get* a Yearbook until Year 11?"

He nodded.

"Well, I was thinking – maybe we could make like ... a virtual one?" I hadn't really thought this through.

"I don't think I understand."

Neither do I, Mr Lutas, I'm freestyling here. And neither did anyone else judging by the confused looks.

279

"Er, yes. Like something to do with that. Like, erm photos and words and things."

Well done me, that narrowed it down to EVERYTHING.

Enthusiastic Tegan enthusiastically nodded with enthusiasm.

"No – I get it! I think it's genius!"

Mikey pushed some paper forward on the table and started drawing.

"A bit like this?" He gestured to the picture of a stick man holding up a sign. "Like a makeshift photo booth, where we can all write messages on signs and hold them up in the photos?"

"Er, yeah?" That worked, I guess. We'd all been in a photo booth just like that when we'd gone out for pizza for Mikey's birthday and they were doing a competition to suggest a new topping. Mikey had written down 'Chips and gravy'. He hadn't won.

"Or –" it was Rachel turn to join in – "or it could be like that thing we did last year in the cinema when we watched that film about that killer vet?"

YES, Rachel, YES! I nodded with so much enthusiasm that Tegan smiled approvingly, even though I didn't think Mr Lutas would have seen a film where someone got suffocated to death with a stuffed chinchilla.

"Basically, you get your picture taken on a posh camera – we could use yours, right Bella?" I shrugged my shoulders in a 'guess so' way, careful not to look at Luke and give away any reminders that might jog his memory about the thing only he knew. "And like Mikey said, we'd all hold up slogans and signs. Then the picture goes straight on to a projector and is beamed up so everyone can see it – really huge, on wall."

Oh yeah! Maybe my idea was genius after all.

I joined back in.

"The big wall above the piano would be perfect! We could make the whole thing look like a real page in a yearbook? A one-night-only yearbook! A nightbook?!"

Mr Lutas mulled it over.

"It sounds an *interrresting* idea. But do you think you have the time ... and skill, to make it work?" Motivational teacher strikes again.

"Totally!" Tegan had a point to prove. I knew how her mind worked – if she could make our idea better than Mr Lutas could have hoped, then maybe, just maybe, he'd let us go to prom after all. She carried on. "It's PERFECT. Luke – you know how to make ramps and stuff, so maybe you could use all your woodwork skills to make, like, a giant real-life frame for people to

281

step into and pose in?"

Wow. Talking to Luke – she really was pulling out all the stops. Even he looked surprised.

"I g-guess I could?" He seemed reluctant, but didn't want to say 'no' in front of a teacher. Shame he didn't, though, as the last thing I wanted was for him to get in Mr Lutas's good books. If there were blank pages to be taken, it was going to be us that got them.

Tegan wasn't finished. "Cool – maybe you could make the signs to hold up too? We'd just need big bits of wood, covered in whiteboard paint for people to write on. They'd need to be big enough to read and able to be wiped clean and re-used through the night. They could have cool handles, or be on sticks . . . or be in speech bubble shapes, or have decoration round the edge to make them look a bit nicer?" She paused for breath. "Sound doable?"

Luke looked a bit overwhelmed, but shrugged his shoulders as if to say 'why not?'. But Tegan had enough momentum for us all.

"Bella, you're on point with your photography, so could you work out what other props we need to make the photos look good – maybe lots of funny cut-out shapes to hold up?" I nodded. She glared at me. I nodded more enthusiastically.

"Deffosoundsamazing. Like, er, big cardboard moustaches, and tiny hats, and er, tufts of nasal hair. . ."

She smiled, not really listening.

"Great, I can do all the fabric stuff, make banners and things – I've probably got some bits I can borrow from Tailor Swiftly, and I'm sure they wouldn't mind lending out a machine – and Rachel can help with any drawing and painting stuff . . . and Mikey can help out with whatever needs doing?" She looked triumphant. "Sound like a plan?"

Mikey gave a double thumbs up.

"Count me in. I'm a dab hand with some scissors, and, er, needle machines?" The fact he didn't know they were called sewing machines suggested he wasn't, but he really would do anything to hang out with Tegan. If only he knew I'd accidentally got him a whole army of fans after last night's *PSSSST*.

WHEN MY FRIEND, MJ, NEEDED HELP LOGGING INTO HIS SCHOOL FOLDER HE WAS V RELUCTANT TO ADMIT HIS PASSWORD. MAYBE COS IT WAS 'DUMBLEDOREISMYKING'. APAZ THE HARRY POTTER BOOKS MADE HIM BLUB SO HARD HIS DAD BANNED THEM FROM THEIR HOUSE.

It'd been my most commented on post yet – if heart eyed emojis count as comments. But all he wanted was for Tegan to like him IRL. And she was still caught up ploting for prom.

"Well in that case, if we'rrre all agreed –" Mr Lutas looked round the group; we murmured various degrees of enthusiasm – "let's spend the rest of this session looking at what we have and coming up with some designs. AND RRREMEMBER –" he hit the table, making us all jump – "whatever we do must be kept secret from your classmates. We don't want to let them down by spoiling their surrrprise."

Rachel flicked her hair over her shoulder. I recognized this move from her mum – it meant she was about to ask for something.

"You can trust us, Mr Lutas. We'll all going to work reeeally hard because you're totally right, it is something everyone looks forward to."

But as annoying as Mr Lutas was, he wasn't stupid.

"Let me stop you right there, Ms Waters. Remember, it's not *me* that caused you to be missing out."

Thwarted.

But Rachel wasn't giving up that quickly. She'd had years of practice of being a one-girl-own-way-getter-er. She could boldly go where no normal person could.

"I know. It was us. And we're really sorry. But maybe, do you think if we work really hard, maybe even put in extra hours, that maybe there *might* be a way of us getting any points to help us go to prom after all?"

We all held our breath.

"Well, Ms Waters, why don't we see? If you all work *rrreally* hard, as you so eloquently put it, then it wouldn't be out of the question, but I guess only time will tell."

Wow. Rachel had managed the unthinkable?! I mentally high-fived her.

"Thank you, Mr Lutas – I'm sure we all will, won't we?"

We nodded, all on-board, even Luke. For the first time this term, we'd found something we agreed on, and got to work.

Despite the total tragedy of making decorations for a prom I currently wasn't going to, as I sketched and cut out and constructed props, I started to enjoy it. Before I knew it, time was up. Time goes fast when you're fashioning stick-on ear hair from paintbrush bristles.

The mood lifted by our progess, and prom-ising news, we packed away quickly. Mr Lutas surveyed what we'd achieved. Even he looked a bit happier.

"I have to say, you have done well today. It is *verrrry* ambitious, but many hands make light work, and in Friday's session we'll be getting some extra help from one of the sixth formers."

ARGH! Way to end on a bombshell. Promshell. *PLEASE* don't let him mean Zac? Zac and Luke and me together was a recipe for disaster – worse than my mum's Parsnip Surprise. I shot Tegan and Rachel a look of distress. Tegan calmly mouthed 'don't worry'.

I took a deep breath and tried to stop a mental freak-out. There was no reason Mr Lutas would choose a student he'd only just met. I *had* to be rational. Especially as there was no way we could dig for more deets in front of Luke.

But I couldn't offload any panic on the others, as Tegan had to run straight to gym and Rachel's mum was waiting outside to take her to a private self-portrait class for the two of them. I waved my goodbyes from the art room and swung by my locker to get my games kit.

School feels so eerie when the lights aren't on. Like it shouldn't really exist when there aren't people forced to be there. My phone lit up the corridor as a message came through.

Hi sis. All OK? Mum's out so I've got tea on.
You back late? X

Result. Clearly the detention letter hadn't arrived yet or Jo would be digging for deets. Phew.

Thx for checking up on me (not). I'm doing
volunteer stuff for prom. Back in 30 x

I wondered if other people had to juggle one and a half mums? Not fair. I grabbed my kit out of my locker and went to stuff it into my school bag. But as I bent over, my locker slammed shut with a bang that bounced off the walls.

"Thought I'd see you here."

It was Luke.

"Haven't you got something better to do than follow me around? Like getting a life?" I instantly regretted snapping.

"I've got *loads* on, but checking up on you is always a number one priority."

I trusted Luke about as far as I could throw him

(which I knew was only twenty-two centimetres because we'd once tried). I picked up my bag to get away. But he grabbed at the strap, pulling me back.

"Shame your 'boyf' wasn't there today. Was looking forward to comparing notes."

I wanted to crawl into my locker and slam the door in his face. But Luke had hold of me and I couldn't get away. I had to answer. It was now or never.

I collected up every bit of courage I could find and looked him straight in the eye. Because as scary as it was, I knew what I had to do. If Luke *did* confront Zac, I'd wave goodbye to any hope of ever sorting things out with him. And Zac would wave ciao to his Italian trip.

I *had* to remember that what Zac thinks of me matters a gazillion times more than whatever Luke does. But it still wasn't going to be any fun giving Luke the ammunition he was so desperate for.

"First things first, Luke, let go of my bag." He didn't move. "Let. Go. Now."

He dropped his hand to his side, startled by the firmness in my voice.

"Right, this is how it is." I swallowed. I couldn't believe what I was about to do. "You were right. I made the whole thing up. The holiday romance. The prom date. The snog. Well, semi-snog. Trying to make everyone believe it by pretending it was all about that sixth former... Even Rach." Luke's eyes were so wide he looked like he'd been stretched. I ignored the grin spreading underneath them.

Deep breath, Bella. Push down the knotting in your stomach. Concentrate on what you have to do.

"I never had a photo – but you knew that. The poor new guy must have been so confused. Bad luck for him, having the same name?"

Luke rubbed his hands together.

"I knew it! I. KNEW. IT. It's what I said from day one. Blobfish and her dream world! I CAN'T WAIT to tell the others."

My heart was beating faster than in the one netball match I'd played in. The reality of this being the main gossip at school tomorrow had smacked me in the face like a cold shower. Still, dragging me down was better than dragging Zac into this. Luke was so excited he'd clenched his fist into a 'yes'.

"I *said* Fishy Balls could never get a guy like that. Well, *any* guy!"

"I got *you*, didn't I?"

Luke's smile vanished. I'd mentioned the Voldemort of chat. The subject that couldn't be named.

"You were nothing but a way to make me and my mates laugh. Remember that."

But neither of us *was* laughing. And maybe that's because there was something that never added up to me. If I *had* just been a joke to him, then why, when no one else was around, had I met his mum – and why had he stuck out an evening with mine?

But I didn't get chance to call him out. We both froze as we heard weird jingling behind us. *Eurgh*. Undeniable Mr Lutas and the jangle of the keys in his pocket he was always fiddling with. Without another word, Luke darted out of sight just as Mr Lutas came out of the geography room. Wonder what he'd been doing in there? Probably looking for Mrs Hitchman. I tried to compose myself, even though my heart was beating so hard it sounded like it had moved to my ears.

"Good work today, Ms Fisherrr."

Wow. A complement from Mr Lutas. Had the paint fumes got to him? Lucky the lockers were beside me in case I fainted.

"I'm glad I caught you before you headed off."

My heart sank. *Now* what had I done?

"It slipped my mind earlier, but after the *episode* in my arrrt room last week, I've been meaning to have a word with you."

I flinched at how mortified he sounded on my behalf. Nothing like a teacher finding *you* an embarrassment.

"I wanted to let you know that this teaching assignment is verrry important to the sixth formers' course, so please can you be. . ." He thought for a while. Probably looking for a teacherly way of saying something intellectual. ". . . *norrrmal*? Especially as Zac will be helping in next detention sessions."

WHAT ARE THE CHANCES? If there was a lottery for losing money, I would totally win it. Now Zac was going to know that, on top of everything else, I was a condiment-squirting-detention-getting saddo. And we'd have to make awkward polite supervisor–student convo in front of everyone. BLEURGH. Although major phew that I'd put a stop to Luke's plan to have it out with him. Had I actually managed to do *something* right?!

But why, out of everyone, was it Zac that was helping? Before I could stop it, that exact question popped out of my mouth. Mr Lutas and I were equally caught off guard by my abruptness.

"Well, we need all the hands on deck we can find. And I guess that's part of the job being my s. . ." Mr Lutas stumbled over his last word, looking embarrassed about what he'd let slip.

Had I heard him right?

OH MY SWEET CHEESES. If only there was a way to UN-HEAR him.

Mum says, when we're stuck for words, that 'the cat has got our tongue'. Right now, a herd of lions must have jumped into my mouth, chewed my tongue off, and pan-fried it up for Mary Berry.

I was so speechless, I wasn't sure I'd say anything again until my thirty-second birthday.

Did Mr Lutas just say 'son'?

TWENTY-TWO

Tegan reckons that if you sleep on something it will always be better in the morning (unless it's a crisp, in which case it would just make crumbs in your bed). But after two more sleeps, I still hadn't got my head anywhere near around Zac being the spawn of the world's worst teacher. Or that Mr Lutas had managed to talk someone into procreating with him. It was completely shuddersome. Last night I'd lost three hours' sleep worrying that in kissing Zac, by seven degrees of spit separation, I'd exchanged saliva with my teacher. It was all too much. When I see Zac in detention later, I'll have to check for signs he'd inherited the over-production of nose-hair gene. Still, he'd probably still look fit with nose hedges.

Despite the worry of the looming Zac encounter, the morning went better than expected. First I had my second MIAGTM sighting of the week, then prom hope took a step forward as Rachel got extra Lutas credit for helping out with his lunchtime art club, and Tegan got full marks in her German test. Partei, partei, partei (as Tegan put it). And I managed the biggest thing of all. Not doing anything disastrous. Although when Rachel whispered 'hello, father-in-law' when Mr Lutas walked into assembly, I kicked her so hard she trod on a Year 7. Tegan said I'd laugh about it one day. But that could only be true if it was the same day I discovered Zac had been born via sperm donation.

Despite lots of whispers and giggles in my direction after Luke made it his life work to make sure everyone knew about my confession, I felt better that I didn't have to worry about him grilling Zac any more. Knowing that after all the drama I'd caused Zac, I'd actually managed to stop some for once, created some sort of positive-vibe superhero cape that helped bounce off all the sly comments from Lou and Luke's mates, who were all desperate to impress them by reminding me how tragic I was.

And there were more good things too. Not worrying about what Luke would say to Zac freed up the worrying bit of my brain to concentrate on what *I* was going to say to him. I'd even ironed my uniform so I seemed a bit more together (well, got Jo to do it, as the only time I'd tried I ended up dropping the iron on the carpet and permanently melting half of one of Mum's slippers into it).

But despite trying to channel Tegan's strength, and Rach's optimism, by the time detention ticked around, I was a total wobbling blancmange of nerves. Rachel had to physically push me through the art room door. But the combination of stumbling over my feet, and stumbling over the sight of Zac, made me do a weird yelp, like a tiny dog that had trodden on a thistle. Everyone, including Zac, turned round. I panic-gestured at my shoe as if that's what had made the squeak. Mr Lutas gave me an entirely unconvinced and alarmingly sympathetic smile. It was very unnerving. Especially as above the alarming smile was an even more alarming nose – an exact replica of the nose I once thought was cute on Zac. And it had been staring me in the face, literally, on Mr Lutas this whole time. How had I never noticed?

Tegan headed straight to the far end of the room

where Zac was helping lift her heavy sewing equipment down from the shelves. It was so hard to make my eyes do anything other than just stare at him, even if it was just his back. I couldn't believe Tegan was so calm standing next to such hotness, but as usual, she was focused on her job. Art is one of the few things she's not amazing at, so she'd played to her strengths and cut and stitched two massive fabric banners – one for the main school entrance, and one for the hall, each with the school name, the year and 'Year 10 Prom' on. She'd stayed late yesterday and come in early today to work on them with the sewing machine she'd borrowed. With Zac's help she proudly unravelled one, and held it up for us to see, totally covering the two of them with her giant creation. Half of the letters were already in place and it looked so A-mazing that an impromptu cheer went up. I crossed my fingers Zac would stay helping her all lesson.

But my fingers clearly need to work on their mind control, as moments later Mr Lutas told Zac to come and lend a hand with my props. Zac didn't show any emotion as he headed over. I brain-shouted at every face muscle I had to behave and not move. Turns out there is nothing funny about making giant eyebrow props when you're having to do it in awkward silence. The giant love heart was even more tricky.

Mr Lutas walked by and smiled approvingly at our work. But I had a feeling it was something else that had put him in this abnormally good mood. And I was right. He clapped his hands, asked us to stop what we were doing and head to the storeroom.

"I wanted to show you something that I think we can all be very prrroud of. Yes, it's a team effort, but someone here has really pulled out all the stops."

Tegan raised an eyebrow – had Mr Lutas been *that* impressed with her early morning stint?

Mr Lutas opened the door to the storeroom. I couldn't help but gasp at what I saw. An amazing 3D wooden photo frame, almost as tall as the ceiling, with the school crest carved into it alongside the date of the prom. Next to it was a giant pile of signs, rough around the edges, but all taking shape. ARGH! Luke must have worked overnight to do all of this! This was the opposite of making a mess of it – he'd made a total tidy of it. How dare he!

Luke looked as pleased with himself as I felt un-pleased. Mr Lutas was positively beaming. He patted Luke on the back.

"Prrrretty impressive stuff, I think you'll agree?"

Zac nodded. But I struggled to be even fake-enthusiastic for Luke. *We* were meant to be getting the glory, not golden-frame, golden-boy douche-boy.

Mr Lutas cleared his throat deliberately dramatically.

"So . . . I think it's to fair to say Luke's earned his place back at prrrom."

Oh double great. Great threepled. Tripled. Whatever. Thanks, Mr Lutas, for playing rrright into his hands. If I knew a bit of after-school woodwork was all it took to win you back round, I could have bought that cheeseboard in that I made (well, Jo did, but I watched).

Eurgh.

Luke hit peak smug-face.

I turned so I couldn't see it and tried to focus on the positive. We had proof prom *was* possible. And I could tell by Rachel and Tegan's faces they were thinking the same. All I could tell from Mikey's face was that he really needed to work on not looking lovingly at Tegan whenever she was in a room. Eager to crack on, everyone headed out. I turned to do the same, but the door swung shut.

Luke stepped into my way.

"Seeing as I'm off to prom, thought we'd better clear the air."

I sighed. Not this again.

"C'mon, you have to stop slamming doors in my face. It's not a thing."

But a third voice spoke up.

"Guys, can we just get back to it?"

I span round. Zac was in here too?! I'd been so busy trying not to look at him, that I'd forgotten to look at him! Well done, eyes.

Luke smirked.

"Don't worry, it'll only take a sec. It was you, Zac, I was after really."

Luke being 'after' Zac was about as reassuring as being told a giant comet 'might' not be about to hit the earth. I looked around desperately. Could I stick two paintbrushes in Zac's ears and block out whatever Luke was about to say!? Hadn't I already given him what he wanted?!

Luke held out his fist as if he wanted Zac to fist-bump it. Zac did not fist-bump it. He just looked annoyed.

"What is it, then?"

Luke scrunched his face as if it was hard for him to say, even though it was obvious he was loving every second.

"Just thought you should know that Bella – this is Bella," he gestured at me, "I think you met her under a table – has spent the whole of this term banging on about an imaginary boy that she allegedly 'had the best snog of her life with'. And, get this, she tried to make out it was YOU. She even told everyone you were going to be her prom date." Luke laughed to himself. "How pathetic, huh? She can't even get herself to prom, let alone get a date to it?!!"

I wanted to purée myself and drain away down the sink. Why did Luke have to humiliate me like this?!

What must Zac think of me?!

I could see in the mirror propped against the wall that I'd gone redder than the paint bottle I was standing next to, which was labelled '100% Maximum Red'.

Zac looked disgusted. So much for me making it up to him at prom/ever.

"Is that all, Luke?" Zac sounded pissed off. Luke replied with a cheery 'uh-huh', not able to hide how happy he was at making me squirm so hard. A prom ticket AND embarrassing me. He really was having the best day.

"I'll leave Bella to give you the full deets. Enjoy!"

Luke gave me a final wink and shut the door.

My heart was racing so fast that the glue-blob on my jumper that looked annoyingly like a nipple, was flapping up and down at an alarming rate. Deep breath, Bella. Focus on trying to explain yourself.

But my mouth wouldn't make words. And I couldn't

make any noise other than small whimpers which wasn't going to resolve much.

Zac lent back against the counter and pushed himself up on to it. I looked awkwardly at my fingernails, but sadly they didn't have conversation starters written on them.

Zac broke the silence.

"So . . . I don't know if you've heard, but I started at that new college?"

HA WHATTING HA.

I put my hands over my face, and managed to say a distorted, "Yes, I am aware," that due to the hand muffling sounded a bit like I said I was a bear.

Not a great start. Deep breath. Take your time.

"To be clear, I am NOT a bear. But I AM sorry. I can't believe what an idiot I've been." I was so panicked everything was splurting out like a yoghurt when you open the lid weirdly. "And that artwork wasn't about you. It was about Zac. Efron? And I don't normally throw food. I mean, why throw it when you can eat it? And my name isn't Bellerina. Although I do think it's a nice gnome. Name! And I didn't tell everyone I snogged you. Or semi-snogged you actually. Well I kind of did, but that was before you were *here*. I swear I haven't said a word to anyone ever since you asked me not to.

Well I've said words, obvs, but not ones about you. I promise! How's Keith the dog? And please tell me you don't like Lou."

Zac said nothing.

I said nothing.

We said nothing.

Nothing was said.

What was he thinking?!

But then something unthinkable happened.

Zac smiled. And he put his hand on my arm. And it made me buzz on the inside just like old times.

He noticed me smile, and quickly took it back, remembering that wasn't what supervisors did.

"Seriously, Bella, have you been bottling up a week's worth of conversation or what?"

"Oh, that's only a *day's* worth. Really." It was actually only an hour's worth. Nipple-blob-glue flapped a little slower. But why was Zac being so nice after what Luke just told him? Wasn't he raging about me putting his Italy trip in danger?

Zac carried on, unphased.

"I seeee. So, where should I begin? Keith's good. Missing me, I hope. But good. And I like the name Bellerina too. But I don't like Lou. Not in that way. She's terrifying."

302

He smiled, his fit, inappropriate-to-fancy smile. Which only made it even fitter. Wow. This was going so much better than I thought. But why?! I had to find out.

"But . . . but what about Luke?"

"What *about* Luke? Between me and you – I think he's a grade A idiot. I mean, he sounded like enough of one when you told me about him at Black Bay."

Oh man. Why hadn't I had the foresight to predict Zac was going to turn up at my school and change the names of the people in my stories even though I'd only just met him?

"But what about what he just said?"

"Well, there's only one thing I can say really. . ."

I auto-paused myself, waiting to find out what.

". . . and that's thank you. For having my back and making out it wasn't true." What the what? "Don't look so freaked out?! Lou spent her entire morning shouting to anyone in earshot about the convo you had with Luke. It's hardly a surprise I got to hear about it."

IN YOUR FACE, LUKE AND LOU, and your lame attempts at causing trouble. Turns out you both did me a favour.

If I wasn't in a confined space with Zac, I'd *totally*

do a victory dance right now. And then collapse with relief that he wasn't mad.

"Anyway, I know I said let's wait till prom to chat, but seeing as we're in a store cupboard, I guess now is as good a time as any for me to explain myself?"

I shook my head confused. As if *he* had any explaining to do?!

"So, my mum got temporarily relocated to Sweden with her work. Did I mention she was Swedish?"

He hadn't, but maybe that would explain why he was so hot. I mean, being Swedish sounded really hot, and I'd only ever met him from Sweden, and he was hot, so therefore they must all be really hot.

"Earth to Bella?" I snapped out of Sweden perving and instead made a mental note to visit there one day. Zac carried on.

"So, I needed to finish my A-levels somewhere, and had arranged to stay with a friend in Birmingham. But then Dad, sorry, Mr Lutas, got involved and at the last minute sorted this placement out instead, so I could stay with him." Zac looked a bit awkward. "Funny thing is, I'd even checked out the names of the sixth formers here, hoping one of them might be you."

He didn't need to say what he was thinking. 'BUT

TURNS OUT YOU HAVEN'T EVEN DONE YOUR GCSES, SO THAT WAS A WASTE OF TIME.'

I couldn't hold in a cringe wince. Zac saw, and shuffled alongside me, so we were now leaning side-by-side. He gave me a full body nudge.

"Oi, don't be like that. What's done is done. And . . . and, I need to come clean about something too. You know that Italy course?"

Oh, here comes the bollocking.

"As if I could forget? Helping your chances was the one thing that made telling Luke I was a compulsive liar the tiniest bit bearable?!"

Remember – I tried!

"Ah, yeah. . ." Zac looked more sheepish than an actual sheep. "Well . . . I've kind of already won the place on it. I found out the morning I started here."

NOS. TRIL. FLARE.

HE WHAT??? He'd told me the exact opposite when he'd messaged me.

"Stop judging me, nose! I only found out hours before I saw you in the art room. And Dad had just given me a massive talk saying I could only go if I proved to him 'I was maturrre enough to make the money worrrth spending.'" He let the info sink a bit.

"That's why nailing this placement was such a big

305

deal to me. Why I had to get full marks. It wasn't the uni testing me – it was Dad. But it's not like when I messaged you, I could have been honest and thrown it all out there – that Mr Lutas was my Dad, and was watching my every move – so I had to think on my feet. Think of another reason I had to keep under the radar." Zac laughed under his breath. "Kind of funny that it was him who let the dad cat out of the bag."

It would be funny, if it wasn't the most dramatic family revelation since any episode of *EastEnders*.

I was speechless.

But I needed to become speech-full.

As rubbish as it was finding out I'd been lied to, I totally understood why he had. And who was I to judge after what I'd done? It was time for me to say my sorry for doing the same.

"Well, thanks for letting me know. And congrats. And happy art trip, I guess?!" Zac grinned, clearly relieved to have his secret out in the open too. But I hadn't finished. "But, I want to say sorry too. I should have just been honest from the start. I guess . . . I guess I was just trying to make you think I was something I wasn't."

"You were dressed as an arrow – you should have let me come to my own conclusions." He was teasing me, but he was right. "People who dress as cardboard road signs are EXACTLY the kind of friends I like. Right up my street."

Friends. The word punched me in the stomach.

The confirmation that while I'd been working on winning him back, Zac had been working on moving on. I was glad he couldn't see how crushed I must look. But he was happy chatting away, unaware every cell in my body had just done a little cry.

"I haven't even told you the best bit." Well he'd certainly told me the worst bit. "But you CAN'T let Dad know I told you. . ."

"Go on. . ."

"Well, last night over dinner he mentioned that if you guys finished all your props by the end of your last session, they were going to let you all go to prom."

Zac held up his hand for a high-five and despite being a JUST A FRIEND, I couldn't help but give it a massive thwack. This *was* most excellent news! What a rollercoaster the last ten minutes had been. Who knew Mr Lutas had a nice side after all?! I couldn't WAIT to tell the others. Although I definitely could wait to tell them Zac and Bella – Zella – was no more.

I stood up so fast I bashed into a mannequin and ended up in a hug-mount with it. Zac laughed. His horsey laugh. And for the first time, it didn't sound as cute as I used to think. Which made me feel all kinds of weird.

Had this week made me feel differently about Zac *too*? But I'd been too caught up in winning him back to notice? Could him being so clear we were friends actually be a bit of a relief? At least this way I could stop pretending I wasn't entirely uncool, and practising a fake birthdate, and revising where places like Singapore are.

Zac reached out his hand to help me untangle myself.

"C'mon, we better get going. They'll be wondering what we're up to. Although, we might as well play Luke at his own game, so try not to look too happy."

"Deal." I shook my face out and concentrated on looking like I'd just been cringed-out by a really fit boy. I was worryingly good at it.

As I pushed the door open, Tegan and Rachel were staring in a way that meant 'OMG, you've just come out of a cupboard encounter with that hotness, are you OK? You have to tell us everything.' I gave them a look back which they could hopefully interpret as, 'Of course I will. It was unbelievable. Like, we didn't snog or anything, in fact I guess the opposite, as we're officially "friends", but obvs he's still totally hot. And we all might get to prom after all. But I have to look moody so Luke thinks he got one up on me.' I think I managed it.

Like a pro, Zac got straight back to work, with no hint of what went down. This only made Tegan give me even more concerned looks, so when Mr Lutas had his back turned I did a full on hand-on-head phew gesture at her. I noticed Luke eyeing me suspiciously so styled it into the 'ow, I've got a bad headache' gesture instead.

As soon as Mr Lutas gave us permission to leave, I bundled Rachel and Tegan as far away from Luke as possible and filled them in. They were gutted that our team effort to win Zac back for me had failed, but they almost vibrated with excitement when I told them the prom news. Rachel maintained an impressively long 'Yeehaaaaaa' without stopping for breath, *and* that was while leaping around in circles. It was so loud that Mikey came bursting into the girls loo, thinking there had been a murder. But when we explained the news, he stopped looking for evidence and led a chorus of 'we've got ninety-nine problems, but prom aint one' instead.

The evening went downhill from there (as in, it got better, as surely going downhill is way better than uphill?). Jo was waiting outside for us, so we scored a free lift home, and chatted at a million miles an hour, making proper plans for prom. But despite my hurried briefing as we got in the car, in all the excitement Rach let slip the 'd' word. Detention. I'd tried to extra-loud-whoop-for-no-reason as she said it, but Jo never misses a trick.

As soon as we were alone, Jo called me out on it. With nowhere to escape, and full of adrenalin from the last hour, I came clean about the whole thing, from the art lesson onwards. Well, obviously I'd tried coming half-clean first, but Jo sussed that there was no way I'd choose to spend extra-curricular fun-afternoon time locked in a room with Zac, Luke and ZAC'S DAD. She almost crashed the car when she'd realized I'd snogged Mr Lutas's son. And then almost crashed it into our house when she couldn't stop laughing that she'd seen my almost-boyfriend's dad's life drawing pictures. I made a mental note to never share that with Zac.

When I went to bed that night, I felt the happiest I had done all term. Yes, I was going to have to work on accepting Zac and I were never going to happen, but prom *was* going to be back on, and it *was* going to be an epic night with the others. I'd just have to appreciate Zac as a supervisor, rather than a snogavisor. Plus mounting the mannequin might make a funny story for *PSSSST*.

But when I opened up the app, in amongst the likes, and comments, and jokes from LilDrummerBoy that always made me snort-laugh, there was something I hadn't seen before. A direct message.

THANKS FOR SHARING YOUR SECRETS
PRUNEFLAPPER. THEY'RE 10/10.

I clicked delete. Obvs just spam.
But there was another one in the thread.

PF NEVER DOES DISAPPOINT.

Why thank you, mystery fan. Although no one had ever abbreviated PruneFlapper to PF before.
But when I looked again my world stopped.
They hadn't written PF. They'd written BF.
Someone out there knew it was me.

TWENTY-THREE

I love Saturdays. It's so nice to wake up and not feel like you have to jump straight out of bed. You can just lie there and wait for it to become the right time to get up. Which might be four p.m. and that'd be totally cool as long as I bang my foot on the floor a couple of times to make Mum think I'm up and I'm doing something constructive in my room, like rearranging my posters.

My phone buzzed loudly. Eurgh. Not like me to set an alarm? But as I fumbled for it, I accidentally answered. It wasn't an alarm, it was Rachel ringing me.

"Halloohowareyou?" Why is there no way of hiding lying-down voice?

"Hi, lazy poo," Rachel teased. "Just wanted to see if you still wanted a lift."

What?

"To go in to town . . . 'member?"

"Errrrrrrr. . ." This was too early for my brain to be functioning.

"To meet up with Tegan?"

Mum put her head round the door and started doing an impression of a teapot. Why did she not understand phone calls were private? I waved her out.

"To go dress shopping for The Prom of the Century. . . You've totally forgotten, haven't you?!"

"No, I *totally* have not forgotten. . ."

Mum was now making a 'T' shape with her hands, whilst helpfully saying 'tea' in a loud whisper. I nodded so she'd go away, sticking a finger in my spare ear.

"And I'm totally getting ready as we speak. Sorry, Mum was being weird. *Go away, Mum.*"

Mum pulled an 'ooh, so you're going out' face. I got out of bed and closed the door, physically pushing her out of the room.

I *had* sort of forgotten a bit about the whole shopping trip, as I'd been a bit pre-occupied with working out who'd messaged me on *PSSSST*. Had it been a typo, or the world's creepiest message? I'd deleted the app and everything on it just in case. Still, I could hardly tell the others what was on my mind, as

I'd never actually got round to telling them about it in the first place.

When Rachel's car pulled up outside thirty minutes later, I still had dripping wet hair and no make-up on. I flung myself on to the backseat gibbering apologies, not realizing it wasn't Rach's dad driving, it was her River Island catalogue modelling HOB, Dan. I threw him the hottest look I could muster via the rear-view mirror (hard when you only have eyeliner on one eye and are impaled on a seatbelt holder). He smiled back politely in a you're-my-little-sister's-friend-and-someone-should-really-tell-you-I-have-a-boyfriend kind of a way. Well, in your face, Dan, someone *has* told me, but little do you know you're just one in a long line of boys that I drool over who will never go out with me. It really doesn't stop me.

Tegan was already waiting when we pulled up at the Elgar Statue. I didn't bother explaining that it was my fault we were late, cos I knew she'd know. And she knew that I knew that she knew.

Last night we'd group-called Mikey and made exact plans on how we were going to get all the props finished on time. Tegan was even giving up gymnastics for the week to make sure the banners got done. So with props-completion fully planned, and tickets guaranteed, today we were going to concentrate on the fun stuff instead. After a term of ups and downs, it felt amazing to finally look forward to our first prom together. All we needed to do was find some serious YAAAAS outfits. We hit the shops up like a military operation.

Group shopping is political. Rachel naturally drifts towards shops that sell dresses for more than my whole year's allowance, so Tegan and I politely pretend to look round and fake-browse socks and keyrings. I need them both with me, though, as when I do finally try stuff on, I rely on their faces more than I do mirrors. Mirrors seem to say, 'Yes, Bella! No one else will be wearing this neon-striped dress!' while their faces say, 'Is glittery-traffic-warden a *thing*?'

But after hours of searching, none of us had found a dress.

"Laaaydeeeez, we've been looking for daaaays now, and no one's got *anything*." Rachel was slumped outside Tegan's changing room and had obvs forgotten the two CDs, one bracelet, new lipstick, stick-on eyelashes and bag of pick'n'mix she'd bought without even noticing.

I held up my little shopping trophy.

"I did buy this nail varnish, but no one's going to

notice my nails if I'm naked everywhere else."

Tegan popped her head out of the curtain. "Guys. Honest opinions. What do you think of this one?"

I clapped my hands like an excited fashion-loving seal as Tegan flung back the curtain like a sexy matador. Woah, she looked HA-MAZ-ING. The fitted, slash neck dress clung to every bit of her body, only stopping at the floor, and she looked so sophis, I swear she was actually gliding around the changing room.

"Wow, Tegan, just wow." I snapped a picture of her. "See? You look increds."

She beamed at our reactions.

"High-five to this. *And* it's in the sale!" Her voice got muffled as she dived back into the changing room and wriggled the dress off over her head. "Maybe I could sew some black tasselly things on the shoulders. But in a good way." She didn't need to clarify; she always had a knack of making things look customized in all the right ways.

We headed to the till happy one of us was sorted. Tegan fished out all of her change.

"Woohoo for me managing to find something I could afford. Mum was a total no-go for lending me any money after she'd got that detention letter!"

I winced.

"You know mine never arrived, right? I'm living in total fear!"

Rachel shook her head.

"You're so jammy. Did you train Mumbles to eat post or something?"

"I wouldn't put it past her. The other day she tried to eat a bee, but it stung her in the mouth and made her look like she'd had doggy botox."

Rachel looked impressed.

"She might be on to something there. Dogs are well wrinkly. Anyway, enough TALK. I'm fading here. Is it TIME yet?!"

Rachel was referring to our ritual, and the answer was 'yes'. So the three of us, Tegan happily swinging her new purchase, headed off to our routine shopping stop-off, Froth, a converted old church with sofas so big you could lie on them. We ordered three hot chocolates (obvs with marshmallows), plus an extra-large bowl of potato wedges and mayonnaise. Surely that ticked all the nutritious food groups? We left on a marshmallow high, with new enthusiasm to attack the racks, only detouring to pop into the shoe shop where a boy Rachel likes works. Turns out they only sell man shoes, so he ended up recommending some slippers for her granddad. By the time we left, Rachel was completely in love. And the proud owner of three pairs of size 11 odour eaters.

"Did. You. See. Him?" Rachel was talking half-speed like some kind of love zombie. I grabbed her hand to stop her walking into a tree, and pulled her into a discount clothes shop before she had time to notice.

"Er, yes, Rach. We were literally standing next to you, and weirdly we didn't have our eyes closed the whole time."

Tegan was more matter of fact.

"I wish that lads we knew were as decent as that. All the ones we know act like they're twelve." Tegan never normally talked about boys unless she was telling us how she slayed them on the pommel horse (which I pointed out sounds like some sort of rubbish jousting). Maybe I should take the opportunity to bring up Mikey again?

"Well *some* of the lads we know are all right." I pretended to think, like this wasn't all one big set up. "I mean –" more fake think – "what about someone like Mikey?"

Tegan laughed. "What *about* him? I've told you a gazillion times, we're nothing but friends." And we've told her a billion times she's wrong. "I mean yeah, you *know* I love hanging out with him, but he sees me as one of the lads. And I'm cool with that. Guys and girls *can* be friends you know, so will you two stop stirring!"

We were back in our no-win sitch. Play unwanted cupid and annoy Tegan, or back off, and get frustrated at what could have been. Rachel went for the second option.

"What about you, Bells? What are we going to do about your boy sitch?" She prodded me accusingly with a coat hanger. "And I don't mean no-go-son-of-a-teacher-man, I mean the original love of your life: MIAGTM. What's going on there?"

I OTT huffed. Boys were a touchy subject with me. Well, technically untouchy, as I'd probably never make physical contact with any of them ever again.

"Absolute zero. Less than zero."

"Well, look," said Rachel, "if we manage to get our dresses sorted before five, Dan can go the long way home, and we can squeeze in a park perv."

Tegan prodded me.

"MIAGTM won't even recognize the car, so we could proper crawl along the hedge."

Rachel grinned.

"Yeah and who knows – he might see you through the window, and chase down the car until you agree to a hot new goalkeeping-based date?"

I spluttered on the chewy fried egg I was eating.

"AS IF, guys! It only takes peeps ten minutes to realize that I'm a human disaster. So I might as well just carry on looking from afar and start planning for when I'm old and take loved-up selfies with my twelve dogs and spend the rest of my time decorating my walls with plates that have paintings of cottages on them."

The others laughed. But it was weirdly comforting to be back to my totally undesirable self. At least I knew how this version of me functioned. Free to squeeze spots on my face and waste my evenings watching slo-mo dog-running videos.

Four exhausting hours of speed shopping later, Rachel finally found the dress, shoes, necklace, strapless bra, perfume and lipstick of her dreams, and I'd managed to convince myself I'd find something back home in my wardrobe. Right on time Dan picked us up, and despite protesting that he felt like a cross between an OAP and a ice-cream seller, he delivered on the world's slowest drive along the playing field. MIAGTM was in full football flow, and I was treated to over two glorious minutes of uninterrupted viewing pleasure before we headed back to Rachel's at normal car speed.

Back in her room we laid out our prom haul, already

a bit giddy with excitement. What on earth were we going to be like next Friday on actual prom day?!

All that was standing between us and the night of our lives was finishing what we'd promised Mr Lutas. And that was going to be a breeze.

Shame it was going to be accompanied by a hurricane of disaster.

TWENTY-FOUR

I had three messages from Tegan – and she'd only sent two the day one of her front teeth had got kicked out by one of her students attempting to do a backflip. Something must be seriously up. But what? And why tell us she wanted to talk, and not just say the thing that she wanted to talk about? It wasn't like I wasn't already on edge, what with today being a guaranteed Luke sighting in our final detention. We agreed to meet outside the post office, and for once I wasn't the last one to arrive. It was a worried-looking Tegan who turned up late.

"Please don't shout."

Not the reassuring first words I was hoping she'd say. Was she moving? Or dating Zac? Or been secretly filming for a Channel 4 documentary on friend groups where one friend is a bit weirder than all the others, and they were going to tell me I was about to be sent to a camp in Ohio for six weeks?

"Enough of the weirdness. What's up?"

She grimaced and looked at her left foot, which was kicking a lamp post.

"Honestly, you're going to kill me."

Rachel put her arm around Tegan affectionately.

"We're honestly not. What. Is. It?"

Tegan took a deep breath.

"So you know when you left yesterday?"

Rachel and I nodded. As planned, we'd finished up our bits of final decoration prep at lunchtime and had popped in to see Tegan after school. She'd been working flat out on the banners, sewing so quickly she looked like she was in fast-forward. "And I still had half the letters for the two big welcome banners to do?"

"That you wouldn't let us help with?" Rachel glared at her, although we'd all agreed that us trying to sew would end up taking Tegan even longer to fix.

"Well, I wish I had."

Uh-oh. This didn't sound good.

"Just after you left, Mum turned up – apparently they needed a stand-in gymnastics teacher, and she said

I'd do it. She didn't even ask! She just dragged me away. We spoke to the caretaker, and he promised I could come back after to finish up, Mum even offered to help. So I *thought* it was under control. But when we came back, everywhere was locked up. . ." Her voice dropped to almost a whisper. "There was nothing I could do."

Rachel looked confused.

"So, what are you saying?"

Tegan patted her eyes like she was trying to block a tear coming out. Although on closer look, they looked like they might have been doing a lot of crying recently.

"That I'm nowhere near finished, and Mr Lutas is going to hit the roof. And after EVERYTHING, I'm totally not getting to prom after all. I've probably ruined it for everyone."

I tried to say something positive, but all I felt was positively gutted. Out of the three of us, Tegan had worked the hardest and deserved to go the most. It was only because she'd been trying to do such an amazing job that she was late finishing. Maybe we could work like maniacs at lunch and get it finished? Because it was all of us going, or none.

But after we got to school, that glimmer of hope got completely un-glimmered. There was a lunchtime exam resit in the art room and it was firmly out of bounds.

By the time detention rolled around, we were defeated. When we walked in, I tried to catch Zac's eye in a way that said, 'Hey, FRIEND. Please don't think that we're not grateful to your dad, just cos we haven't finished everything, but Tegan had a gym-ergency.' I *think* Zac interpreted it as 'hello'.

When Mr Lutas arrived, he was the most upbeat I'd ever seen him. He got even more worryingly joyous after he unlocked the storeroom and saw inside. Was he actively looking forward to moaning at Tegan? I knew his good side couldn't have been rrrrreal.

"Gather round, gather rrround. It's time to see the results of our little prrroject."

Mikey gave us an excited thumbs-up. Tegan hadn't been able to warn him what was about to happen. Luke just looked like his usual annoying self. He was going to love this.

Mr Lutas cleared his throat, like he was about to deliver the kind of defining speech we'd recount to future generations. Or at least post quotes from on the internet.

"I have to say, I am VERRRY disappointed in ALL of you."

I braced for impact.

"Because if you'd only worked as hard as you have

these last few weeks in the rest of the term, you'd be a bunch of grade-A students all rrrrrrround."

Er, what?

He pushed the door fully open. Inside was the wooden picture frame, but now it was sprayed gold and surrounded by finished signs, all different shapes, sizes and designs. Luke must have worked 24/7 to get them finished. Damn his skills. I wish his woodwork would not have worked.

But there was something even more weird above them. There, dangling from the ceiling, were the banners that Tegan hadn't finished. Except they were. All the letters sewn on, and all finished to perfection.

I dug my elbow into her ribs. If this had been a joke, it was a really weird and unfunny one, which would technically make it not one. But she looked more baffled than me.

"Wasn't me!" She mouthed behind Mr Lutas's back.

"So ... I take back what I said last week. I'm delighted to say that you have all fully earned your tickets to prrrom. I'm sure you're as excited as Zac and I to see it all in action!"

I wasn't sure how, but we'd done it. We'd all done it. Together. Not quite the way I'd dreamt of, but I was going to prom, and so were my friends. And so was Zac. Even if he was my new supervisor friend. I think the technical term for what happened next was 'whooping'. Tegan, Rachel and I flung our arms around each other and jumped around in a tiny circle, while Mikey awkwardly tried to join in but ended up sort of patting us on the back like upright dogs. Zac couldn't hide his massive grin, and as we hopped around, even Mr Lutas' face began to contort into something unrecognizable. Oh gosh. Was he actually smiling too?! And was I accidentally smiling back at him because I was so relieved?

Hello, weirdest school incident of my life. People are *so* confusing. We should totally do lessons in them, and not stuff like history, which you can just look up on the internet.

But there was *one* person who wasn't clapping along. Luke. Despite all of his efforts to ruin it, Tegan, Rachel and I had ended the terms as friends – friends who were going to prom. IN YOUR FACE, PUKE.

"Simmer down. Come on. . ." Mr Lutas flapped his hands up and down to wind down the jumping, but just looked more like he was at a really fast hip-hop gig. "While I'm very imprrressed you got it done in the nick of time, there is one more thing to do." He reached up to the top shelf and pulled down a dusty projector.

"See what it looks like in action! Bella, have you got your camera?"

I nodded and ran to my bag. "And get those special pens for the signs while you're there. Luke left them on the side."

I spotted the pile of pens by Luke's things, stuffed them in my pocket and grabbed the sponges beside them. Mr Lutas then talked through how the logistics and set-up would work, before leaving us alone with Zac to do a dress rehearsal with the props.

I played with my camera settings, as Tegan set up my tripod, laughing at Mikey who was pulling major poses in the frame.

"Don't laugh at a genius at work, please, Tegan." He stuck his tongue out and his fingers up. "Just call me Mikey Cyrus." He then attempted some sort of bum wiggle that looked suspiciously like he might have practised way too many times in the privacy of his own home.

Luke looked away, disgusted and, ignoring my snort-laughing, handed out his signs and the sponges to wipe them clean.

"Here, guess we might as well use these. See how they look when they've got stuff on them." He couldn't have sounded more unenthusiastic. It was annoying how good all his signs looked – my favourite was a giant thought-bubble shaped one, and a big arrow that reminded me of the first time I met Zac. I grabbed them both.

Ignoring Luke's standard bad mood, I handed out the pens and we all got sketching.

Rachel went first, and pretended to pout as she held up her sign. It was star-shaped and had gold polka dots all around the edge. In the middle, on the whiteboard-painted area, she'd written 'HANDS OFF HOB'. Tegan almost cried with laughter as I snapped away on my camera, pretending not to get the Dan reference. The props all looked so cool on my screen. It *had* been a good idea after all!

I waited till last for my turn. I'd used the two biggest signs. On one I'd drawn a pigeon. And on the other a massive bird poo. Luke looked bemused. But it wasn't for his benefit. Zac couldn't help but grin. It was a nice to have something to look back and smile about.

Together we all flicked through the pictures on my camera. They looked awesome – the rest of our year was going to LOVE it, especially when they were projected up on the wall. Hyped that we'd pulled it off, we started to pack everything up to be taken to the hall. But as Tegan and I were folding up her banner, there was a yell from the storeroom.

"BELLA. What the HELL have you done?!"

It was Luke. And he was raging.

But what *had* I done?! We ran to see what the problem was. Luke was crouched on the floor, signs around his feet, sponge in his hand, furious look on his face.

"I can't believe you'd do this, you absolute..."

Zac barged in and cut him off before he could say something he definitely shouldn't.

"Oi. Language. What's up?"

Luke shoved my arrow sign into Zac's chest. "This."

Zac took hold of it, but like me, couldn't see the problem.

Luke pointed the other sign right at me.

"She did this on purpose. I KNOW she did."

"Did *what* exactly?"

Luke rubbed at the sign.

"Gave everyone permanent markers." He kicked one of the signs with his foot. "These are RUINED."

Permanent? But I'd just grabbed what Mr Lutas told me to?

"No, that can't be right."

I picked up Rachel's sign and rubbed at it with my

jumper and thumb, like my mum does to my face when I've forgotten to check for over friendly-toothpaste.

But her words didn't budge. All that was disappearing was my good mood. What *had* I done?

"Luke. This was a mistake. Honest. A mistake."

Annoying Luke was normally the most fun I could have in the day, but this didn't feel right. This was an accident. I didn't mean to ruin his signs. To ruin *our* project.

"You don't have an honest bit in your body, Blob. So quit pretending this isn't your way of getting back at me."

He threw one of the signs against the wall in frustration.

I looked above where it landed to where I'd put the wipe-clean pens down. And my stomach knotted. They were *still* there. Next to a half-empty box of permanent-markers I must have grabbed when I'd handed them out. What. An. Idiot.

I pointed to the mix-up.

"Honestly, I'm SO sorry. Look, I must have grabbed the wrong ones. I had NO idea?!"

Luke didn't react. He looked gutted. As much as I hated him for it, I knew he'd put his heart and soul into this project. He dropped his head into his hands.

Zac put a supervisor-ly hand on his back.

"C'mon, surely we can sort this out?"

Luke threw his shoulder up, throwing Zac's hand off.

"Well, unless you want to give up every second of *your* spare time to repair them with skills you *don't* have, then no, I guess there's nothing you can do." He looked up at me. "You've gone too far this time, Blob. And you know it."

The room was silent. No one knew what to say. Especially me. I apologized on loop, but Luke didn't want to hear it. I even offered to help sand the signs down and repaint them. It wasn't much, but as it was all I could do I left Luke with my camera so he could use the pictures we'd just taken as a base for any new designs he was going to have to repaint. With conversation going nowhere, Zac ushered the rest of us out, to finish up the packing up and head home. When we left, Luke was still working away in the storeroom.

I felt like poo, but the others were buzzing about prom being officially on, and only 48 hours away. By the time we bundled into Jo's car, despite still feeling guilty, it was getting tough not to let the others' excitement rub off on me. Not letting Jo get a word in edgeways, our words spilled over each others', as we tried to work out what had happened. Rachel reckoned that the accident was karma (or korma, as she originally said) for everything Luke had done to me this term. Tegan was more concerned with who fixed her banners, and thought it might have been Zac and Mr Lutas. I tried picturing them in a high-speed emergency sewing fest, and figured a more logical explanation was that it was a ghost. Of a Victorian seamstress. Who liked end-of-term parties. Tegan even made me feel better about Zac being our prom supervisor when she pointed out that it could never have worked between us as one day I would have HAD to have dinner with his dad and there's no way I could ever make casual teach-chat whilst chewing on a fish finger. Or have a shower in the same place that Mr Lutas got naked.

Despite this cheery evidence, Jo sistey-sensed I was secretly still a bit glum and suggested I plug my music in. Three songs into my freshly made 'Prom-bably the Best Playlist In The World ... Ever' and I'd finally started to put Luke's accusations behind me. By five songs we were all screaming along, tone deaf but happy. MIAGTM was even out playing football. Before I could stop him, Mikey wound down the back window, just as the speakers blared out, 'I want to kissy kiss your face, boi.' I dived down in my seat, whilst shouting insults at Mikey, who just waved regally at the entire pitch who were now staring in our direction. Honestly, did that boy not know girl code?!

Once they'd all been dropped off, the car seemed way too quiet.

"So it all worked out then?"

Jo seemed pleased for me.

"Uh-huh. So can I now please get stressed about what to wear instead?"

"Most unsubtle hint to borrow clothes EVER."

"That's cos it wasn't. Although *now you've offered*?"

"I didn't."

But she *might* if I play my cards right? "How was training?"

"You know."

I didn't, as the last type of training I'd ever done was nappy training and thankfully I didn't remember that.

"Looking forward to tour?"

"I guess." She didn't sound as enthusiastic as normal. But I needed her onside and had enthusiasm for us both.

"Well, maybe I could come and check out one of your races?"

She scrunched up her face.

"Errr, did I hear that right? Did you just volunteer

to come and watch me RUN?"

I can't believe she was so unbelieving of my cunning plan to pretend to be in interested in athletics in return for wardrobe services. How unreasonable.

She pulled up on the drive and switched off the engine. Mum waved from the kitchen window. I didn't need to hear to know she was dancing to ABBA. This usually meant we'd be eating something Swedish-themed. Or just burnt as she'd got too distracted. We once found a beetroot she'd left in the oven for two days. It looked like a cannonball.

When we sat down to eat, Mum had lived up to expectation – some trout with Swedish ligonberry sauce (except she couldn't find ligonberries so had used strawberry jam) with charcoaled beetroot. It was weirdly tasty, and I wolfed it down as I listened to Mum's stories of upcycling her used cotton-wool pads into tiny beds for homeless hamsters. After dinner we went through to the lounge and watched a programme on ghost hunting. Maybe I should invite them to our school to check for any paranormal sewing activity? I huffed loudly when Jo ducked out leaving just Mum and me. Mum never asked *her* why she couldn't 'respect family time' as she snuck upstairs, no questions asked, probably to video-chat with her uni mates.

But when Jo came back down I realized I'd got her all wrong. Because she was clutching an armful of clothes.

"C'mon then. We've only got two evenings to get you prom-ready. She chucked the dresses on the table. "So which one's gonna make you Bell-a of the ball?"

She'd even brought down the mega-expensive one she worked all Christmas to save up for.

She smiled at me and held it out. And before I knew what I was doing, I was giving my big sister an even bigger hug.

CHAPTER

TWENTY-FIVE

I think my lungs are exploding. They're definitely on fire. We near on sprinted home to Rachel's house after the bell finally rang, even though we had all that extra stuff to carry home from art. I donated my cheese and pineapple sculpture to the bin – I'd only got a B anyway, dammit.

I'm hoping that lying, huffing, starfished on Rachel's bed might help the sweating and pinkness subside. I look like a piece of ham that's been left in a sandwich bag overnight. And tonight, of all nights, is the night I need to look HOT, not HAM. Tonight is THE night. Prom night.

As Tegan sang to herself in Rachel's en-suite shower, I continued to pant, freaking out that I was running out of time to get ready (while not actually starting to get ready in any way). I swear, if my mind and body met in real life they wouldn't be friends. In the same amount of time, Rachel managed to paint all twenty of her body nails and drink her Mum's 'prom-mocktail'. Our glasses even had alphabet ice cubes that spelt out our names (although my L and A had melted together by the time she gave it to me so it sort of said BELT).

When Tegan came out of the bathroom, she set up station in front of the mirror. A buzzing Rachel jumped next to me on the bed, causing me to rocket up and spill my drink in my hair. Oh well, that bit could just be sticky.

"I can't believe it's TONIGHT! You know what this means, right?" She didn't give us time to answer. "Obvs party of the year. But also – only one week of surviving school left. Then it's summer summer SUMMER!!"

Tegan yelled 'freedom' followed by an even louder 'ow' as she almost gauged her eye out with a blue mascara.

"Have either of you two seen the guest list? I wanna know who's coming?!"

I shook my head, which is hard when applying eyelash glue.

"Just imagine. *Anyone* could be there. PJBJ.

338

Shoe-boy. . ." She looked dreamily into space as if we were going to Paris, not a prom. "Just think, Bella. Someone could have invited MIAGTM? As a mate date."

If someone *had* brought MIAGTM as a real date, I'm sure I'd be morally allowed to use my newfound detention glue-gun skills to permanently attach them to a toilet. I tried not to scrunch my face up thinking about it, as it was making putting on my fake eyelashes extra hard (even at the best of times I tend to glue one eye shut and I really don't want to look like a prom pirate).

I broke it to Rachel gently.

"Sorry to disappoint, but I haven't heard anyone mention his name." I corrected myself. "Not that I know what it is."

"He probably wasn't christened MIAGTM?" Rachel sounded like she thought this was genuinely helpful. "So what *would* you do if he was there?"

I went to answer, but was luckily saved by the yell as Rachel's mum shouted up to tell us to get a move on and that we 'better be bringing our major sass game'. I was trying, but felt a bit more sausage than sass-age.

After thirty minutes of mirror gymnastics, we looked at the end result. My trial run with Jo yesterday had paid off – I'd achieved something that resembled 'average human girl going out of the house'. Not Rachel, or Tegan level, but 'Bella on a good day', which I'll take.

"Wit-woo, don't you all look grown up?" Rachel's mum whistled as we came down the stairs. She was being proud-mum paparazzi, taking shots of us walking, not even giving me time to breathe in or tilt my less-good eyebrow away from the camera. She patted us into photo formation on the stairs. In my/Jo's green dress I felt like a mermaid with legs – or is that just a maid?

Rachel had a tight white boob-tube dress on, with toeless silver shoes. Sounds gross, and a little bit angel-esque, but it really worked. Only two per cent of the world can get away with tight white clothing – Rachel was one of them, Olympic ice-skaters are the rest. However, at her own peril she'd dismissed our warnings that using ten shovels of glitter may have rendered her unsnoggable, unless the boy wanted to look like a piece of tinsel. Tegan had piled her braids up, and with her smoky eyes her blue dress looked even more show-stopping than it did in the shop, the customised tassels making it look like something out of *Vogue*. I loved my friends to pieces, but I did sometimes feel like they were a premier-league football team and I was the furry animal mascot that accompanied them.

Outside a car beeped. Rachel's dad was already waiting, sitting behind the wheel of their freshly polished car, dressed in hat and tie (her dad, not the car. I don't think cars can have hats, unless you count roof racks, but I don't.)

He got out on to the gravel and opened the back door for us.

"Ladies, I am your driver tonight. Please take your places."

"Why, thank you, sir!" I tried to daintily step in but caught my heel in my dress and splatted on the back seat. Classic mascot move.

"*I have a feeling tonight's gonna be a good, good night.*" Tegan sang as she got in, physically pushing me along the leather seat, my dress making me slide like a tray in the canteen. "Maybe even superlatively good."

"Totally. Although I'm not sure what superlatively means. Imagine if I've managed to psychiatrically will MIAGTM to turn up with all of my positive vibes?!" Rachel said dreamily. Tegan whispered 'psychic-ly' under her breath.

"Marry?" I snorted. "Who cares about *marry* any more?! Just as long as I snog his face off! Although then he'd be MIAGTSTFO!"

341

I cackled at Tegan.

Rachel's dad slammed the driver's door closed, reminding us that he had ears. Must move convo on to something more dad-appropriate.

"Seriously though. For me, tonight isn't about anything but you guys." I gave them my cheesiest smile.

"Awwwwwww, thanks matey." Tegan stretched her arm around me and gave my shoulders a squeeze. "Same here."

Mr Allen made dad eye contact with Tegan via the mirror. "I thought you were in a relationship, or whatever you girls say, with that nice boy . . . Michael?!"

Rachel cried 'NO' and rammed her fingers in her ears at her dad's off-parental-piste outburst. Tegan looked shocked.

"He's not my boyf! You're as bad as these two. I mean, yeah, he's great, but he's just not that –" she searched around for words – "well, he doesn't like me that way, and even if he did, he's just too –" she paused – "boy."

Rachel's dad shook his head.

"Women. Young or old, I will never understand them."

"Shurrup, Dad. We're one hundred per cent not un-understandable!"

Rachel flicked her hair back and pretended not to notice that she'd coated the headrest with glitter. By the time we pulled up at school, the entire front seat looked like it had been given a disco makeover.

We clambered out of the car, getting our first glimpse of the decorations in action. It was exciting to see everything we'd worked so hard for finally up and in action. Tegan's amazing banners hung over the gates and above the doors – the ghost must be well chuffed. The streamers Rachel and Mikey had made were rustling as they dangled down the entire length of the corridor. Everywhere you looked there were our tiny details that had transformed the school from lesson hell to party paradise. Standing arm-in-arm with my friends, watching everyone else be blown away by what we'd achieved, I couldn't be any happier. It had taken a term, but I'd finally managed to do *something* right.

We threw our heads back and strutted through the doors and into the hall. Hello, world, we're here! And yes, my left ankle did just give way slightly, but let's all pretend that didn't happen.

The room looked way bigger without the usual school stuff in there. Music was blaring out and everyone was clumped round the edges in their own groups. Credit to Luke, the giant frame looked amazing. And he'd managed to make a whole new set of signs. People were already posing with them, writing massive messages as my camera clicked away. At the far end of the hall, the pictures were being projected on to the wall and they looked awesome. Although I didn't know how I felt seeing Lou's nostril the size of a balloon. Oh well.

I scanned round the room checking out who was already here, carefully not making eye contact with the cluster of teachers at the back of the room. Is cluster the right word? Maybe 'a dullness of teachers' would be better? Standing in the middle of the dullness, next to a couple of the other sixth-form supervisors, but still sticking out like a sexy sore thumb, was Zac. If my brain could talk, it would say 'swoon'. Major swoon. Zac in a suit was too good for this party. For any party. Except maybe a 'top ten most fit and amazing people in the world' party. And I'd never be invited to that, so I'd never know. He put his hand up and gave me a little wave.

If someone had told me back in Black Bay that this would be where we'd end up, I would have thought they were mad. But they would have then pointed out that I was a one-shoe-d arrow-wearing weirdo, so who was I to judge?

The sixth-form girls next to Zac were all over-laughing at his jokes. Maybe they found international cinema as hilarious as he did? They looked so much more at ease with him than I ever did, battling to get his attention, probably talking about college, and things like changing gear and crosswords and whatever else you do when you're seventeen. But I didn't feel jealous. Because now Zac was my back-having-prom-getting-into-hot-friend instead. Which felt way better than having him as a date because he thought I was someone I wasn't.

I waved back. The girls shot me evils. I shot them smiles.

Tegan grabbed my hand and pulled me outside to the school garden.

Seconds later Mikey appeared with his best mate, Jay. "Fashionably late, I see." Mikey was wearing a suit two sizes too big – a classic case of dad-borrowing. He couldn't take his eyes off Tegan. "Wow, you look *incredible.*"

He was so obvious! I kicked my toe into his shoe, yelping as my flesh made direct contact with his heel. Yet another reason to only ever wear trainers.

"Err, yeah, you ALL look incredible. *Standard.*"

Tegan put her hand up to her ear as she honed in

on the music, completely missing what Mikey said. His face went all sad like a balloon that's a week old.

"Can you guys hear that? It's Tay-Tay! Who's with me?" She didn't stick around for an answer, and ran off towards the music and laughter in the hall, waving us to follow. Rachel and I chased after her, wobbling as our heels got stuck in the grass, the boys acting as our human stabilizers.

After over an hour of dancing like no one was watching (which unfortunately they were as I pioneered both the 'shaving the beard' arm move and 'grooming the disobedient pug' skank), the DJ announced there was only ten minutes till he'd be crowning prom prince and princess. As the girls rushed to touch up their make-up, and the guys rushed to get to the back of the room to pretend they didn't care, the queue for the frame disappeared. Seeing our chance, we charged over, and squeezed ourselves in for one massive picture.

"Coming throooough!" Mikey squodged himself into the middle of us, held up a sign on which he'd scrawled 'Prom Crew 4 Eva', and pulled his best duck face. Tegan and I did peace signs, and Rachel blew a kiss at the camera. From across the room Zac smiled over at us.

"Cheeeeese!" we yelled, hugging and happy to be together. Our image popped up on the wall. We looked so huge, so smiley. Mikey pointed up. "Finally frame-ous."

We collapsed into laughs as the moody upper-sixth photographer asked us to politely get out of the way.

A hand tapped me on the shoulder.

"Looking good, guys!" I span round in time for Zac to wink at me. "Although not enough bird poo for my liking."

The others laughed, getting the reference, seeing as they'd heard about it in such detail they'd practically been there. Zac stepped to the side so he could talk to me away from the group.

"So, Bells, I don't know if I told you, but I'm off next week. So once term's done, I'm outta here."

I figured that would be the case but it was still gross hearing it.

"That sucks. It's been kind of ace having you here." I corrected myself. "Also like totally awful in places, but mainly ace."

He laughed in agreement.

"Couldn't have put it better myself. It's definitely been . . . memorable."

"Thanks for all your help, anyway. Especially the getting-to-prom tip off."

Zac nodded over to his dad.

"It's him you should be thanking. Don't let him know, but I think he was secretly trying to help all along."

I nose-snorted. Always good to leave Zac with some hot mental images AND noises.

"Erm, this IS your dad we're talking about?"

"Yes, the very same one who sweet-talked his latest student into letting you all come. I heard it getting heated in our lounge."

What on earth was he talking about? Zac clocked my confusion.

"Mrs Hitchman?! Did you not know he teaches her and her husband still-life drawing? I reckon that's the only reason she said yes to you coming!"

So *that's* why I'd kept on spotting them together. Why she'd helped Mr Lutas get Zac here so quickly. Well, wasn't Mr Lutas a dark horse? And the kind of dark horse that wasn't actually having an illicit affair with our headmistress after all. If horses even had affairs.

Mr Lutas stared over at us, like he knew we were talking about him. Zac turned his back on his dad and gestured for me to get in the photo frame with him. He really had gone renegade now he only had five term days left. But as we stepped in to pose, I spotted Luke in a dark corner. Watching.

But I wasn't going to let him ruin my night. He'd done more than enough ruining already this term. I checked with Zac, and as the photographer snapped away, I made a heart shape with my hands at the camera for old time's sake.

As the picture got projected up, I continued to ignore Luke's ever-growing scowl. That's what happens when a player gets played.

Zac nudged me in the ribs – I tensed any muscle I knew how to move. His dad was striding over.

Mr Lutas nodded up at the photo.

"I can't believe you'd do that."

Uh-oh. My heart-shaped cringey-ness didn't seem as funny four-metres high. I wished both the real me and the giant photo me would disappear.

"I would have hoped you, Zacharrry, of all people, could have got that composition a *little* better?" Oh ha-di-ha. "Although Miss Fisher, one word of advice. . ."

Oh goodness, what now? Please don't let it be about sculpting cheese.

"Choose your holiday rrromances more wisely. You can meet some *verrry* strange people in caravan parks."

Mr Lutas winked at me the way Zac had done minutes earlier, and laughed. SO HE KNEW?!

"Did you really think I was born yesterrrday, Ms Fisher? Give me some credit!" He was loving how much I WAS NOT DEALING WITH THIS. "And while you're at it, you should give a serious amount of credit to that young man too."

Mr Lutas nodded his head across the room, and with a big smile for both Zac and me, he walked away. He'd nodded at Mikey. Who was in an impromptu dance-off with Jay as they tried, and failed, to recreate an entire Justin Bieber routine (Mikey looked more like my mum trying to do yoga when she's pulled a muscle in her back). I turned back to Zac, but as I did, Luke barged through us both, knocking me sideways as he rushed to speak to the photographer. He was obviously still mad at me for the signs, although I was surprised that he didn't give Zac a bit more respect. But I didn't want to waste any more time on him than I already had done.

"I can't actually deal with your dad knowing about us, so can we pretend he never said that, and can you explain about the Mikey thing instead?"

Zac looked sheepish. "M-bee."

I prodded him with the sharp end of one of the signs.

"We've seen what happens when we're not straight with each other." I prodded him a bit harder. "Spill!"

"Oiii! OK." He searched for the words. "I guess Dad just meant that, hypothetically, if say he'd maybe got a text from the caretaker saying he was going to close the school up, but hypothetically he knew that someone needed to get back in to work on something, he might, you know, tell his son. And his son, in this scenario, might mention it to someone he might have bumped into that evening. Someone who might have wanted to help, and might have, say, hidden from said caretaker, and stayed overnight to finish the job?"

Oh. My. Endangered. COD.

Was Zac telling me that, hypothetically, the person who was currently dancing like an injured puppet had been the one to finish up Tegan's signs? That unhypothetically Mikey had spent a whole night behind a sewing machine to get Tegan to prom? This was so big. SEW big.

Zac laughed. He looked relieved to have let that cat out of the bag. Although goodness knows who puts cats in bags.

"Close your mouth, goldfish. I thought you might have figured it out?" I wasn't going to admit that I was so far away from figuring it out, I'd concluded it was actually a fictional spectre.

"Well he *was* yawning all day. But I do that most days and I don't have a super-hero sewing alter ego."

Zac looked happy for the subject to move on.

"Talking of alter egos, Velvet Badger have got a gig in July. In Birmingham. I wondered if you and the others wanted to come?"

Nostril flare struck again. I would LOVE that. And I loved that after all that had happened, Zac was up for being proper friends, even after term finished. But as I went to try and regain control of my face, and tell him we were one big 'yes', loud laughs broke out over the music. Please don't let Mikey be attempting a headspin again – last time he'd broken his own nose with his knee.

Along with the rest of the room, Zac and I turned to see what was happening. It deffo wasn't Mikey, as people had stopped dancing and were looking up at the projections. The picture had no people in – just one big hand-written sign. I read what was written on it.

I instantly wished I hadn't.

They were words I'd seen before.

WOULD YOU GET A FAKE PERIOD FOR TWO YEARS
RATHER THAN 'FESS UP? THAT'S WHAT MY FRIEND
R DID AFTER SHE YELLED 'CAN I BORROW A TOWEL?'

My dress felt like it had morphed into a straight jacket, stopping any breath going in. I frantically scanned the room for the others. PLEASE don't let them have noticed. But Tegan and Rachel were shoulder-to-shoulder, staring up at the screen.

A new photo popped up. And it was another sign. Just as big.

MY FRIEND TEE USED TO GET SO HYPED
PLAYING HIDE AND SEEK THAT WHENEVER
SHE HID, SHE WEED HERSELF.

The room began to spin. What was happening?! Why were my secrets on the wall?! Why wouldn't everyone stop laughing?!

Another one came up.

WANT TO MAKE MJ BLUB? JUST ASK HIM
WHAT HAPPENS AT THE END OF HARRY POTTER.
**SHAME HE CAN'T GET A LOVE POTION FOR
HIS REAL-LIFE HERMIONE - TEE.**

Had the music stopped or had my ears sealed over with horror? The whole prom was now staring at the projections. Except Tegan, who was storming over, looking like her world was falling apart. Which was exactly how I felt. I'd never told ANYONE these secrets. Anyone but *PSSSST*. So why were they now on my school wall?! Who was doing this?! And how could I stop anyone figuring out they were about me and my friends?!

Very slowly, Tegan spoke.

"Was. This. YOU?"

I didn't know what to say.

"Bella. Was this you?"

I felt so guilty I wanted to be sick on the spot. But that wouldn't help me blend in and stop people realizing this was something to do with me, and figuring out who these stupid secrets were about.

"No. I mean . . . maybe?"

Rachel pushed her way through the hysterical crowd.

"Can *someone* tell me what's going on?"

Tegan pointed at me.

"Ask her."

EVER WONDERED WHY ONLY ONE OF OUR

TEACHERRRS GETS TO TAKE HIS STUDENTS ON FORRREIGN TRIPS? COULD IT HAVE ANYTHING TO DO WITH HIM PAYING EXTRA CURRICULARRR VISITS TO A PERSON WHO HELPS HIM GET AHEAD? (AKA OUR HEAD MISTRESS)

A bang came from the corner of the room as a furious Mrs Hitchman stormed out of the door, chased by a stern-looking Mr Lutas. Zac followed. As did a wave of sniggers. If there's one thing people love more than a student scandal, it's a teacher one.

HOW DO YOU KNOW THAT THE FITTEST SIXTH FORMER IN THE WORLD IS EX-ZAC-TLY THAT? WHEN YOU FIND OUT HIS DAD IS THE WEIRDEST TEACHERRR AND STILL WANT TO SNOG HIS FACE OFF AGAIN. THEN PUT HIS FACE BACK ON. THEN RE-SNOG IT OFF.

My stomach knotted so hard I wasn't sure how I was still standing upright. They *were* the words I'd posted on *PSSSST*, but I'd never used names?! Zac had been added in. But only Tegan, Rach, Zac and I knew the truth about what really happened at Black Bay, and surely it couldn't be one of them doing this?!

Was this an actual nightmare? Please someone tell me it's a nightmare. Mum, wake me up with a cup of tea. PLEASE. Mumbles, lick my face. ANYTHING!!

I'd never heard so much laughter in the hall. The DJ had turned the music off, as all dancing had stopped in favour of pointing fingers round the room, trying to figure out who each story was about. *Please* don't let anyone work it out. I will never moan about anything ever again, including a weirdly long eyebrow hair I have, if someone, anyone, makes this stop before more damage is done.

What could I do?! Deep breath, Bella. Think logically. Or just think at all. I needed to stop anyone getting any proof that they came from me. Then I *could* still protect the others. But I had to stop anything else going up. Anymore clues.

I barged my way over to the projector. Where *was* that stupid plug?

But I was too late. With one click the final picture came up. It was someone I knew all too well. Luke. And with a smile he was holding the worst sign yet.

THANKS BELLA FISHER FOR THE LOLS.
HAPPY PROM ☺

CHAPTER

TWENTY-SIX

"So let me get this straight?" From the other side of the cubicle door, Tegan repeated herself for the fourth time. Between tears I cringed for the eighty-ninth.

I'd done my best to explain what had happened. Why it had happened. Even though I still had no real idea how. The first time they looked shocked. The second time they looked baffled. They third time they looked so angry I thought I was going to see myself ugly crying in the mirror above the sink. To preserve any dignity, I'd run into the loo and locked myself in.

I could almost see their fury seeping under the door. But it was nothing I didn't deserve.

Tegan was quiet angry – the scariest kind.

"You told EVERYONE the stuff we promised to tell NO ONE."

I nodded my head. But that's not so useful from behind a door.

"Sort of."

"Sort of yes, or sort of no?" She was raging – and I couldn't blame her. It wasn't a leap for people to work out Tee was her, and R was Rachel. And Mikey probably wasn't going to speak to me ever again. Not now the whole school had shouted things like 'Snivel-us Snape,' 'Nothing Ron with crying' and 'Snogwarts' as he'd run after Tegan. She'd brushed him away, mortified that her private life had now become so public. Please, please don't let me have damaged their friendship for good.

I, Bella Fisher, am like human-disaster-Velcro that life-ruining just clings to. Can I at least stick to just messing up my own stuff from now on? Maybe I should become a nun after all. Plus, those robey things look really expandable if I comfort eat for the next forty years.

I took a deep breath.

"I WISH I could explain it. But I can't. *PSSSST* was just a silly thing I did after we all fell out. I only did it to find Zac. But then people started liking my stuff, and I kept going. It said it was all anonymous. I never used names. I swear! I thought it was totally harmless. I didn't feel like real people could see them?!"

It sounded stupid now. Who did I *think* had been liking everything?

As I apologized for the forty-seventh, forty-eighth and forty-ninth time, I messaged Jo. I needed her to come and save me before I attempted escaping from school via the toilet pipe thing.

Rachel peered under the door.

"I don't get it, Bella. Why would you do this? I thought we were all friends again?"

"We ARE all friends."

Tegan butted in.

"Weird thing for a friend to do, don't you think?"

"But that's the problem. I DON'T think. And I should. I will! In fact, I'm thinking RIGHT NOW. I'm thinking what a total idiot I've been."

If *only* I hadn't gone to Black Bay. None of this would have happened. I'd only used that stupid app to try and track down Zac.

"I know you hate me right now, and I TOTALLY GET IT. I hate me too! But please, please, please can you at least think about forgiving me? It was a weird, out-of-control accident. Like my whole entire life. I'd do ANYTHING to make it up to you. You guys are EVERYTHING to me."

But nothing came back except silence, until Tegan cleared her throat.

"There's no point in talking now. Rachel and I don't want to miss out on *all* the fun cos of you."

But if I'd learnt one thing this term it was to not give up on my friends. Yes, I'd messed up, but I *knew* I could put it right. I banged the door with my hand.

"NO. I'm not letting this happen. This is NOT ruining us. I CAN be a good friend. I will be."

But Tegan sounded broken.

"Good friends are people you can trust. C'mon, Rach."

The bathroom door swung shut as they left me alone.

I stayed alone, in my bad-mood cubicle – moodicle – until Jo messaged to say she'd arrived. I tried to wipe the mascara away from under my eyes, but smeared it up into the world's biggest eyeliner flicks. Oh well. I couldn't be any more humiliated than I already was.

Ignoring the no-running-in-corridors rule, I sprinted as fast as I could (not fast) towards the secret path through the bushes that led down to the school gates. I didn't want to risk bumping into anyone.

But the one person I most wanted to avoid was taking a time-out too.

"Leaving so soon?"

If I hadn't been wearing Jo's ring that Grandma gave her, I swear I might have attempted my first ever punch, right into Luke's face. I know violence doesn't solve anything, but seeing Luke face down in a pile of twigs and crisp wrappers would at least cheer me up.

"Have I ever told you what a complete and utter douchebag you are?"

He laughed.

"Every day."

But I couldn't find anything to laugh about. Why had he done this? How had he done this?! And why drag Tegan, Rachel, Mikey and worst of all Zac, down with me? Zac had never even had anything to do with him.

"So what? You're now some sort of internet stalker, are you?" I shook my head. "You're pathetic."

He smiled. "But you made it so easy for me."

I definitely hadn't. Easy was things like eating a pack of five supermarket doughnuts, not finding someone on an anonymous app that he shouldn't even know about.

"How so, stalker?"

"Let me break it down for you." He said it like I was three and he was teaching me my first words. "First off, you showed me the app in the library, so I knew you were on it." Crapballs. That must have been when I almost showed him that picture of Zac. How could I have been so careless?! "Then, as literally *everyone* knows, when you sign up, it shows you the people who are nearby." Everyone it seems, except me. "And cos of all your likes, and the fact we live three streets away, it meant you were the first person that came up."

What the what? When I'd signed up it only offered random follow suggestions. Although – my heart sank – I *had* been on that motorway in the middle of nowhere. Maybe there had been nobody nearby *to* suggest. So hold up. Did this mean I'd accidentally been sharing my closest guarded secrets with people who lived the closest to me? How was this a good idea for an app?!

But that still didn't explain how he'd linked PruneFlapper with me? Or discovered the truth about Zac? I'd been so careful to protect everyone.

"I'm not buying it, Luke. It doesn't add up."

"It adds up fine to me. I thought it was you when I saw that ankle bracelet on your profile pic." My profile pic was just my feet on the windowsill at Black Bay? Surely Luke wasn't that observant? "And then there was the er, time of the month thing, which y'know I *could* have thought was about someone we knew." AKA – he totally knew it was about him, and I'd just wound him up even more. "And then last week when you posted about the camera, I knew it HAD to be you. It was way too big a coincidence."

For someone whose mum spent her whole time trying to channel good energy, I sure had the worst luck. The one secret Luke knew about me was one of the final ones I'd posted up. The one person who I'd been posting most about had been the one person to piece it all together. I could kick myself. But I was bad enough on two feet, and falling over wasn't going to help this situation.

"But *why,* Luke? Why do this?"

"What, despite you ruining my work?"

I cut him off.

"Which I didn't do."

"Whatever. And posting that stupid story about me. And –" he flinched as if not sure to carry on, but not quite able to stop himself – "and lying to me about Zac."

"But I *told you* the truth. I made it all up. Which you took great joy in telling the whole freakin' school."

"I saw the pictures, Bella. You really should be more careful what you keep on your memory card."

Kicking myself wasn't enough. Could I please run back and forth into this large tree? Had I actually been so stressed out about the sign situation that I'd handed over my camera to Luke, complete with all my pictures?

But it was weird. Luke didn't look cross. He looked a version of . . . upset. The exact same way he'd looked when I'd told him I thought we should see each other less. The exact same way he'd looked when he saw my OTT heart-pose pic with Zac. Right before he'd shared all my secrets.

Could Mikey be right? *Was* Luke more bothered by our break-up than I'd ever imagined? I shook that thought right out of my head. Because it didn't matter to me why he'd done what he'd done. He hadn't just hurt me, he'd hurt my friends. And done it in the most public way possible. He was pathetic. So pathetic that I finally realized what I should have done weeks ago. That whatever Luke said or did from now on couldn't hurt me any more. So I needed to stop wasting any more time on him, and focus on un-doing his damage and making it up to the people I love.

Without bothering to reply, I pushed past him, ran to Jo's car and threw myself on to the front seat. I hoped she would forgive me for the mascara stain on her dress where my tears had pooled between my legs. As she drove away the lights flashed out of the hall, silhouetting Tegan and Rachel dancing. I guess I was happy they were putting Luke's stunt behind them. As long as I didn't get put behind them too. I tried not think about what Zac and Mr Lutas were in deep conversation about at the side of the hall, and not panic that Mikey was sitting alone at the edge of the room. But it was hard when at the exact same moment he messaged me to say thanks for blowing any chance with Tegan he ever had. I switched my phone off. I HAD to fix this.

Jo did me the favour of not making conversation the entire way home. When we arrived, she even popped into the kitchen to chat to Mum, giving me the distraction I needed to retreat to my room un-interrogated.

I stayed fully clothed under my duvet until I heard her knock. She slid under the covers beside me, not even doing a double-take at me wearing her dress as my new PJs.

"C'mon then. Hit me with it. Whatever you say will just be between you, me, and that rather fit poster of Louis." Last week I'd turned it on its side so when I wake up and open my eyes it's like he's lying next to me (but without the danger of him getting a faceful of my morning breath).

Jo tucked a loose bit of hair behind my ear.

I didn't know where to start.

But before I knew it, I'd finished. Every detail, every *single* detail from Zac, through to detention, through to Luke's stupid threats, through to me accidentally winding him up so much he'd ruined everything for everyone.

"So, on the positive side. . ."

I snorted. The only positive side to this was, if I restarted life, and just used this whole thing as a terrible dress rehearsal (in actual terrible dresses too) I could get back to a normal functioning fifteen-year-old by the time I'm thirty.

"As I was saying, *oinker,* at least everything's out there now. It's not like any more surprises can be lurking."

But there was something I *hadn't* told her. And I was done with secrets.

"Well. Nor quite. There *is* something I need to tell you."

She raised her eyebrows.

I felt like I was having an out-of-body experience, watching myself about to say something but not actually sure I could make all my speaking muscles do the saying.

But I had to come clean. For Jo to help, she needed to know everything. I wanted a no-sister-secret-zone, whatever the consequences.

"It's about the camera I won."

"The one you never let me borrow? What's it got to do with me?"

Brace, Bella. One last thing and you can be officially empty of lies.

"Well, the photo that I won with wasn't the one I showed you and mum. The photo of Mumbles where her jowl had flapped into her eye as she jumped over a puddle?"

Her eyebrow went up.

"Go on..."

"Well, that was Photo1. The one I sent through on email to enter was actually Picture1. It was just an accident. A total accident, cos I was about to miss the deadline."

"And what *exactly* was Picture1?"

This was where it got awkward. And maybe illegal.

"That arty one you took of an athletic track?"

AKA the photo that was up in Jo's room. That she'd taken.

"No way?!?"

Yes way, an award-winning accident.

"I'm *so* sorry! It was a TOTAL accident. And I only realized when I walked up to collect the prize and they suddenly put it up on the screen behind me. And then I didn't know what to do, so I didn't do anything. And I've been dying about it ever since."

I held my breath. Was Jo going to go summon Mum up here?

"Well, in that case –" she lifted up one of the mugs of tea she'd brought up for us – "here's to me being a prize-winning photographer too! Who knew?!"

She clinked her mug against mine and smiled.

And I smiled back.

Relieved. Happy. And not hiding anything any more. Except the stain on her dress.

I'd survived a full sister confessional.

"So, now you've got everything off your chest – except for my dress and YES I've noticed that stain." Oops. "Maybe it's my turn to come clean."

I didn't understand. How could someone who never did anything wrong have something to own up to? She plumped up my pillow and sat cross-legged.

"Remember at Christmas – how I did all the cooking for a month, including Christmas dinner?"

"Of course I remember. It was incrediballs!" It was also the first time since Dad left that we'd not had spaghetti hoops on Christmas Day.

"Well fanks, sis. But had you never wondered why I was doing it? And not even moaning about it?"

Woah. I hadn't. I just thought she was sucking up as usual.

"It was because I was grounded."

I spluttered my tea back into the cup, like an Italian water feature, but without a tiny stone penis on show.

"You what?!"

This was like finding out the Easter bunny is actually real and lives in a giant burrow in Herefordshire.

"Yup. Y'know this athletics tour? Well, when they sent letters out about the teams I realized they'd mixed up some details —" she buried her head in her hands — "and that they'd made me a whole lot faster than I'd really been. And that . . . that maybe I shouldn't have quite been on the team after all."

SUPERGULP.

"Oh. My. Jonas. What did you do?!"

"That's the thing. I didn't do anything. Not for a whole term. But when I came home for Christmas, I *had* to tell Mum. I couldn't deal with the stress any more."

369

How did I not know any of this?! All this time I'd been annoyed at her for being the mega-sis, and actually she'd been mega-in-trouble sis?!

"Andwhatdidshesay?!"

"She marched me out of the house and straight to the club. And made me tell them their mistake. It was the most embarrassing thing I've ever done." This was a big claim, as we'd both once had to do a photoshoot for Mum's friend's neon yoga clothes range. "Mum didn't even get changed out of her kaftan and slippers."

I would say I was speechless, but I couldn't, as I was speechless.

"They only let me keep my tour place, cos they appreciated that I'd 'fessed up, and then it turned out my time was good enough to qualify anyway, as one of the others had got injured."

So *that's* why she'd been so shifty talking about tour?! No wonder she'd kept it to herself.

"Mum didn't want me telling you cos she hates the principle of karma not sorting life out and having to resort to normal-person punishment. But I'd always thought you'd figured it out?"

I ABSOLUTELY hadn't. I thought she was just buttering Mum up. Via delicious broccoli-soup skills.

"Wow. I had NO idea."

"That's why I hid the letter from Mum. I couldn't face up to having to swallow any of your attempts at cooking. Or deal with your moaning."

"*What* letter?"

"The detention one in my room. Unless you want it back? I recognized the school logo."

WHAT THE WHAT?! So my detention letter *had* arrived! And she'd hidden it?! I'd never seen this side of Jo before. And I liked it.

I gave her a massive 'thank you' hug, smearing mascara on her cheek. She rolled me back on to my side of the bed and grabbed the tissue out of my hand to wipe it off.

"C'mon, panda eyes. Enough about me. How about we work out what to do to fix this mess you're in. I've had quite enough of you moping about the house for one year."

She was right. If I had been able to tell Jo the thing I'd been dreading, I could do anything. And that definitely included proving to Tegan and Rachel that I was the friend they thought I was.

"Yup, with one clever person, and one ... well, me ... we must be able to fix at least *something?*."

But as I finished my sentence, I yawned. It was

gone midnight and I'd shed all my energy when I saw those stupid pictures from Luke.

Jo and I agreed to carry the convo on in the morning, and true to her word she woke me up at nine a.m. with some toast – heavy on the butter, light on the Marmite, just how I liked it.

She even brought a laptop. She meant serious business.

As we talked, it became clearer and clearer to me what I needed to do. I needed to prove to Rachel and Tegan that I could be trusted. And that they were more important to me than what anyone else thought. But I wasn't sure how.

Jo opened her laptop, and shut down her uni work. As she did I got a brainwave of EXACTLY what I had to do.

It wasn't going to be easy, in fact it was going to be mortifyingly awful. But with her help, I might be able to pull it off.

It was time I, Bella Fisher, risked it all.

CHAPTER

TWENTY-SEVEN

To everyone else it was the last day of term.

To me, it was D-day. D-isaster day. Or D-on't You See I Was Just An Idiot But It Won't Happen Again So Forgive Me? day.

I'd been building up to it all week. It wasn't that Tegan, Rachel and Mikey hadn't been speaking to me. They had. It was just that it was *just that*. Speaking. Not laughing. Not arranging to meet. Not messaging me in the evenings with pictures of vegetables that look like bands. Jo said they were being 'civil' but the only civil I knew was 'civil war', so that didn't sound too reassuring.

Normally, the whole school filed into assembly silent with boredom, but as it was our last one for months, everyone was massively un-silent with complete and utter un-boredom, and the teachers weren't even bothering to try and shut us up. They were as ready for the summer as we were.

I sat down next to Rachel, accidentally catching her hair with my watch. She told me it was fine, which meant it wasn't, as she'd normally just yank my ponytail in retaliation and laugh.

I rocked back and forth on my chair, full of nervous energy as Mrs Hitchman did her yearly tradition – a look back over the whole school year. I hoped she didn't hear the sniggers as she described the Christmas play as a traditional 'affair'. People had been talking about her and Mr Lutas all week. I'd been trying to correct them, but who wants the truth when gossip is more entertaining?

But I wasn't listening to Mrs Hitchman droning on about the success of the first-ever pacifist boxing team. All I could think about was what was coming up. *Could I actually do this?!* I wanted to lie flat on the floor and hyperventilate with fear, but the dust might suffocate me and that would be even more embarrassing. *Could I not think of an emergency Plan B?* I looked at the others sitting beside me. *Nope.* They were my best friends in the whole world, and I'd let them down. This was something I *had* to do.

Despite never being more scared in my life, thinking about the tiny possibility that I could make things right gave me the boost I needed (sadly just a mental one, and not a chocolate one, which would have calmed my nerves more).

Mrs Hitchman clapped her hands together and my ears tuned back into what she was saying.

"So, as you can all agree, it's been yet another exceptional year."

Not one person made any noise that could be construed as agreement. Unless you counted a sneeze from Mikey, but I didn't. Ignoring the silence, she carried on.

"So, enough from me."

"More than enough, actually," Mikey whispered. I inwardly winced at yet another of his attempts to make Tegan laugh and get back in her good books. It was my fault he was out of them.

"Now it's time for MY favourite school tradition. Hearing from YOU."

Mrs Hitchman smiled out at us, as if, for the first time ever, hands would fly in the air and we'd all clamber to share our most personal moments with a room full of people who would despise you for dragging out the painful assembly for even longer. What was it that they put in the staffroom coffee that made teachers so delusional?

But this year, one hand did go up. And when it did, Tegan, Mikey and Rachel looked like they'd seen a ghost (and not the one that finished Tegan's banners, because that had turned out to be Mikey, not that Tegan had given me an opportunity to tell her).

The hand was shaking with nerves.

The hand was mine.

I couldn't believe I was doing this.

An excited, and fair to say surprised, Mrs Hitchman called me up to the stage. I tried to block out all the evils that were being thrown up at me from everyone aged sub-teacher. My legs felt so wobbly, I was worried I was going to have to crawl the last few steps.

The whole hall was the hushed, excited silence you only ever heard (or didn't hear, seeing as it was a silence) when someone was about to do something so mortifying it could lead to a permanent change in nickname. For someone who was too self-conscious to go bowling or play Jenga, this was unbearable.

Deep breath, Bella.

The IT teacher nodded at me. She had the file I'd emailed last night ready to put up on the screen.

Was it too late to turn back and pretend this was

the first-ever case of delayed sleepwalking? The bit of my brain that made this plan shouted at me to carry on. The rest of my brain told me to stop shouting at myself, and turn and run and never look back. My legs, which didn't have a brain, made the final decision by hardly managing to walk forward, let alone run away.

I saw the concern on Tegan's face. Fingers crossed this wasn't going to just make matters worse. But with two hours left of term, this was the last chance I had to put things right. There was no going back.

I stepped up to the microphone. Here goes nothing. "IS THIS THING ON?"

My voice boomed around the room. The back row looked at each other, already on the verge of laughter. Say something cool to win them back round.

"YES IT IS."

I took a deep breath and remembered what Jo had said in practice. Not the bit about me looking like a Jack Russell when I was panicking, but the bit about trying to blur out everyone in the room except for the three people I cared about most.

"So, erm, here we are."

Mrs Hitchman nodded encouragingly.

"Here I am."

The voice that echoed back at me sounded like a

complete stranger. Could I be the first girl to experience their voice breaking? In front of an entire school.

One of the sixth formers did a 'get on with it' tap on their watch. Must blur harder.

"So ... you might not know me. Or maybe you do. . . I was the one who accidentally got that massive blu-tac ball stuck in my hair last year? It was HUGE! Honestly, you have NO idea how hard it was to get out." *No, Bella.* Get back to what you practised.

"Aaaaanyway. I'm here to tell you the truth. About this year."

I paused.

"About me. Bella Fisher."

I heard a voice shout out 'AKA Fishy Balls' and a small group laugh, but I had too much to think about without bothering to care what Luke did.

Tegan and Rachel looked nervous. If only I could discreetly reassure them this was all for them. But as I had about 250 pairs of eyes on me, which is like 500 individual eyes, there was no way I could.

I gestured for the first picture to go up. Jo had spent the week helping me make them. A ripple of laughter went round the room as a picture of me beamed up – complete with bird poo. Zac had sent me the original when I'd told him what I was planning. After I'd explained about *PSSSST* and he'd accepted my apology for what went down at prom. When he'd given me his landline number so I could ring and do the same with his dad, who'd had to patch up things with Mrs Hitchman. Possibly the most awkward phone call I will ever have, especially when Mr Lutas said 'Thank you for rrrrrrecitfying the matter' and I misheard and asked him what rectal-fying meant.

Zac gave me a massive thumbs-up from the back of the room, which gave me the lift I needed to get back on track. I was going to miss him.

"Sooooo, this is me." I guess they could tell that by the fact I am me, and the person in the photo was also me. "And I wanted to take a couple of minutes to clear some things up. Because I've made some really bad decisions this term, and the people who have been the absolute best, and the most innocent-er-ist, have been the ones who have got hurt."

The faces staring up at me looked as confused as when an interpretive dance group had come in to assembly to perform a routine about the dangers of plastic bags.

"I'm here to give you the truth behind some of the things you might have heard these last few weeks. Especially the ones from prom." Tegan and Rachel looked like they wanted to bolt out the door. But they HAD to stay. To hear what I'd been working on all week. My plan to stop everyone laughing at them, and focus it on the only person who deserved it – me.

"First up – me. This term I've been trying hard to be a better student, to be more, er, normal. But guess what? I have no idea what normal is. For example, this –" I gestured at the screen – "isn't even the worst photo of me. Not by a long way!"

I probably shouldn't have said that so proudly. I nodded for the next picture to come up – me freaking out when I got a Kinder Egg toy container stuck on my chin.

"See? I'm a total doofball. And this is what I'd be like ALL the time if I didn't have the best friends in the world to help me get through every day." I smiled apologetically at Tegan and Rachel. "And not get things stuck on my face. "

Mrs Hitchman did a 'please don't say doofball again' cough. Must win her back round.

"Like Mrs Hitchman said, it's fair to say this year has been a bit exceptional."

Her smile returned.

"An exceptional disaster."

Her smile disappeared.

"So, here's what else you need to know about me. Because if there's one thing I've learnt this term, it's that secrets, and pretending to be things you're not, only lead to bigger problems. And potentially poo on your head." This time I looked at Luke. He had his trademark scowl on. And I was delighted. Because if I told everyone everything, he would have nothing more to try and ruin my life with, and nothing more to hurt my friends with. I smiled.

"Fact one." The screen clicked on to a picture of one of the pieces of art I'd done before Christmas.

"I am terrible at art. I once got an A for this picture of my cat. However, Mr Lutas, I need to tell you something." He raised an eyebrow. "It's not really my cat called 'Cat'. I was just under pressure when you asked. It was meant to be my dog, Mumbles. And she's not even a cat-like dog because all she does is sniff trouser areas."

Mr Lutas didn't smile. *Oh no.* Had I made things worse?!

"Sorry. Not the point. The point is, that Mr Lutas deserves a massive shout-out for making someone like me able to do something like this."

A picture of the prom decorations went up. A few vaguely impressed 'ohhhhs' went round from the years who hadn't seen them.

"Cool, huh? Who knew I had it in me? Such PROM-ise?!" I waited for laughs. But only two came. One from Zac. One from Mikey. But that's all I needed. I beamed at them both.

"So put your hands together for Mr Lutas, who pulls this off every year, just for us."

Luckily the room clapped, giving me time to compose myself. I wiped my hand sweat on my skirt and carried on.

"And we need another round of applause for the lady who lets it all happen." I nodded towards Mrs Hitchman. "Who I also happen to know is a dab hand with a paintbrush, along with her very happy husband. Who is very happy. With her. As a wife."

A confused round of forced applause splattered through the room. Mrs Hitchman looked mortified. Zac pretended to put his head in his hands. Oh well, it was the thought that counted.

"And a final thank you should go to the sixth formers who've given up their time to supervise us." A few hands clapped. "Especially Zac," the claps got joined by wolfwhistles and whoops, "who as you all know by now is Mr Lutas's son. But you may not know — because even Mr Lutas doesn't — that Zac has spent his last week here giving up his evenings to create a brand-new space for us." For the first time since I'd met him, I saw Zac go red. "So give it up for Zac, and his conspirator-Mrs Hitchman, who've created St Mary's first-ever band rehearsal room!"

The hall burst into applause led by Mr Lutas, who was staring at Zac, positively glowing with pride.

"Pretty cool, huh? If anyone wants more info, Zac's put full deets on the music board." I paused as the clapping died down. But I couldn't buy more time. I had to get on with the hardest part.

"So, back to business. Here's fact two. This year there's been loads of gossip about me and my friends. So I wanted you to know what the actual truth was." I looked directly at Rachel and Tegan. "I really hope this is OK?!"

The next picture clicked up, of the three of us. I gulped so loudly it sounded like one of the speakers had popped.

"This person here —" I pointed at Tegan's face — "is probably the most cleverest —" that wasn't right — "cleverer —" oh no — "*intelligent* person I've ever met and has been an amazing friend to me since day one. Despite having zero spare time, as she's always off doing incredible things like winning national gymnastic competitions —" there were murmurs of impressed surprise at this discovery – "she always finds time to help ANYONE with ANY problem they have. And she didn't give up on me this term, even when I was a total cowbag and refused to give her a second chance. So I wanted to take this assembly to say a huge thank you to her, and a thanks for holding out for me. She really is the best friend you could wish for." I hesitated, scared at what was coming next.

"Which is why she never told anyone my lowest moment. . ." Here goes.

"When I was seven and she was staying over, I was a bit confused about . . . stuff. So, over dinner I asked my mum whether. . ." Tegan's jaw dropped open. Yes, I was about to share *that* secret. There was no going back. ". . . whether I could practise kissing with her. As in, yes, snog my mum."

The room gasped. Mrs Hitchman glared at me so hard I thought part of me was going to melt.

"OBVIOUSLY I DIDN'T KNOW WHAT IT WAS, I'M NOT A WEIRDO." Woah, I stepped back from the mic after almost deafening everyone. This revelation must NOT be the last thing that 250 people hear before a lifetime of silence. "AND SHE SAID NO." Still too loud. "But still. That's not the kind of thing you want the world to know. Although now you do."

I couldn't look at Tegan in case she was even more mad with me than before I started.

"And this, on the right, is Rachel. You all probably know her as 'fittest girl in the school'." I felt a twinge of pride with how offended Lou looked at the general whisperings of agreement. "Which is cool." Sorry-not-sorry, Lou. "But she's also kind and generous and always looking out for other people. In fact, on more than one occasion she's taken the wrap for something that wasn't her at all."

They didn't need the specifics, did they? But as I peered off stage, I realized that if I was going for total honesty, that's exactly what I needed to do. It was now or never.

"OK, full disclosure. One time I'd had this spot, and all through maths it had been sort of straining to get out. Like my dog, when she's on the lead. But a spot?"

Mrs Hitchman steadied herself like she was in the early stages of fainting. Maybe I should have gone with *never*.

"Anyway, I was squeezing it, and got WAY too into, and somehow leaned on the sink. Which then fell off, and then kind of flooded the entire girls' loos. And before I could stop her, Rachel said it was her! Because

385

I was already on a warning. And I didn't even manage to squeeze it properly. The spot. Not Rachel."

Wow. So this is what disgusted silence sounds like. Rachel looked like she was in shock. Jo *had* warned me to spare the finer details of it, but something about being up here had opened my mouth floodgates and I couldn't seem to stop anything.

"So yes, you might have heard some gossip, or seen something silly at prom, but take it from me – knowing one tiny thing about someone doesn't mean you know that person at all. So don't waste your time wondering who said what, and which rumours are true. Because I GUARANTEE that every single person in this room has said something funny, or been misunderstood, or put their foot in it, or crushed on someone we shouldn't." I smiled at Mikey. "But I'm here to say, SO WHAT? NONE of that is bad. That's part of being normal. The only *really* bad thing is something that *I* am guilty of – and that's betraying someone's trust, especially when they're the best friends in the world."

You could hear a pin drop. Although no one really carries (let alone drops) pins.

As painful as this was, I felt a little buzz of pride that for once I wasn't hiding behind anything. "So, I wanted to say sorry to Rachel and Tegan – and what the heck, Mikey, Zac, Mr Lutas and Mrs Hitchman too – as that's exactly what I did. And I will never do it again. Starting from now. Because there's one last thing you need to know."

My final two pictures popped up.

"I didn't win the camera that you all wanted. *This* was my picture." Mumbles flapping face looked even more glorious four-metres high. "This *amazing* one," I pointed at Jo's athletics pic, "was my sister's. It was an honest mix-up, but I should have come clean." I smiled apologetically at Mr Lutas. "I didn't do the right thing then, but better late than never. So, if anyone wants to use it, I've given the camera back, and you can sign it out from the library."

A few people clapped. Mostly people just sat rigid, stunned at how their end-of-term assembly had turned into something that you normally saw on ITV when you were off sick. But I didn't care cos there were four people who were cheering, whistling and making more noise than the whole school put together. Rachel, Tegan, Mikey and Zac. My friends.

Dignity 0. Life 1.

Wow. Had I, Bella Fisher, made a sort-of almost good decision?!

Mrs Hitchman beckoned me off stage. And I let the whooping and clapping continue as I returned back to my chair, to be greeted by the world's biggest bear hug with Rachel and Tegan, complete with pile-on from Mikey. Thank goodness this was end of term assembly, or we'd probably get re-grounded.

But I didn't care if I got told off. *I'd done it.* My plan hadn't gone quite to plan, but I'd got there. And I'd got my friends back.

The rest of the afternoon was a mixture of being called 'assembly girl', 'poo head' and 'mum snogger'. And 'Fishy Balls', but I was used to that. It was also full of new hellos to people who had never spoken to me (but who now thought I could be useful to know, as however bad their lives got, not being me was a reliable ego-boost) and goodbyes to ones I wished were staying longer. But that was made easier by the four Velvet Badger tickets that were now in my bag.

When the final bell of the final day finally went, Tegan and Rachel were waiting for me at Bum Tree. Rachel was dangling what looked like a massive tissue in the air, and it was getting dodgy looks from everyone who walked past.

"Errrr, why are you waving some pants at me?"

She grinned.

"Tegan's idea. Start the summer off with a dirty knickers party."

Tegan laughed.

"How many times? It's 'dirty laundry'!"

I still didn't get it.

"Can you put them away? People are staring." Not that that was a new thing for me today. "Someone please explain?!"

As we walked to Tegan's house that's exactly what she did.

In honour of my assembly life-re-assembly, Tegan had decided we were kicking summer off in style, starting with a dirty laundry party. An evening of all of us sharing all the secrets we'd *ever* had, and not told each other, so we could reset any not-knowings to zero. In Tegan's words, it was a tribute to me 'being a total nerd burger in front of the whole school, who we were now stuck with for life, as no one else was going to ever run the risk of befriending you'.

We sat in a circle in her garden, enjoying the warm evening as we flicked open our cans of Diet Coke, tore into our Haribo, and pledged to 'fess up to everything. No secret too big or too small. Tegan went first. Although I couldn't imagine someone like her having *anything* to hide.

"OK, first things first. An apology to Rachel." Well, this was interesting already. She closed her eyes as if too embarrassed to witness Rachel's reaction. "It's not *just* Bella who likes cookers. Or should I say . . . your HOB."

I ALWAYS KNEW I WASN'T THE ONLY ONE WHO THOUGHT DAN WAS HOT?! And Tegan always made out I was so inapprops!! I squealed "I KNEW IT!" as Rachel stuck her tongue out, accidentally flopping out a half-chewed chewy cola bottle on to my knee. Once I'd picked it off, and they'd finished laughing (and I'd dug out that picture of Dan that was almost so fit that surely even Rachel couldn't deny it, although she still did), Tegan composed her best serious face for round two.

"Ready for more?" We both nodded.

"OK. Here goes. One time at a massive gymnastics comp, I wanted to look older. Like more serious?" I said, "Uh-huh" but didn't really understand as to me Tegan always did that effortlessly. "So, I stuck cotton wool balls down my leotard."

No biggie, she'd already told us that ages ago.

"Thing is. . ." A grin crept back on to what was meant to be her serious face. "I had to do a particularly aggressive triple backflip. And as I did, they all flew out. Right in the judges' faces." I snorted at the image of Tegan's exploding fluff chest. Between the kind of laugh that you need to bend over for, she tried to eek out the final details.

"I didn't want to lose points. So ... so I, told ... them ... they ... were ... for ... m-m-medicinal ... boob ... sweat ... purposes!"

I officially crossed the line between 'laughing' and 'laughing so hard I cried'. It actually hurt. Could sides *actually* split? This was so un-Tegan like?! My muscles ached with being too entertained. This was basically exercise.

But the laughing didn't let up. I had to curl into a foetal position to be able to deal with Rachel's description of her emergency A&E trip. She'd always told us it happened after she fell off one of her mum's exercise balls. But apparently the real story was that she was listening so hard at Dan's door – to his convo with his fit friend – that when they opened it unexpectedly, the handle caught in her hoop earring and ripped it out. Fit friend ended up driving her to hospital as she blubbed in the passenger's seat, wearing a pair of pink earmuffs to stem the blood flow. Glam.

We stayed in the garden talking, chewing, laughing and snort-laughing until there was almost no light left in the evening. Turns out however well we thought we knew each other, we all still had a whole heap of funny things we thought we'd never be able to tell other humans. I felt so happy (and full of sweets) I could almost pop. But it wasn't just because I'd found out that the others were almost as rubbish at life as I was. It was because this terrible term had somehow term-inated with us being better friends than ever.

As Tegan was about to launch into her final story, her dad shouted that she had a visitor. Flustered, she leapt up and ran into the house, faster than me when my mum tries to drag me into her 'Suppleness and Sexuality' workshops. Rachel and I gave each other a look meaning we'd both clocked something was up. Tegan never got flummoxed by anything.

When she came back, instead of walking straight back out she knocked on the back door, and poked her head outside.

"So, er, there's one last thing I haven't told you guys."

I sat bolt upright.

Had she ordered surprise pizza for us all? I was ready and willing to deal with THAT news. Even if it was evil mushroom.

"Don't be mad. But, I . . . I guess it's time you met someone. . ." She hid behind the door to compose herself before popping her head back out. "Meet my . . . my boyfriend."

I took such a massive breath of surprise that I inhaled an entire daddy-longlegs that had been in mid-flight. RIP DLL. Rachel grabbed my hand. So it was news to her too. This was news of the century. And that included when Louis Tomlinson's baby was born.

I craned my neck to see round the door. Who WAS this person Tegan had kept secret?! Who had won over the girl who wasn't bothered by any boy (except Rachel's brother, but he had a boyf so she couldn't have him anyway). *Gulp.* It was going to be *our* friend duty to totally start hanging out with him. He'd better be AMAZING. Amazing enough to deserve Tegan. But not so amazing that we also became obsessed with him and it all got awkward. Please tell me it's not Zac?!

Tegan pushed the door open. And grinned.

And it all fell in to place.

Her boyfriend stepped forward.

And he was smiling so hard it looked like he'd just found out he'd won a lifetime of Chomps.

I approved. And from Rachel massive smile, so did she.

"Surprise!" Mikey winked at us.

And with that he scooped Tegan into his arms and planted a massive kiss on her cheek.

TWENTY-EiGHT

"So how was it then?"

Jo hadn't been home when I got back from the dirty-laundry-party night. Still, I'd been in so much shock over the Mikey revelation that I would have struggled with sentences anyway. I swear I was happier than if *I'd* found a major perfect boyfriend of my own.

This morning, while I'd spent hours building up the energy to think about getting out of bed, my over-achieving sister had already gone out for athletics training. Now she was back and perched on a stool eating what looked like flakes of charcoal (which turned out to be roasted Brussel-sprout leaves she'd discovered in the oven). After all the help she'd given me, Jo was desperate to hear all about how yesterday's big reveal had gone.

But this convo required a clothes cuddle. I ran up and pulled on my extra-fluffy dressing gown over my PJs, regardless of the fact that it was the middle of the day. I tromped back downstairs three at a time and jumped up on to the stool next to her.

"Wellllll, basically it was like the worst thing ever. But also the best, and now everything is great. So thank you. Loads. And I'm going to see Velvet Badger. And you can come."

"Think I'll pass, thanks." Jo had moved on to chopping vegetables and lime jelly into tiny cubes. "Don't ask – Mum's read that eating green food improves life expectancy, so all we've got is this or gherkins."

I'd take gherkins every time.

"Your loss. They're like the best guitar band EVER. Although Keith's not well at the moment. And he's the guitar." Out of habit I shoved whatever food was nearest into my mouth, which turned out to be some jelly and celery (jellery?). I tried unsuccessfully to pretend I was enjoying it.

"Anyway, Mikey and Tegan are basically going to get married. They're TOTALLY TOGETHER. And it's beyond cute. And Rachel and I will be bridesmaids. Although I don't really want to have to stand next to her wearing the same dress for compare and contrast reasons. Although Tegan doesn't believe in marriage so maybe they'll just have a commitment ceremony and I'll be OK."

Once Jo had deciphered what I was getting at, she looked genuinely pleased.

"Oh, ace! So Tegan finally realized what a decent bloke he was?"

Well, kind of. It was more that after I'd fled prom, Zac had spilled the beans about Mikey's prom-saving late-night secret sew fest. Guess he'd got bored of listening to me witter on about how amazing they'd be together. And that's what had made her finally see Mikey in the way we'd all done for ages. She'd just been waiting for the right time to tell us.

Jo put the remains of her chopping in the fridge and closed the door.

"So did you manage to do the speech like we practised?"

I nodded. She didn't need to know that I'd also told everyone about my mega-spot. Or done an accidental mucous bubble out of my left nostril when I panick-breathed too heavily.

NAMASTE.

A man's voice boomed out Mum's favourite yoga greeting. It took me a second to figure out what was going on before remembering that she had reset our doorbell to it a few weeks ago to 'encourage positive arrivals'. All it encouraged was me forgetting what it was and arriving too late at the door to actually answer it.

Mum's footsteps clunked towards it, so Jo and I carried on our chat.

"So, anyway." I grabbed my camera out of my bag and plonked it on the counter. "I added something in. I came clean about the camera comp! And Mr Lutas was well imprrrrrressed and said I should keep it for the summer and hand it over next term. Which is a TOTAL RESULT."

"Bella!" Mum flung the kitchen door open. She was wearing the stripy kaftan that makes her look like a human packet of fruit pastilles.

"What?"

"There's someone at the door for you."

"Er, who?" Not like her not to tell me.

"I don't know." She lowered her voice. "But he's A BOY."

'He's' do tend to be.

Jo's eyebrows shot up.

"Is it *Luke*?!?"

I had no idea. But today not even he could bring me down. I hopped out of the room, high-fiving Mum on my way out with a 'namaste', not even bothering to check my reflection in the microwave to see if I had small flecks of jelly on my top lip (I did).

"Hey hey, namaste!" I sang happily at the door, flinging it open.

But it wasn't Luke standing there. What was standing there was a complete surprise in person form. And oh my holy moly, WHY WAS I WEARING PYJAMAS WITH TEDDY BEARS ON THEM? At three in the afternoon. On a Saturday.

"What are YOU doing here?!" I couldn't tell who was more embarrassed. Him or me? I DEFINITELY scooped the award for most embarrass*ing*.

For some reason, standing there, on my doorstep, totally unannounced, was MIAGTM. Football boy. Boy of my dreams. The man who, as his name suggested, I was going to marry. And there he was. Just standing there, with his mega smile, not flinching at my teddy bear attire. In his gorgeous baggy jeans, in his baggy undone hoodie. Looking entirely hot.

And I'd just sung in his face.

And he'd just met my mum.

As my mouth gawped open, a small blob of jelly flopped on to my bottom lip. Was it too late to run back in and check for other morsels?

"Er . . . I guess I'm just standing here trying to say hello?" He looked like he might turn and leave at any second. Which he probably should do as I looked like I was mid-electric-shock. Although he also totally shouldn't do, as ideally I'd put him in a plant pot and keep him here for life. "Or even a namaste?"

Fact. Our doorstep has never encountered anything so hot. And that includes the time my mum threw a snood out that had gone up in flames after she'd tried to experiment with an ear candle. But why was he here? Was it another goalkeeper crisis? Or was he here to report my dog for crimes against groin-sniffing?

"How do you know where I house? Sorry, live?" Goodbye, ability to speak.

"I saw it on your dog's tag when we were chatting about colon?"

"COLON?"

I splurted the word so hard a jelly projectile hurtled towards MIAGTM and landed on a small tuft of hair just in front of his ear.

"Your football league? Hope that's OK. It sounds weird now I've said it outloud."

Oh my goodness. The jelly blob was still clinging on. Do not look at it whatever you do, Bella. He must not know!

"No, course, that's fine. Is that why you're ear?" ARGH. "Here? Colon?"

Quick, Bella, speak more before he dwells on why I was thinking about his ear and reclassifies me as a gelatinous spurting pyjama blob. "Cos I don't play any more. We weren't going anywhere. In Colon. So we made a quick exit. I hung up my boobs."

"Boobs?" He looked startled.

I spluttered. "BOOTS."

This was a disaster. And I hadn't brushed my hair for seventeen hours. And I probably had a whole jelly on my head and didn't even know.

"Riiiight." He stepped up a step, and lent on the doorframe. Oh My Crusted Cod. He was touching my house. That basically counted as *me*. Although, ARGH. I angled my body to try and hide the ABBA Benny cut-out. He/it could be the final straw.

"I'm actually around here loads cos I have my drum lessons round the corner."

What the what?! MIAGTM loiters near me?! I bet I've only not seen him here because I've been out trying to get a glimpse of him elsewhere. Damn myself.

"Drums?!" *Great*. Another unauthorized mouth outburst. Why wasn't Jo getting my telepathic vibes to come out and throw a sheet over me to stop this madness. "That's..." say something normal. Just be honest. "Fit." NOT THAT HONEST. "... ting! FITTING. For a drummer. Like you."

Of course he drummed. He ONLY did fit things. It was only non-interesting people like me that had to do non-fit things like brush teeth or change pillowcases.

"Yeah... so I was hoping to see you around..."

I nodded dumbly like those nodding dogs people put on windscreens. *He'd been hoping to see ME?!?!* If my brain actually popped with dealing with this, would it ooze out of my ears, or would he just think it was more flying jelly?

"... cos I'd wanted to tell you something."

"I'M IN MY PYJAMAS."

For some reason I just stated the obvious. Loudly. In his face.

"Erm, yes. You are. But no, that's not it. The thing is... It's me."

He was almost as baffling as me.

"What is?"

"LilDrummerBoy? The one that had been writing?"

Oh. My. Holy. Codballs. This was too much. HE

was LilDrummerBoy? Reading my innermost thoughts on *PSSSST*? Laughing at my inability to be normal?! Being non-normal himself?! I was so speechless, I worried I'd forgotten all words. But then I realized I was thinking with words, so calmed down a bit.

MIAGTM looked super awkward.

"I thought you knew. You kept chatting back . . . but then you disappeared offline." Disappeared?! More like deleted to save any shred of dignity. "I'd been wanting to talk to you about it, say a proper hello ever since that day we chatted about football. When you showed me the pics of you and your friend with Sellotape on your faces?"

FOR THE MENTAL RECORD, MIAGTM, I DIDN'T SHOW YOU, YOU ACCIDENTALLY SAW.

"That was not ME, it was just someone who looked like me. And someone who looked like my friend. Together. That both happened to be on my phone."

He looked unconvinced.

"Err, well, either way, it was around then that you put that football story up on *PSSSST* and I realized it was you that I was following. Online! Not in real life or anything. You'd been in my feed ever since I'd signed up, when I was waiting for my drumming lesson to start. It'd recommended you cos you were nearby." OK

WORLD I GET THE MEMO. I REALLY AM THE ONLY PERSON WHO DIDN'T GET HOW *PSSSST* WORKS. "I thought you were dead funny."

Hang on, so all along MIAGTM had been chatting to me on *PSSSST* and I'd thought he was a general randomer, as opposed to a non-random major hottie?

"But you do realize I'm in my pyjamas, right?"

"Erm, yes," he looked me up and down. "I can *still* see that. . . Anyway, despite the fact your mum thinks I'm insane, your dog thinks my, er, trousers smell, and not forgetting, I made you think you had an online stalker for the last couple of months . . . would you be up for hanging out with me? Maybe tomorrow? Maybe at six?"

Can. Not. Deal. Was he asking me out? To HANG.

"Tomorrow? Six?" All I could muster was repetition. I needed an interpreter. If only Benny was real. I couldn't speak. "I'm in my pyjamas."

Wow, Bella. If your knockout style hadn't impressed him enough, your grade-A chat will really seal the deal.

"Yes, I still, *still* know that. So, how about I come and call for you? Would you be around?"

There was only one thing I could say. Quite literally – I could only remember ten words.

"Yes. Cool." I tried to think of more words. "One thing though. . ."

"Yup?" Concern flashed across his freckled face.

"Please don't ask me to catch any footballs."

"Agreed. And you – can you maybe not wear that teddy print in public again? It's a bit ... last season. Though the horse slippers? They can stay."

BUMFLAPS. I hadn't even noticed those! I thought horseshoes were meant to bring you good luck?!

"So, see you here tomorrow? Same place – different outfits?"

I nodded, trying to hold back what I think was a one hundred per cent mega dreamy smile that was trying to invade my face.

MIAGTM turned to leave, but stopped in his tracks.

"Oh, one last thing before I go."

What? Please don't tell me now this was all a joke?! Please no. I couldn't flee whilst wearing these slippers; the fake horse tails on my heels were too much of a trip hazard.

But instead he just put his left hand out towards me, his blue eyes looking straight into mine.

"I'm Adam. Pleased to meet you."

MIAGTM finally had a name.

ACKNOWLEDGEMENTS

Books are weird – because there's a name on the cover, it seems like they might be the work of one person. But it's ALL LIES. They're a team effort. But, if all the names of all the amazing people who made it happen went on the cover, then book covers would be a whole lot less fun to look at. So I shall try and put some of them here instead.

To my real life MIAGTM/MIDMBITHMHGCATW TATETM (Man I Did Marry, Because I Think He Must Have Got Confused And Then Was Too Awkward To Ever Tell Me), Chris. You are a bottomless pit of wonderfulness (and emergency tea), and my calm in any storm. Thank you for making me know love at first sight is real, and for still making me cry-snort with laughter every day.

And an indescribably huge thank you to the person who began it all when they believed in this book when it really wasn't one. You make me (and everyone) feel non-stupid when I don't have a clue what I'm doing (AKA all the time). Your patience is a thing of wonder – as are your nails, and well, just you. Gemma, thanks for loving love, and loving Bells, and letting me be a part of the amazing world you help create for so many people. And thank you for introducing me to Team Cooper. How can such talented people be so nice?

Lucy Rogers – ERM, WHAT? Have you actually made this happen?! How can someone so wonderful and wonderfully together ever identify with such awkwardness? You are a person of too many talents (and most excellent imaginary timekeeping). Fishy Balls and I couldn't have found an editor who gets us more than you do. Thank you for knowing exactly what was needed EVERY. SINGLE. TIME. What a total HELL YEAH-ditor (does that work?!) (no). And thank you for welcoming me into the world of the Scholastic crew (Jamie Gregory! Cover designer of dreams!), who have been amazing every awkward step of the way.

A big massive dollop of love to my first reader, who ALWAYS makes time, even though she's busy overachieving on all fronts, Jessica Hitchrod/man. You're more excellent than you will ever let me say. And an over-familiar body hug to the insanely talented Ali – the best person I could have ever learnt from (thanks for helping me reign in all the exclamation marks!!!!!).

And thank you to all my incredible friends for waiting for me to un-hermit/inspiring me with life disasters. You are too funny, too smart and too good-looking to hang out with me. But if I write your names here, YOU CAN NEVER LEAVE ME. Pam (we NEED a character called Escherichia), Tina Bean (where is Australia anyway?), Rosanna (Brit and I can't WAIT to read your book), Becky and Sarah (I know April Fools is the first of one month…), James (housemate for life), Yasmine, Anna, Vicki, Trev (thank you for reading way back when & making it real), and the whole Switch crew (HIGH FIVE!) (Tom B, I'm probably crying right now). And of course NYC BG Julie (bet you don't make it this far), Dan (take it easel, baby), the rest of the N-Unit – Matt, Mikey, Lyndon, Jono, Katie, Vivek and

David – team MTV ISR (more stories please VM), and the Gornell crew (I won a whole new rad fam!).

But none of this could have happened without the people who were there when I was Bella's age (and way more awkward than she will ever be). My amazing family who always believe anything is possible; Moomin, Daddles and the best big sister imaginable, Becca. I couldn't be more overjoyed that Chris, Ian and Rose have joined the club too. Thank you for being my wall of arms and bringing so much magic into the everyday.

And finally, finally, a massive shout-out to anyone who has ever felt like Bella does, AKA the best people in the world. Because being super awkward means you're super awesome – and one day you might get to write a book about it.